...raries and Information...

'This is a wonderfully **tense** story, full of characters who may or may not be telling the truth. **Compellingly creepy** – not one to read while home alone'
Glamour

'A beautiful read, brimming with **intrigue and suspense** . . . It's an incredibly accomplished debut, a real **heart-racing chiller**, and I genuinely didn't want it to end!'
Samantha Hayes, author of *Until You're Mine*

'A tense, claustrophobic, and **deeply unsettling** novel about the damage a disturbed teenager threatens to wreak on one woman's life'
Penny Hancock, author of *Tideline*

'A **stunning** debut psychological thriller'
Sun

'*Don't Stand So Close* is a **heady cocktail** . . . Obsession, repression and delusion twist their tentacles throughout Luana Lewis's **riveting and remarkable** debut'
Elizabeth Forbes, author of *Nearest Thing to Crazy*

'An assured debut novel that will have you **turning the pages** to discover the truth'
Paula Daly, author of *Just What Kind of Mother Are You?*

Also by Luana Lewis

Don't Stand So Close

and published by Corgi

FORGET ME NOT

LUANA LEWIS

CORGI BOOKS

TRANSWORLD PUBLISHERS
61–63 Uxbridge Road, London W5 5SA
www.transworldbooks.co.uk

Transworld is part of the Penguin Random House group of companies
whose addresses can be found at global.penguinrandomhouse.com

Penguin
Random House
UK

First published in Great Britain in 2015 by Corgi
an imprint of Transworld Publishers

A CIP catalogue record for this book
is available from the British Library.

ISBN
9780552169547

Typeset in 11/14pt Sabon by Falcon Oast Graphic Art Ltd.
Printed and bound by CPI Group (UK) Ltd, Croydon, CR0 4YY.

Penguin Random House is committed to a sustainable
future for our business, our readers and our planet. This book is made from
Forest Stewardship Council® certified paper.

MIX
Paper from
responsible sources
FSC® C018179

1 3 5 7 9 10 8 6 4 2

To the Alhadeff women,
Leonara, Fortunee, Esther and Norma

Prologue

The day she died

She lies crumpled at my feet.

Her right arm is flung out to the side, as though she's trying to reach out to me, as though she might still grab hold of me with those cherry-red fingernails.

She is naked beneath her dressing gown. I kneel down and try to pull the edges of her robe closer together, to cover her, to give her some dignity, at least. I run my fingers through the soft black strands of her hair. My hand comes away sticky with her blood.

'I'm so sorry,' I say.

I kiss her, one last time. Her sweet, fresh smell mingles with the metallic odour of death.

After years of practice, I am able to split myself in two: the part of me that acts spliced clean apart from the part that feels. In this way, I stay quite calm while I inflict pain. And the woman that lies destroyed on the floor is not a mother, or a wife, or a daughter.

I stand up and take a last look around this room where she died. Grey veins tear through the marble floor and slither up the walls. The taps glitter a too-bright gold. The surfaces are hard, the edges sharp.

I turn my back on her and I leave her all alone.

I am not really here. I never was.

Chapter 1

Two weeks later

The strange thing about DS Cole's questions is that I have answered most of them before. Not here, though; not at a police station, in a cramped and windowless interview room with scuffed walls.

I reach up to rub my right temple.

'Are you all right, Rose?'

'Another headache,' I say.

DS Cole nods, as though she understands, as though she sympathizes with my pain. 'Would you like a glass of water?'

'No, thank you.' I brace my hands against the old wooden table between us and I cross my legs, tight. The tension helps me focus. 'Please go on. I won't pass out on you, I promise.'

It's strange also, how the tables have turned. I'm supposed to be the one on the other side of this table. The one who delivers bad news – the worst possible news – to devastated parents. But now here I sit and my side of this conversation is a dark place from which there is no escape.

DS Cole speaks clearly and slowly. 'I'd like you to tell me about any contact you had with Vivien in the days before she died.'

She waits, patiently, for me to begin.

'The last time I saw her was on the Sunday,' I say. 'It was my granddaughter's eighth birthday that weekend and Vivien had a few people over to the house, four or five of Lexi's friends from school, and their parents. There was a young woman painting the children's faces, butterflies and tigers and so on, and a bouncy castle in the garden. I was at the house for around an hour and a half, I suppose.'

DS Cole is young, somewhere in her late twenties. Younger than my daughter was when she died. Sometimes, as I look at her, she reminds me of one of those figure-ground pictures they used to show us in school, the ones that don't settle, that change depending on how you're looking at them. She's an attractive young woman, with large, deep-set eyes and a peroxide-blonde fringe draped low over her eyebrows; but when I look again, she's almost boyish with razor-short back and sides and a strong, sharp-angled jaw. Her body, too, won't be pinned down one way or another. She's slim and flat-chested inside her tailored shirt, her coat-hanger shoulders narrowing down to small hips.

'When you think back to that day,' she goes on, 'did

you notice anything unusual, anything that might have pointed to the fact that Vivien was unhappy or distressed?'

'There is one thing that stays with me,' I say. 'Vivien asked if she could speak to me in private, upstairs. She told me she wasn't happy with the advice she'd been given by her fertility specialist, and that she wanted a second opinion. She asked if I could recommend someone.'

'And what did you say?'

'I said I would make some enquiries. I work with several consultants at the neonatal unit. But I also told her I wasn't convinced it was a good idea to change. In my opinion, the person she'd been seeing – Mrs Murad – is superb.'

'Did Vivien say why she was unhappy with the advice she'd been given?'

'We only spoke briefly, and she didn't go into detail. Afterwards, she was busy, distracted, running around and sorting out the children, the cake, the entertainers. My attention was really on my granddaughter.'

DS Cole nods. Apparently she's satisfied.

'How would you describe Vivien's mood that day?' she says.

'In hindsight, maybe the fact that she mentioned the issue with Mrs Murad was some sort of clue, but I really didn't notice anything out of the ordinary. She and Ben had been trying for a second baby for years, and she wasn't obviously upset when we spoke. Not that I picked up, anyway. But then it was her daughter's birthday party, and she had guests, and it was important to her to keep up appearances.'

DS Cole has a clipboard in front of her and she lifts it, consulting her notes, formulating her next question.

'And that was the last time you saw her?' she says.

'Yes.'

I remain very still. My legs are crossed, my hands folded one on top of the other on my lap.

'You had no contact during that week? After the birthday party?'

'No.'

'Was that unusual?'

'No.'

DS Cole really does have a way of asking the same thing, over and over again. It's disconcerting, the way she behaves as though we've never had this conversation. She lays her clipboard down and pushes her chair out, further away from the table. As she crosses her legs, I notice her shoes: tan brogues with pointy toes.

'If we can focus on the Friday,' she says. She pauses, watching my reaction. 'Are you sure I can't offer you a glass of water?'

Though my mouth is dry, I don't want to delay. I want this over with. 'I'm fine,' I say. 'Please, go on.'

'I'd like to take you through what we know. There might be something else you remember, or something you remember differently.'

'All right.' The muscles in my face stiffen and it's an effort to speak.

'We know Vivien walked her daughter to school on that Friday morning,' she says. 'And that after dropping Alexandra off at the school gates, Vivien went for a run. She took her usual route, through Regent's Park. The waitress in the café remembers serving her. She says Vivien was there most mornings and that she stood out, because she was very attractive, and in good shape. But there was heavy fog and visibility was poor, so we don't have any reported sightings of your daughter on her way back from the park to her house on Blackthorn Road. We assume she went straight home, because that's what she usually did.'

I look down at my hands, resting in my lap, with their short nails and their chafed skin. Years of rigorous hand-washing have taken their toll. Vivien's hands were always so soft, her skin like silk, her nails painted a daring red or an elegant beige.

'Vivien didn't contact you that morning?' DS Cole says.

'No. But I had a phone call, from Mrs Murad's secretary, to say she hadn't arrived for her appointment.'

'And do you know why Mrs Murad's office would call you, instead of her husband?'

'I assumed they'd tried Ben's phone and couldn't reach him. And Mrs Murad and I know each other well, we work in the same hospital. I manage the neonatal unit, so we see several babies who are conceived as a result of fertility treatment.'

DS Cole leans forward, pushing her fringe out of her eyes and resting her elbows on her knees. 'So what did you do, when you got the phone call about the missed appointment?'

'I told Mrs Murad's secretary I didn't know where Vivien was. Then I tried to phone her myself, but her mobile went straight to voicemail.'

'Had Vivien done that before, not turned up for appointments?'

'I don't really know, but I'd say it wasn't like her. Vivien was an extremely organized person, she liked everything to be planned well in advance. But then we didn't have that many arrangements and we didn't see each other that often, so I can't really be sure.'

DS Cole looks up from her clipboard. I wonder if she judges me. I wonder if she's close to her own mother, or if she understands how difficult things can be.

'Did you think about contacting Ben, when you got the phone call about Vivien's missed appointment?'

'No. It didn't occur to me. Ben is always so busy and he often travels for work. I assumed Mrs Murad's rooms had tried him already and had no luck. I had no reason to think . . .'

There is no point in finishing my sentence.

'Did you consider popping over to Vivien's house to check up on her?'

I shake my head. 'No, I wouldn't have thought that

was a good idea. Vivien didn't appreciate spur-of-the-moment visits from anyone, least of all me. She hated surprises. I assumed she'd had something important to deal with and that she'd reschedule her appointment when she was ready.'

My right hand creeps over my left. I want to dig my nails in deep, to distract myself from the pain in my head, but DS Cole is watching me so I don't.

'I do wonder, if I had gone straight over there, whether she might still be alive.'

'I'm sorry,' DS Cole says.

Since my daughter died, I find people apologize to me constantly.

DS Cole looks at me for a few moments and then smiles, a small, sad smile of commiseration. I clear my throat.

'Do you remember what you did, after the phone call from Mrs Murad's secretary?'

I've been through all of this before, more than once, and it gets easier each time. Each time I repeat this story, I'm that much more removed.

'I was at home, it was my day off. I cleaned the kitchen, I ran the dishwasher, I did a load of laundry – I remember I washed all of my uniforms for the week. I went out for a walk, to pick up some groceries, and when I got back I tried to call Vivien again, but she still wasn't picking up. I had an arrangement in the early evening – a friend of mine had bought us tickets to a play. So I took a bus up to Hampstead and walked around a bit before meeting Wendy for an early dinner.

And then, after the performance, on the bus home, I switched on my phone and I saw I had nine missed calls from my son-in-law.'

I pause.

'I'm a little confused,' I say, 'because I've told you all of this before. Has something happened, DS Cole?'

I know there are times when police keep information back – a piece of evidence, perhaps. I wonder if there are things about my daughter's death that DS Cole knows but does not share with me.

'Well,' she says, considering her words carefully, 'as you know, we're still not sure about the cause of death. Vivien's body was found in her bathroom that afternoon, and she'd sustained an injury to her head. While we don't think this injury was severe enough to have caused her death, we need to understand what happened to her. We have to consider the possibility that Vivien was assaulted.'

DS Cole is doing everything she can to avoid using the word murder, but still, I hear it loud and clear. I see it, written on these grubby, windowless walls in capital letters. As she speaks, my vision blurs around the edges. I seem to be staring at her from far away, as though we're standing at opposite ends of a long, dark tunnel.

'Rose, are you *sure* you're all right?'

My bones are heavy inside my skin and it takes an effort to nod my head. I look away from her, down at the floor for a few moments, until my vision clears.

'A pair of diamond earrings is missing from the house,

16

though the rest of Vivien's jewellery, including the engagement ring she was wearing, is all accounted for. There was no sign of forced entry at the property either, but it's possible someone might have approached your daughter on the street as she came back from her run, and forced her to let them inside.'

When I try to swallow, it feels as though something's got stuck. I clear my throat.

'We also have to consider the possibility that your daughter let someone into the house,' DS Coles says. 'Someone she knew.'

I nod. A terrible image hovers at the periphery of my vision and I try my best to block it out, but it won't leave me. The image grows larger and I teeter at the edge of a crater, my thoughts fragmenting.

'In the weeks before Vivien died,' DS Cole says, 'did she mention anything that might have happened to upset or alarm her? Someone behaving strangely? Even something minor that might have seemed unimportant at the time?'

'I don't remember anything like that. But as I say, if there was something upsetting her, I'm not the person she would have turned to.'

'And who would she turn to?'

'Her husband.'

'Did you ever suspect your daughter might be seeing someone else?' she says.

The question blindsides me. I haven't been asked this before.

'DS Cole, do you know something?'

'These are standard questions,' she says. 'I have to ask.'

'I see. Well, the truth is I don't know. But it's unlikely. I can't imagine Vivien doing anything to jeopardize her marriage.'

DS Cole gives me a regretful, tight-lipped smile.

'So you can't release her body to us?' I say.

She shakes her head. 'I'm sorry,' she says again.

I start as she leans forward and gives my hand a gentle squeeze. I try not to flinch.

I remember the last time my daughter touched me. We were standing in the entrance hall of the house on Blackthorn Road. Vivien put her arms around me, she hugged me. I remember my own arms stayed limp at my sides. That was eight years ago.

Chapter 2

It's dark by the time my interview with DS Cole is over. The bus stop is right outside the police station; I wait twenty minutes for mine to arrive and the journey home is slow and tedious, stop-start through the London rush hour. I sit up at the top, where the windows of the bus are shut tight and the glass mists over with the breath of so many people crammed together. Everywhere I go feels airless.

I disembark opposite Cambridge Court and cross over to reach the front door of the building. Leaves litter the concrete steps. The paint on the lintel is cracked and a spiderweb hangs down across the corner of the doorway. Inside, the air is stale with the fug of bin bags left out too long.

While I fumble for my keys on the fourth floor, the dogs across the hallway begin yapping.

My own flat is silent. I close the door behind me and I slip off my coat and hang it carefully on its hook. I run my hands down the pale-pink cashmere, smoothing it out, so it hangs straight. The coat was a gift from Vivien on my fiftieth birthday. There was no party and no family celebration; I worked that day. Ben, Vivien and Lexi were away on holiday in France, but she had the coat delivered to me. With roses and champagne.

How bizarre it is, to know my daughter will never age.

I pull off my boots. Then I stand still for a few moments, unsure what to do next. I can see through into the kitchen, where one plate, one knife, one fork and a single glass are laid out to dry next to the stainless-steel sink.

On my fridge, secured with four round magnets, is a child's drawing. It is a picture of a small ginger-haired girl standing next to her small, dark-haired mother. The figures are squashed into the bottom right-hand corner of the page, and my granddaughter has signed her name in capital letters across the top: *LEXI*.

I need to see her.

I turn back to the front door. I pull on my coat and my boots, I pick up my bag and my keys, and I leave.

On the ten-minute walk to Vivien's house, the rain is soft and persistent. By the time I reach number sixty-three Blackthorn Road, my hair lies damp and limp against my skull. My coat is covered in tiny droplets of water, glistening under the orange streetlights.

The stucco-fronted Victorian villa is set back behind wrought-iron railings. The steps leading up to the front door are marble; the rounded topiaries, one on each side of the front door, are a matching pair. Two Range Rovers lie quietly on the driveway, like slumbering guard dogs. The shutters on all four floors are closed, but light seeps out through the ground-floor windows.

I press the buzzer, looking directly into the camera. Before long, the lock on the gate snaps open and I walk along the short path and climb the shallow steps. I'm expecting to see my son-in-law at the front door and so I'm caught off guard when his driver opens up instead. Isaac is a man of around my age, solidly built and shaven-headed. We've met a handful of times before, but only briefly. The last time we saw each other was at Lexi's birthday party, where, like me, he hovered around the edges; he was helping guests with coats and parking permits. I remember Vivien insisting he have a piece of cake, handing him a pink paper plate, laughing.

He ushers me in out of the rain. 'Ben's upstairs; he's putting Alexandra to bed,' he says. 'Here, let me take your coat.'

'Thank you.' I shrug off the damp cashmere and hand it to him. I've already left muddy footprints all over Vivien's Victorian chequerboard floor.

Isaac opens the cupboard next to the front door and slips my coat onto a hanger. Inside, I catch a glimpse of Vivien's black fur – the goatskin – still hanging in its place. On the floor of the cupboard, there are three pairs of navy wellington boots arranged in order of size.

'I was hoping to see Lexi before she fell asleep.

21

Do you think I can pop upstairs to say goodnight?'

'I think it's probably better if you wait down here.' Isaac looks somewhat uncomfortable as he says this.

'Of course,' I say.

I'm disappointed but not surprised. I understand that spontaneous visits are still not welcome.

It looks as though Isaac was just about to leave the house: he's wearing a long tan mackintosh. But it appears that now he's going to wait, watching over me until Ben comes downstairs. I run my hands over my wet hair, trying to smooth it down.

Isaac is looking at me, as though there's something he wants to say. I imagine a little softness in his eyes.

'I wanted to say how sorry I am,' he says. 'I can't imagine . . .' His sentence trails off into silence.

'Do you have children, Isaac?'

'I have stepdaughters. Twins.'

'Then you probably can imagine,' I say.

I didn't intend to but I've made him uncomfortable. I'm irritated at not being allowed to do something so simple as go upstairs and kiss my granddaughter good-night. He looks away, glancing hopefully upstairs, but there's no sign of Ben.

We stand, awkwardly, in the middle of the entrance hall. Isaac has his hands clasped in front of him, his feet apart. I smooth my hair down again.

Vivien is everywhere around us. Each object has been chosen with great care. Tall glass vases, silver picture frames and stone sculptures are positioned just so. On the walls, bold oil paintings hang alongside charcoal sketches. Everything clashes and yet fits together.

I hear the creak of Lexi's door on the first floor and I look up. My son-in-law stands at the top of the stairs, staring back at me.

In the living room, Ben presses his palm flat against a panel in the wall and it opens to reveal a mirrored cabinet filled with glasses of different shapes and sizes, and row upon row of bottles. The Bell's Special Reserve, already two-thirds empty, stands forward from the rest. Ben half-fills his glass with whisky. He doesn't bother to replace the lid of the bottle.

'Would you like a drink?' he says, half-turning towards me but not quite looking at me.

'A glass of water, thank you.'

After all these years, the two of us are polite strangers, our connection to each other oddly tenuous in Vivien's absence. Ben leans down to open the fridge in a cupboard under the drinks cabinet. He takes out a bottle of Perrier and pours.

'How is Lexi?' I say.

'She's fast asleep.' He walks over and hands me a glass of cold, fizzing water. 'I try to keep to her routine,' he says. 'Vivien always had her in bed by seven-thirty.'

'Of course. Routine is so important. But what I meant was, how is she in herself?'

'I'm not sure. She eats the food I put in front of her. She goes to school. The school counsellor says to follow

23

her lead, to answer questions as she asks them, not to push her to talk until she's ready.'

'That sounds sensible. I'm glad you have their support.'

The silence between us rankles as we stand facing each other. I'm glad I have the glass to hold on to, something to do with my hands.

Ben is less imposing in the flesh than in the many likenesses of him that smile from newspapers and web pages. He's not the sort of man you would pick out of a crowd: of average height, not much taller than I am, his wiry brown hair is shot through with grey and he has a hint of middle-aged spread. Vivien used to say that because he is soft-spoken and unassuming, people tend to underestimate him. She used to say he reminded her of a teddy bear.

Thirsty, my mouth dry again, I take a sip of icy water.

At this moment, Ben does not look like a cuddly toy. He looks like hell. His eyes are dull and bruised and he's aged ten years in the weeks since she died. But then I imagine I don't look so great myself.

'Does Lexi ask about her mother?' I say.

'She does. Every day. When I fetched her from school yesterday, she asked if Vivien was waiting for us at home. I explained it, all over again. I told her that her mother can't ever come back. She seemed to understand. Then a few hours later, she asked again. She wanted to know if Vivien would be home in time to read her a story before bed. They say children don't really understand what death is at her age.'

He takes a deep drink of his whisky. Another dark, deep gap falls between our words, between us.

On the large leather-topped desk at the opposite end of the room there is a silver-framed photograph of Vivien. She is smiling, her head tilted, coquettish, to the right. Her dark hair hangs poker straight to her shoulders and the ruffles of her blouse are buttoned demurely right up to her throat.

I blurt out, 'Do you think you should still be living here?'

'We're not moving,' Ben says. 'This is our home, Vivien and the architect practically rebuilt it from the ground up.'

He takes another drink, looking into the bottom of his whisky glass as though he might find salvation there. He leaves my side to pour himself another, and once again he's generous with the Special Reserve. In all the years I've known him, I've never seen him drink more than a couple of glasses of wine. I don't like the way he's drinking now, but I'm not about to antagonize him by suggesting he stop.

There are practicalities, I suppose. The size of the mortgage, the reality of selling such a house so soon after an unexplained death. Perhaps Ben has to live here for reasons I am not privy to, not burdened with.

I walk over to the back window. Vivien has planted a row of trees along the back wall, in an attempt to screen out the ugly brown-brick council buildings behind, though the saplings don't quite manage it, they aren't tall enough yet. There are tiny lights buried in neat lines all around the edges of the compact square of lawn. A stone lion is mounted on the side wall, under a flood-light. His mouth is open in a silent scream.

Ben has come to stand beside me.

'DS Cole asked me to go in to the station for an interview this afternoon,' I say.

We make eye contact in the window across our rip-pled reflections as he takes yet another, deeper drink.

'What did she want?' he says.

'I don't really know. She went over exactly the same ground we've covered before. When I saw Vivien in the week before she died, what she said to me, what I did that Friday.'

I'm not sure whether to say that DS Cole talked about the head injury, and a possible intruder. I decide it's better to say nothing. If Ben is fearful, if that's part of the reason he's drinking, I don't want to exacerbate his anxiety.

'I assume they're keeping in touch with you?'

He nods.

'If you're worried about your granddaughter's safety,' he says, 'you should know I'm in touch with a security firm. We're putting in a more sophisticated security system. Isaac is overseeing all of it.'

The bitterness in his voice is unlike the Ben I knew before. Ben who was Vivien's rock, always on an even keel and so easy-going. Ben who was warm where Vivien was cold. For Lexi's sake, I don't want to see him change.

'I trust you to keep Lexi safe, Ben. I didn't mean it that way.'

Though he couldn't keep Vivien safe. This conversation is a minefield.

'I can't imagine what it must be like for you, to sleep in that bed, to use that bathroom – what it will be like for Lexi, as she grows older, to know—'

I stop speaking because I fear I'm making things worse, for him and between us.

'I don't know which is worse,' Ben says, 'to think someone hurt her or to know she committed suicide. Isn't that bizarre? Part of me would prefer murder. Then I don't have to deal with the fact that she made the decision to leave us.'

'No,' I say, 'I don't think that's bizarre at all.'

'There's no evidence of an intruder,' he says, 'and I don't believe there was one. I think I didn't see what was in front of me.'

'What do you mean?'

'I mean, I should have known. I should have done something to help her.'

'You can't blame yourself.'

'Oh, I can.'

This room is too warm and I feel a familiar thudding headache coming on. From the corner behind me, a statue watches over us: a bird carved from black stone with an enormous hooked beak, so tall it reaches almost to the ceiling. How I hate this house. I worry about Ben and Lexi, as though the traces of what happened upstairs might poison them too.

I notice in his reflection in the glass in front of me that Ben is wearing a white shirt over black suit trousers. His tie hangs loose around his neck. He must be spending time in the office already.

'Who will look after Lexi when you need to go back to work full time?' I say.

'Isaac is helping me out for the time being.'

'Really?'

'He has adult daughters of his own. He's wonderful with her.'

'It sounds like you've come to rely on him a great deal.'

He nods.

'Ben, Lexi is eight years old. She needs a woman in her life.'

Ben does not say anything, but I imagine I can read his thoughts. His own mother died before he and Vivien even met, and so Lexi never knew her paternal grandmother. I feel sure Ben is thinking of her now, and wishing his own mother were standing beside him instead of me. I'm sure he believes his own mother would have done a much better job of loving Lexi. I am someone Lexi sees briefly at birthdays and at Christmas time. I am her grandmother in name, but not much more.

'I'm looking into hiring a nanny,' he says. He places his drink down on the coffee table. He begins fiddling with his wedding ring. 'Rose,' he sighs, 'why exactly are you here?'

'I want to help,' I say. 'I can take time off work. I can pick up Lexi from school. I can stay to help with her homework. I can cook. Anything you need. You only have to ask.'

'I appreciate the offer,' he says, though his tone says something different.

'Is there a problem, with what I've said?' I ask him.

'Lexi isn't used to spending time with you.'

I could say the same about him, but I don't, I manage to keep myself in check. Ben is in pain. He's grieving and he's powerless. I have to be patient.

'Ben, I promise you, my priority now is Lexi. My career comes second. I've stepped down as manager of the unit.'

'Lexi is my priority too.'

'Yes, of course. I didn't mean to imply anything different. I'm sorry,' I say. 'I'm not expressing myself very well. I think you know what I'm trying to say. I'm really not trying to make you angry.'

'Do I sound angry?' he says.

'Yes. And understandably so.'

'I am angry. Angry that I've lost my wife and that Lexi is going to grow up without her mother. And I'm angry at you, Rose. Angry that you disappeared from our lives after Lexi was born, after all we'd gone through in that pregnancy and at a time when Vivien really, really needed you. I don't have any right to criticize you, Rose, and I have enormous respect for you, raising Vivien as a single parent and still managing to have the career you've had. But Lexi is so vulnerable. And she barely knows you.'

I want to protest at the unfairness of what he's saying, but I don't.

'Please give me a chance,' is all I say.

'I'm trying to give Lexi some sense of a normal life,' he says, 'and to minimize the damage here. I really don't know what you want from us and whether your relationship with my daughter is going to help her or make things worse. I worry that you're using Lexi to deal with the guilt you feel for neglecting your own daughter all these years. Do you understand what I'm saying?'

'I do.'

Ben is in pain, his face mapped out with loneliness and regret. He is doing the best he can for his daughter and he believes I have no heart.

I have to be careful, because Ben holds all the cards. I'm frightened of being unimportant and of being discarded, and I see all too clearly that my place in my granddaughter's life is far from secure. I have not understood until now that I might lose Lexi, too. I could lose everything. I have to tread carefully. So I don't argue with him and I don't defend myself and though I feel the pressure of the tears behind my eyes, I do not cry.

'Well?' he says. 'Where have you been for the last eight years?'

'We all do things we regret.' I sound weak. Shallow.

'Look,' he says, his voice softening. 'All I can think of is what it would have meant to Vivien to have your support with Lexi all these years. She needed you.'

'I know this isn't the right time,' I say, 'everything is so raw and Lexi is your priority, rightly so. But one day, I'd like to explain. We can sit down and talk properly.'

He picks up his glass and returns to the drinks cabinet for a refill. There's no point in beginning this conversation now, no point trying to reason with him or persuade him of anything. He can't be thinking straight after all that whisky.

'Vivien was so lucky to have you,' I say.

My daughter has crept back into the room. She is with us in the curves of the armchair and the lines of the charcoal sketches, in the polished silver of the picture frames. She is in the air we breathe, in the sensual mix of whisky and gardenia. She is the strong glass and steel frame that has been grafted onto the spine of this old house.

Ben returns to my side, at the window, and we stand in a more amiable silence as we stare out at Vivien's twinkling lights. After a few moments, I ask him the question I've been wanting to ask since I stepped through the front door of this cursed house. I ask if I may go upstairs to see my granddaughter.

To my relief, he says yes. As long as I do not wake her.

The walls of the square landing on the first floor are covered with family photographs: Lexi on the day she came home from the hospital, Lexi in Ben's arms, Lexi as a toddler taking her first steps. There is one shot of the family together, as they pose on a beach. It is a beautiful photograph, because they are all laughing.

All three doors up here stand slightly ajar. Red and pink letters on the middle door announce: *Alexandra's Room*. I wait in the doorway until my eyes adjust to the darkness and I can make out the sleeping figure of my granddaughter.

I step into the room and move closer, slowly, until I'm standing at the edge of her bed. Lexi is on her side, curled up, her eyes closed and her right hand cupping her chin in a pose that reminds me of her mother when she was little. A strip of light from the landing falls across her face, illuminating a skin so pallid as to be almost translucent.

She's so still I feel afraid, just the way I did when she was a tiny baby in an incubator and I feared she would stop breathing. I place my hand against her back, against her cotton pyjama top, and I feel her chest move up and down with each breath.

I want to run my fingers through her ginger curls but I stop myself because I don't want to wake her. Her sleep is peaceful.

Lexi's quilt has fallen to the floor. I pick it up and lay it gently over her small body. The fabric is a delicate grey and there are little white stars embroidered around the edges. The same fabric has been used for the curtains and the upholstery of the armchair in the corner of the room.

As I look around, at the drawings on the walls, signed illustrations from *Matilda*, I think about how much time and thought my daughter put into the decoration of her only child's bedroom. Somehow, her careful choice of bedding and curtains and etchings feels like an accusation: Vivien succeeded where I failed. Each phase of Lexi's life has been documented and celebrated, portraits taken, birthdays celebrated. It's as though Vivien was trying to replace everything she missed out on while I was working twelve-hour shifts at the hospital. As though she wanted to show me my failings.

I cannot stop myself; I bend down and kiss Lexi's plump cheek. She still has that innocent, baby smell. I want to keep watch over her always, as though by watching I might keep her from any more suffering.

Chapter 3

The gate clangs shut behind me. When I look back at the house, Ben has already closed the gloss-black front door.

Blackthorn Road is hushed as I begin my walk back to Cambridge Court. I pass a row of ivy-clad houses secured behind high gates and then a new build, still under construction, a board outside promising an indoor cinema and a basement swimming pool. The night is milder than it should be at this time of year and the air is lush with the smell of wet earth.

As I reach the corner, I see a woman walking towards me. She's looking down at the pavement and the hood of her raincoat is drawn up over her head. We draw closer, we exchange a glance. And then we stop.

'Rose!' she says.

'Cleo?' I take a step back, not quite trusting my own eyes. It has been so many years since I saw her last that I wonder if I have conjured her up, my daughter's oldest friend.

Cleo hesitates, then she holds her arms outstretched, before she rushes at me and enfolds me in an embrace. The vigour of her grip convinces me she is real.

'I'm so sorry,' she says. Her voice is muffled, her mouth pressed against my shoulder.

We're standing in front of a house with a low white wall and over Cleo's shoulder, I can see inside, through the window and into a well-lit kitchen. A young woman is standing at the sink, filling a kettle. She carries on with her life as normal, safe and sound in her own home, her children asleep upstairs, no doubt.

Cleo feels me tense up and she lets me go. She tucks her hands back into the pockets of her raincoat. 'I'm so sorry,' she says, again. 'I don't know what to say to you.'

'Don't worry, there's nothing anyone can say.'

Cleo fiddles with her hairline, pulling loose a strand of fine brown hair. She was the same way as a child, always fidgeting.

'I can't believe she's not here any more,' she says. 'I remember being in the Reception classroom and looking at her and thinking that Vivien was the prettiest girl I'd ever seen. She looked like a pixie, with her big eyes and her black hair.'

Her eyes fill with tears. Mine feel so dry.

Cleo's family lived on the ground floor of Cambridge Court and she and Vivien were in the same class at St Leonard's all the way through infant and junior school. Cleo was an intense, intelligent little girl, but I also recall stains on her school uniform, dirt under her fingernails, lice infestations. My daughter was the ballerina princess, her hair combed back in a tight bun and traces of glitter still lingering on her cheekbones.

You should be kind to her, Vivien, I hear myself say. I asked my daughter to take pity on Cleo, but Vivien went further; she genuinely liked her.

I was never sure how I felt about Vivien and Cleo's friendship. Maybe it was the way the two of them would lock Vivien's door when Cleo visited, as though there were secrets they wanted to keep from me. I worried, sometimes, that during the hours spent in Vivien's bedroom, behind closed doors, my daughter might manipulate Cleo, might take advantage of Cleo's adoration. I suspected Vivien would copy Cleo's homework and that several of Vivien's school projects might in fact have been the result of Cleo's best efforts.

'I'm surprised to see you here,' I say. 'I thought you and Vivien lost touch years ago?'

'We did, but I needed to pay my respects.'

'So you're on your way to see Ben?' It's not my intention, but my words come out sounding like an accusation.

Cleo doesn't appear to notice. 'I've thought of you, and of Ben and Alexandra, every single day since she died,' she says.

Although the diffuse orange streetlight is forgiving, something bothers me about Cleo's face. Something's not quite right, though I'm not sure what it is. Perhaps it bothers me that she's wearing rather a lot of make-up for a condolence visit. Her lips are a deep red, her eyebrows drawn in in a dark brown and her eyelashes are thick with mascara.

'I'm sorry, Cleo, I'm tired and I need to get home. It was good to see you.' I take a step away from her.

'Are you still working such long hours?'

'I've cut back. I stood down as manager of the unit.'

'Please,' she says, 'I want you to call me if there's anything you need.'

Cleo has a messenger bag across her chest and she opens it and pulls out a leather card holder. She slips out a business card and hands it to me.

Cleo Baker. Translator.

I tuck it into my coat pocket.

She looks as though she's about to embrace me again, but I draw back, raise my hand in a half-wave and walk on. After a few steps, I stop. I turn back and watch as Cleo walks towards my daughter's house. She presses the buzzer on the side of the gate. Pushes it open. Disappears inside.

Chapter 4

Inside the Intensive Care ward the lights are dimmed and my blue-gloved hands are pushed through the holes in the side of the incubator as I tuck little Kelsey back into her nest. Kelsey was born yesterday and I've been with her since my shift began. A twenty-five weeker, she's ventilated, with a blue tube strapped down across her cheeks and obscuring most of her face. Her head is the size of a peach and her lobster-red body is covered with bubble-wrap. Her eyes are still fused shut and her ears, without cartilage, curl in on themselves.

It's been an eventful shift. Kelsey's heartbeat has been erratic and she's had a suspected brain bleed. There have already been endless X-rays and paediatrician consults. She is a sad case. Not often, but sometimes, I fear we do more harm than good. These babies teeter on the edge of life, scientific miracles – or perhaps experiments – facing futures that may involve suffering and disability. In truth, as I look down at Kelsey, and the needles and tubes that poke at her see-through skin, I wonder if it is cruel to keep her alive.

I'm tired, that's all. Worn out. I don't usually feel this way. Usually, I'm proud of what we do here. My experience over the last decades counts for something, and I believe that after each shift the baby I've been caring for feels better. I carry out many of the procedures myself: I intubated Kelsey and later I inserted the cannula for the antibiotic when her temperature rose, so she didn't have to wait hours, deteriorating, until a consultant became available. I sense the best time for these procedures, I try to wait until the babies are calm and relaxed; it's different from when the doctors do it, then it's an attack, an assault by a stranger that comes out of-the blue.

Here on the ward my thoughts are clear and my head free of pain. Work is my respite. But now, I need a break. Carefully, I withdraw my arms from the holes in the incubator and peel off my gloves.

Outside in the bright corridor the door to Wendy's office, my old office, is closed. No doubt she's in there behind her desk, working her way through a stack of paperwork. I don't regret stepping down as manager. I don't envy my old friend the administrative load that leeches this work of joy and human contact.

I think about going in to talk to Wendy, but I know she will ask why I have withdrawn from her. She will look at me in that way of hers that brings all of my pain right up to the surface and I'm in no mood to break down. So I walk a few steps further and place my hand on the aluminium door handle of the staffroom. But I can't open that one, either. There are too many of Vivien's gifts inside: the ice-dispensing fridge-freezer, the wall-mounted television, the deep sofas, the weekly deliveries of tea, coffee and fruit that somehow continue even after she's gone.

Instead, I make my way down the corridor to the last door on the right, to Special Care, or Graduation Ward, as I always think of it. In here there are no ventilators and no X-ray machines; the lights are on and the curtains are wide open. By the time the babies are moved here, they are bigger and more robust.

Only one cot out of the six is occupied today, by Yusuf, our long-stay resident. Compared to the rest of our babies, Yusuf is a giant. He still has gastro-intestinal problems, and a yellow nasal feeding tube runs down his nose and through into his stomach. I walk over to him, say hello, and check that the tube is sited properly.

His head is elongated, flattened on each side so that his cheeks and forehead bulge. He has been lying on a mattress for more than six months. I stroke his thick black hair as he looks up into my eyes. I can't resist his serious face, so I reach in and lift him out of his cot. His misshapen head rests heavy against my chest as he cuddles into me. Yusuf knows me well.

He seldom has visitors to provide him with the stimulation and human interaction he needs. The nurses know this and we make much more of a fuss of babies like him, the ones whose mothers don't come. The fluffy toy dog in his cot, with the long black ears, is a gift from Wendy.

I take him over to the window and I show him the view. 'Look,' I say, 'see the cars. There's a blue one. And a red one.'

He sucks on his fist as I rock from side to side and pat his back. I drift far away too and I jump when I hear the sound of Andrew Lissauer's voice behind me.

'Rose? Can we talk?'

The parents' suite is adjacent to the Weissman Unit and consists of a double bedroom, a bathroom and a small kitchen area with a dining table. The space is decorated like a mid-range hotel, all neutrals and IKEA furnishings. Parents can stay here overnight, they can 'room in' when they're too anxious to go home and leave their babies on the unit, when they fear the worst as their child teeters between life and death. Or, they can stay when they're transitioning, getting ready to go home and spend their first night in sole charge of their still-fragile baby. In here, they can press the call button and a nurse will be with them in seconds.

'How are you?' Andrew says, as we sit across from each other at the table for two.

It's the first thing people ask me. I dread this question.

'I'm fine,' I say.

Andrew looks sceptical as he adjusts his wire-rimmed

41

glasses, pushing them higher up his nose. He's the consultant neonatologist on our ward, a kind man. We've worked together for twenty years, during which time he married someone else and had three daughters, and his hair turned silver. In a few months' time, he's going to retire.

'How is Alexandra doing?' he says.

Another question I dread.

'She's all right, as far as we can tell, but I don't think she fully understands what's happened. On the surface, everything is normal. Underneath, I really don't know.'

I'm annoyed that the table top is sticky and full of coffee stains. I stand up and move over to the sink, because I need some distance from Andrew and from his compassion. I wet a piece of kitchen roll, but I can't find any detergent. I wipe the table, cleaning it as best I can, glad of something to do that doesn't involve looking at him.

I must talk to Wendy, because the cleaning staff are neglecting this suite, they don't bother to come in here unless someone complains. These rooms are important; they should be treated with respect. This suite is supposed to be our pride and joy, part of our cutting-edge facilities, a complement to our developmental care plan and our holistic approach.

These rooms are Vivien's legacy.

I crumple the piece of kitchen roll and toss it into the small stainless-steel bin, which is of course overflowing.

I sit down again and now I have no choice but to look at Andrew. He is a favourite amongst the parents, and amongst the staff, too. Over the years I've seen other consultants develop a certain detachment from their patients in order to deal with the emotional intensity of their jobs, but not Andrew.

'I think Ben is completely lost without Vivien,' I say. 'They stayed in a hotel for a couple of days, while the police were busy at the house. But now he's taken Lexi back to live there and I think it's a huge mistake.'

As I look into Andrew's gentle brown eyes, I well up. I dig my fingernails hard into the back of my left hand until the tears recede.

'How is the police investigation going?' he says.

'They still aren't sure about the cause of death.'

'I talked to Mrs Murad,' he says. 'She's been trying to reach you. She mentioned she had a difficult consultation with Vivien.'

'I haven't had a chance to talk to her yet.'

'Fertility treatment can be so brutal,' Andrew says. 'And Vivien had such a rough time of it. All those rounds of IVF, then the loss of Lexi's twin. Our treatments take their toll, don't they?'

'And then we send people home,' I say, 'as though nothing ever happened and we hope they'll be able to get on with their lives.'

I infer, from what he's said, that he and Mrs Murad believe Vivien took her own life. As Vivien's doctors, they may have been more intuitive, may have known more about my daughter's state of mind than I did myself.

'Vivien adored you,' I say. 'She was eternally grateful that you saved Lexi's life.'

I reach out and pat his sleeve. I notice how thin his wrists are, how the sharp bones protrude.

'There's something we discussed at the staff meeting,' Andrew says, 'and I hope you'll be pleased.'

He gestures towards the door of the parents' suite and my hand drops from his arm. I don't think he noticed my touch, my fingers resting on the sleeve of his jacket. I pull my hand back into my lap.

'We'd like to put up a plaque outside these rooms,' he says. 'We want to name this *The Vivien Kaye Parents' Suite*.'

He clasps his hands in front of him on the now almost-clean birch-veneer table top. I tuck my hair back behind my ears and pat it down. I clear my throat. Andrew can see I'm too overwhelmed to speak and so he carries on talking.

'I know Vivien wanted to remain an anonymous donor, but we would like to give her the acknowledgement she deserves. We want to honour her memory. And when you and Ben feel ready, we'd like to have an official naming ceremony. What do you think?'

'Thank you.'

Andrew keeps on talking in his gentle voice.

'Many of the staff were here when Alexandra was on

the ward. We all remember the family very fondly.'

He's waiting for some sort of response and I manage to pull myself together.

'This is incredibly moving,' I say.

But I am an imposter. An actress, failing to play the part of Vivien's mother and struggling in the role of Lexi's grandmother. How do I explain to Andrew that the plaque is only going to serve as a painful reminder of my failings, of Vivien's, and of everything else that went wrong, of a catastrophe that began right here, in my haven, my place of work?

Vivien

Eight years ago

Alexandra has been home from the hospital for seven days. She's in her Moses basket, which is balanced on the sofa in the living room. She lies on her back with her little arms flung up above her head and her hands in fists. Every now and again she makes little sucking noises with her mouth. My mother has swaddled her in a cotton blanket, the one covered in giraffes; she's left us alone together while she goes to stock up on baby formula.

I lean in closer. Alexandra smells sour, of curdled milk. There are patches of flaky, dry skin between her eyes and on her cheeks, from some sort of rash she always seems to have. I ease off the white cotton cap covering her head. Her hair, the little there is of it, is a strawberry-blonde fuzz. Her colouring is nothing like mine, or Ben's.

She was in the Weissman Unit for three months, and somehow I still feel as though she belongs to the nurses, instead of to me. I feel as though I need their permission to touch her, as though I need to check with them that I'm handling her the right way, that I'm not doing any harm.

I watch my sleeping daughter and I remind myself how much easier my life will be from now on. No more injections, no more hormones, no more painful and humiliating procedures. No more scrutiny of my diet, or questioning looks from doctors. No more pumping myself full of food and struggling with that too-full, too-rich, sick feeling. My duty done.

I try to feel something. Love, fondness, anything. I try to tell myself she is *mine*. I don't understand the blankness inside me. I know this is not the way a mother is supposed to feel. But then I don't feel like a mother, I feel like a detached observer.

On impulse, I reach into the Moses basket and I loosen the blanket and lift her out. I hold her close. She tenses, drawing up her legs and screwing her eyes tighter shut.

I lay her back down on the sofa, not too close to the edge. Her eyes flicker open, then close again. She is making unhappy, niggling noises.

I open the poppers of her Babygro and I undo her nappy; perhaps it's too tight. I examine every inch of her, convinced I'm going to find something wrong, some sign of my failure.

Her face contorts and she begins to scream. I manage to dress her again but it isn't easy, I have to force her stiff arms and legs back into the Babygro. Her crying grows shrill; she's panicking, like an animal stuck in a trap. I put her back in the basket and tuck the blanket around her, but she won't stop.

I don't know how to swaddle her, I can't do it the way Rose can.

Her crying makes me anxious. Useless. Angry.

I lift her up again and pace up and down the living room, bouncing her harder than I should. She yells her head off, despite all the bouncing, and her crying drowns out my thoughts. I don't know what to do. Her screams are so loud I think I had better put her down again, because I feel, just for a second, as though I'd like to throw her against the plate-glass window.

Back in her basket, her face has turned puce. Now some of her screams are silent, as though she's choking.

As I listen to the sound of her unhappiness, I search inside my own heart but I find only a cold, empty space. I feel nothing, only a wish for her to be quiet. I cannot comfort her. She must hate me, I think.

I have to get away from her or I don't know what I might do.

I leave her alone in the living room, just for a few minutes, while I go down to the kitchen to make up a bottle. Perhaps she's hungry, again. Rose says I should use the sling, that I should carry Alexandra with me, close to my chest, but I don't like that contraption and I can't master all of the straps. Alexandra will be all right on her own until I get back. Crying never killed anyone.

The relief hits me the minute I leave the room and close the door behind me, the minute I put some distance between me and the small, miserable baby on the sofa.

Chapter 5

I have asked Isaac to have dinner with me. I contacted him out of the blue, having obtained his mobile number from Ben's secretary, and he was gracious enough to accept my invitation without sounding surprised and without asking questions. There are some advantages, I suppose, to being a bereaved parent. Perhaps those who have not lost so much feel they owe you a debt. At least, that's what I'm hoping.

We've arranged to meet at the small Italian place at the top of the hill, near the Underground in Hampstead. The night is a murky dark and headlights bounce off the wet tarmac. As I'm crossing the road, I catch a glimpse of Isaac's close-shaven head in the glow of the street-light, but his craggy face is mostly in shadow. He waits for me under a large umbrella and his mackintosh is slick with rain. We greet each other with an awkward hello. He opens the door to let me through first.

The restaurant is warm and smells of garlic and wine.

Red-checked cloths cover the tables. We're seated in the corner, and I'm relieved the place is not too full or too noisy.

Isaac is on the inside. Ben relies on him, and he spends time with Lexi. I need his help. And so I try to muster whatever remnants of charm I once possessed in order to make him my ally. I force myself to make small talk.

'How do you find it,' Isaac asks me, 'working twelve-hour shifts, changing your sleep patterns from night to day?'

'I barely notice it any more. You get used to it. And now it means I have a couple of days a week free. What I'd really like is to be able to help Ben, with Lexi . . .' I look up but Isaac doesn't comment, doesn't react one way or another. 'But Ben doesn't seem too keen on the idea,' I say.

Isaac lifts his glass and I do the same. Since Vivien died, I feel I'm playing some sort of imitation game: I'm an empty shell, impersonating the mannerisms of the live people around me. So we sip Peroni from frosted glasses. The beer is cold and delicious.

'Sometimes it can be isolating,' I say, 'to be awake while everyone else is asleep. It's as though I exist in a different world. And it's not very good for a social life. Most of us end up becoming friends with colleagues on the ward, so it gets quite insular. But I'm lucky, I work with amazing people.'

'I know what you mean,' he says. 'I used to work as a night editor on a news service. I would get to the office at six in the evening and work until four the next morning.'

He's taken me by surprise. 'So how did you end up working as a driver for Ben?'

'Actually, it wasn't Ben who hired me. It was Vivien. I used to deliver her groceries,' he says with a smile.

'You've lost me completely,' I say.

'She didn't tell you?' Isaac is looking at me in that serious, considered way of his.

'No, she didn't tell me,' I say. 'But then there were lots of things we didn't discuss. You've probably worked out that we weren't particularly close.'

I drink my beer. My thoughts swirl and loosen in a not unpleasant way, and the anxiety, the sense of danger that is my permanent companion, settles a fraction.

'So how did you go from journalism to delivering my daughter's groceries?' I say.

'It's a long story.'

'I'd like to hear it.'

It's true, I do want to hear his story. I would like nothing better than to think of something other than myself and my granddaughter, even for a few minutes. Maybe this is selfish, to wish for relief from my pain.

The waiter is passing, and I signal to him. When he comes over I order us another two beers.

'I advanced in the old world of journalism when there was no online content,' Isaac says. 'There was the wonderful newspaper model which provided jobs and profit. At heart I'm a storyteller, and that was an environment where all I had to do was write a great story. Later, I was a good editor. I didn't have to worry about being a commercial operator, the money took care of itself. People paid to advertise in newspapers, and the newspaper owner paid us to work there. Then the internet changed everything. Suddenly content was everywhere, put together by journalists, by non-journalists, by amateurs, by anyone who had something to say. The commercial model that had kept journalists employed fell apart.'

'You mean you lost your job?'

'Not exactly. I worked in newsrooms around the world for thirty-odd years, I moved around a lot as a foreign correspondent. But in the last fifteen years, I ended up settling down in London – partner, children, mortgage – and almost by mistake, I started climbing the corporate ladder. I ended up in a management job I hated and by the time I was fifty I was miserable as all hell. Then I was offered a way out – I was head-hunted for a start-up, an internet content provider. And I thought all I had to do was be a great storyteller again to get a chunk of that new money. But I was wrong. Because there is no clear commercial model for the internet, and everyone is trying something new every day.'

He pauses, rubbing the back of his neck with his left hand. I notice he lifts his glass with his left hand, too.

'You have to be everything,' he says. 'You have to be a technologist, a content person, a marketer, and you have to be financially savvy just to stay afloat. And most journalists are not all of those things. There's this image I have in my mind . . .'

He becomes animated and begins to speak with his hands, drawing pictures in the air in front of him. 'Picture a big, beautiful, placid dam,' he says.

'Okay.' I do.

'The water is still. There's barely a ripple, almost nothing moves – that's old journalism. Then suddenly, out of nowhere, a huge hole is punched in the side of the dam. The water is gushing out; it's spreading everywhere, going in different directions. That's the image I get when I imagine the effect the internet had on the old media. Everything was disrupted. It went from a peaceful, settled situation where there was certainty, to chaos. I don't know what comes next. No one knows where the water will eventually come to rest.'

'So your internet start-up failed?'

'Spectacularly.' He grins, but there's regret too. 'We needed better technology, we needed to be commercial people and marketers and we were none of those things. I won't bore you with the details, but to cut a long story short, it was a disaster. I took my pension as a lump sum and invested it in the start-up, which sadly – or predictably, depending how you look at it – folded soon after I joined. So I found myself with no skills of any use in the world outside of a newsroom.'

'Couldn't you go back to your old job?'

'My old world has disappeared. A fifty-something

man who doesn't have the skills for the internet world is not exactly employable. There are younger, hungrier people who have a multitude of skills, and they tend to come cheaper. I'd held all these positions, I was used to being important – and I was stunned to find myself over the hill and unemployable. My wife, understandably, thought I'd been an idiot to walk out on a job that provided absolute security.'

'So what happened?'

'We were middle-aged and in a position where with only Helena's income, we couldn't quite make the mortgage payments. I wasn't exactly fun to be around and she couldn't stand me moping around the house all day. I really needed a job and Waitrose offered me one. Driving for them got me out of the house. It paid. Blackthorn Road was on my route. And your daughter was a real charmer.'

He lifts his beer, and we toast to Vivien's memory. They must have been fond of each other and that is somehow a comfort.

'So how exactly did Vivien come to hire you?'

He smiles at me and I find him charming when he smiles.

'She'd always book the delivery slot between nine and ten at night, and she'd most often be home alone. I'd end up carrying her groceries right the way down to the basement for her, unpacking them too and helping her put them away. Even though I was always late for my next drop-off. After a couple of visits I knew where everything was.'

Isaac laughs, as do I, at the thought of Vivien's sense of entitlement.

'She always was a night owl,' I say. 'She loved to stay up until the early hours. After Lexi was born, she used to say she felt her day only began when her daughter went to sleep.'

'I think Vivien wanted a bit more freedom,' Isaac says. 'She was looking for someone she could trust to drive Alexandra to and from school, and take her to her tutors or wherever it was she needed to be. She'd been offered an interior design project but she couldn't commit to it because Ben could never guarantee he'd be around to help with Alexandra. She didn't want to hire a nanny. So a few months after we met, she offered me a position as their driver.'

He pauses and looks at me. 'Vivien was very kind to me,' he says. 'She threw me a lifeline.'

'I think she knew how to spot a good man.' I help myself to a piece of bread, dizzy, from beer and from nerves.

The waiter delivers our plates, piled high with pasta in seafood sauce and we turn our attention to negotiating our spaghetti. I'm hungry and I don't have my daughter's self-control, but I'm eating more slowly than usual, like a teenager on a first date. I'm relieved my blouse is patterned with red flowers, so the flecks of tomato sauce won't show. Isaac too has chosen a sensible black shirt.

'Do you mind if I ask about Vivien's father?' he says.

I put down my fork. After the beer, my words flow more freely than they should. It's my turn to confess my mistakes.

'Her father was a registrar on the neonatal ward where I was training. He was married when I fell pregnant, and he was Malaysian, from a very conservative family. He didn't want anything more to do with me and Vivien never had any contact with him. That's really all I want to say.'

Isaac nods, paying me close attention. *At heart I'm a storyteller*, he said. And there is a story in the premature death of a wealthy St John's Wood socialite. I wonder, for a moment, if it's me he's interested in or my daughter's story. Perhaps I am being mined for information. I promised myself, the day Vivien died, not to answer any questions.

Then I dismiss these thoughts as part of the paranoia that goes hand-in-hand with my grief. Ben trusts Isaac. Vivien trusted him. I make up my mind to trust him too.

'I'm sorry,' he says, picking up on my discomfort. 'I didn't mean to pry. I feel like I was talking about myself too much. I'm interested in you.'

I give him a taut smile. 'I was attractive too, once,' I say. 'And young and very stupid.'

'You're still attractive.'

He pauses. We both concentrate on our pasta.

'Was there anyone else,' he says, 'after Vivien's father?'

'No one important. Just me and my daughter.' I don't like the sour edge that taints my voice.

I glance over at Isaac's hand. He's not wearing a wedding ring though he mentioned his wife.

'How about you?' I say.

'Separated. Helena has gone down to Devon to stay with my stepdaughter. She's just had a baby.'

'How did you two meet?'

'Like you, most of my social life happens through work. I was bureau chief for Reuters in Johannesburg and she was a foreign correspondent.'

'You mentioned your stepdaughters the other night at the house?' I say.

He nods. 'Yes, the twins. Abigail and Chloe. When Helena and I got together, they were eighteen months old.'

I look down at my empty plate and I feel ashamed. I still have an appetite – for food, for men – while my daughter lies cold in the mortuary. I feel a distinct pulse of pain on the right side of my head and I reach up and press hard on my temple. I push my plate to one side. As I do, I'm sure Isaac catches sight of the bruises to the back of my hand, but he's tactful enough not to ask about them.

I massage the site of the pain and I drink some water. When I look at Isaac, I notice the tiniest fleck of tomato sauce just to the right of his mouth. I reach out and wipe it away with the tip of my serviette. My thumb brushes his lips. Isaac looks surprised, he wasn't expecting me to be so bold.

We've finished the pasta, the bread and the beer, and Isaac motions to the waiter, who has been ignoring us in favour of a table of eight on the opposite side of the restaurant. When he comes over, somewhat begrudgingly, we ask him to clear the plates and order two coffees. I ask for more water.

The dinner is almost at its end. It's time. I cannot leave before asking for his help.

'Isaac,' I say, 'I invited you to have dinner with me tonight because I have something to ask of you. A favour. I thought, given the fact that you're a father, you'd understand.'

He nods. I try to tell if he is disappointed I have an ulterior motive, but I can't read his expression. I am reluctant to have to plead for a stranger's help.

'I know Ben relies on you to help him with Lexi,' I say. 'He also mentioned you're overseeing security at the house. So he obviously trusts you. I, on the other hand, have a more distant relationship with my son-in-law. Things were complicated between Vivien and me, I don't know if she ever said anything?'

He shakes his head.

'Ben resents the fact that I wasn't around more and I didn't give Vivien more support. I wasn't your traditional granny; I've always been very committed to my career. So understandably, I suppose, Ben is rather cautious about letting me spend time with my granddaughter. And I think maybe he's also directing some of his anger about Vivien's death my way. So, my point is, I was wondering if you might put in a good word for me.'

'What exactly is it you'd like me to say?'

'I want to spend time with Lexi. I thought I could pick her up from school a couple of afternoons a week, maybe walk her back to my flat, give her an early dinner and then bring her home. It would give us a chance to bond and it would give Ben a break.'

'Ben's been picking her up himself most days,' Isaac says.

'I know, I'm sure he has it all sorted for now. But Ben has always been ambitious, and there will come a point where he needs to focus his attention on his business again. You said yourself he wasn't home before ten o'clock most nights, that's when you and Vivien started talking. Vivien once mentioned it wasn't unusual for him to leave the house before six in the morning. I imagine in the long run his investment firm isn't going to thrive if he's only half present.'

The waiter places our coffees down and hands the bill to Isaac. I put my card down next to his. So far Isaac hasn't commented on what I've said. I wait, impatient, as we split the bill and each of us enters our codes into the pin machine. Finally, the waiter leaves us alone again.

'Ben is going to have to find a new equilibrium without Vivien there to care for his daughter,' I say. 'And I think it's better for Lexi to be looked after by her grandmother, rather than a nanny. I've given up my job as manager of the ward. I don't know how else I can prove to Ben that I'm serious. What I'm asking of you is to talk to him. Put in a good word. Ask him to give me a chance.'

'I'll see what I can do,' he says.

'Thank you.'

I'm not entirely sure what Isaac thinks of me. He seems a little distant now I've asked him for a favour; now the conversation has turned to Ben and Lexi. But I could be misreading him. The distance I perceive may exist only in my own guilt-ridden imagination.

Our coffee cups are empty. The party of eight has departed and we are the only people left in the restaurant. The waiter lounges, bored and yawning, against the till. My throat is dry again and my head throbs, as if to remind me who I am. My daughter didn't get to live to her fortieth birthday, and tonight, sitting at this table with Isaac, I've felt happy to be alive. I'm a monster. It's time to leave but I don't want to go home alone.

My living room faces onto the main road and so the windows are always shut. Even so, the drone of traffic is ever present and the air is stale. The fumes find a way to creep inside. An electric heater sits in the cavity where there was once a fireplace, and the two bars glow a fierce orange. I forgot to switch it off before I left for dinner.

On the mantelpiece, above the heater, there is a photograph of Ben and Vivien on their wedding day. Their kiss is captured in black and white. Vivien is sylph-like in satin, her dark hair pulled back, her face turned up to her husband's. A bouquet of white roses tied with a satin ribbon dangles from her right hand.

Next to their wedding photograph is Lexi's latest school portrait. She is unsmiling, a pale-skinned, ginger-haired child wearing a green blazer. There are several more photographs of my granddaughter scattered around the room, and in these a chubby baby becomes a sturdy toddler and then a pensive schoolgirl.

I walk down the passage, trailing my hand along the Artexed walls that threaten to close in on me as I anticipate the long loneliness of the night ahead.

I open the door to Vivien's room. Here, the frosted window faces onto a narrow driveway, behind which is a row of red-brick garages. The light never reaches this room, no matter what the season or time of day. Vivien would complain about the smell, and the damp so persistent that when she put her hand flat against a certain spot on her bedroom wall her palm came away wet.

Her white-painted bedstead still takes pride of place in the centre of the room. The bed linen with lace edging is the same as it was when she slept here last. On the bedside table, her beloved pink-furred Alice band is draped over the small lamp.

I see myself, on a cold, dark school morning, shaking her awake and turning on the light. I set a cup of tea down on the bedside table, next to the Alice band. I think about all those mornings when I hurried her into her school uniform, and shunted her off to a childminder, hours before school even opened, so I could be at the hospital in time for handover. I don't want to think about all the afternoons I wasn't there to fetch her from school, how I would pick her up, exhausted, from the childminder's at night.

In the darkness, I see the shape of my sleeping child. She lies on her side, one hand cupping her chin. Strands of black hair fall across her face.

Chapter 6

At eleven o'clock the next morning, Intensive Care is quiet. There are only twelve babies with us on the unit, and at full capacity we can take up to eighteen. Radhika is looking after the set of newborn twins, while I'm caring for David, our twenty-eight weeker. David's father is beside the incubator, his finger inside one of his son's tiny fists. He has that shell-shocked look all the parents have when they first come in here. His wife is still on the labour ward downstairs, she hasn't made it up yet.

'Rose?' Wendy hovers at the door. She beckons to me and her sombre expression tells me she is not the bearer of good news.

For the sake of Jonas's father, I smile as I secure my notes in place next to the incubator. I walk across the ward with slow, calm steps.

'There's a DS Cole here to see you,' Wendy says. She keeps her voice down.

I'm thrown for a moment as one of my worlds collides with the other.

'I'll take over here,' Wendy says. 'There's no rush.'

'Thank you.'

She pats my shoulder as I walk past her.

'Also,' she calls after me, 'Mrs Murad's left another message for you.'

DS Cole is waiting outside the front door of the unit, in the area where visitors hang their coats, pull blue plastic coverings over their shoes and disinfect their hands.

She wears a long herringbone coat over a tailored white shirt, and I notice how the tweed tapers a little at the waist, so that somehow the masculine fabric emphasizes her femininity. Her dark roots show – deliberately, I think – under her peroxided fringe.

'I'm so sorry to bother you at work, Rose,' she says. 'I have a few more questions you might be able to help me with.'

'Of course.' I try not to look annoyed at the intrusion. She's only doing her job.

I grab my coat, the one Vivien gave to me for my fiftieth birthday, the one I have barely taken off in recent weeks, and pull it over my scrubs. I change into a different pair of trainers. I suggest we go down to the ground floor to get a coffee and I lead the way to the lift, then through the warren of bridges and passages that connect the various buildings. We don't make small talk.

The café is near the front exit and a continuous flow of people passes in and out of the glass doors. It's draughty and we huddle inside our coats. DS Cole leans down and searches inside her satchel, a bag made of green canvas. She takes out a notebook, which she opens on a fresh page. Then she lays a ballpoint pen down along the centre fold. She leans forward, looking out at me from under her fringe.

'I know you mentioned in our last interview that your relationship with your daughter wasn't a very close one,' she says, 'but I wondered whether you knew that Vivien was taking antidepressants?'

'I wasn't aware of what, if any, medication she was taking.'

Yet again, I feel as though I've been judged and found wanting.

'I wondered if you knew whether your daughter was unhappy about anything in particular?'

'I don't think depression is about being unhappy,' I say. 'Depression is an illness.'

'But something might have triggered her illness.'

I don't say anything at all; I wait for her to go on.

'Mr Kaye has told us that Vivien started taking antidepressants around three months ago,' she says. 'Would you have any thoughts about why she began taking antidepressants at this particular time?'

'I really don't know. She didn't share those kinds of things with me. Vivien was a very private person, so I doubt she would have wanted people to know she was unhappy.'

'Not even her own mother?'

She has sharp eyes, DS Cole. And she's no fool. I tell myself she doesn't mean it as an accusation.

'If I had to guess,' I say, 'I'd say that the depression might have been linked to her difficulty conceiving a second baby. She'd been having fertility treatment for several years. But as I say, that's really just a guess. Vivien didn't discuss the details of her treatment with me.'

A cleaner wearing bright purple gloves mops the floor around us. I watch him, hypnotized by the rhythm of the mop, moving smoothly, back and forth, over the damp floor, sweeping away the dirt and the debris.

'In fact,' I say, 'my impression was always that it was Ben who really wanted a second child, and that Vivien was more anxious about letting him down than about not being able to fall pregnant.'

'Did Vivien ever talk about her marriage?' DS Cole says.

The conversation seems to have made an about-turn. I pause as I try to catch up with where this interview is headed.

'For example,' she goes on, 'would Vivien have told you if she and Ben were having difficulties? Arguing?'

'She didn't talk about her marriage,' I say. 'I don't think there was much to say, because I assumed it was all going well. Ben and Vivien were always close, a tight unit. And no, Vivien didn't tell me about any arguments.'

The cleaner is now emptying see-through dustbin bags into a large black bin on wheels.

'As I said, Vivien was a private person. She was generally very reserved, and I think people who didn't know her well might sometimes have mistaken her reticence for rudeness. She could seem stand-offish. Is any of this relevant?'

I have no idea what DS Cole is looking for. My mouth is dry again and I take a sip from my bottle of water. DS Cole waits in silence, as if to encourage me to keep talking. But she doesn't write anything down.

'Ben and Vivien were devoted to each other,' I say. 'They'd been married for ten years and from what I could see, their marriage was a strong one. One of those that would have lasted.'

For the first time, DS Cole looks uncomfortable. She rubs the cropped hair at the back of her neck.

'In this type of investigation,' she says, 'a certain amount of sensitive information tends to come to light, regardless of whether or not it's relevant to our inquiry.'

'I see.' I tap my fingertips against the Formica table top and look across at the kiosk, where a bored teenager with dyed-black hair and eyebrow piercings is texting on her mobile phone.

DS Cole changes her position in the chair, pressing her hands down on the seat on either side of her. 'A witness has come forward to say they saw Vivien and Ben having an argument,' she says. 'This would have been on the day before Vivien died, while she and Ben were visiting a jewellery shop. We also have information that Ben didn't spend the night at home. He checked into a hotel overnight.'

'I don't know what to say. I'm . . . I'm shocked.'

'You didn't know?' DS Cole says.

'No. Are you sure about all of this?'

She nods.

'I'm not surprised to hear they argued, but I find it hard to believe that Ben would walk out on Vivien and Lexi. That would be completely unlike him.'

My daughter spent her last night on earth alone.

'But if your daughter was a private person, then there are things she may not have shared with you?'

'Yes. But then I know Ben, and I've seen the way he is with his wife and daughter. He was devoted to them. They were his life. Ben puts his family before everything.'

I can't tell whether DS Cole is convinced by what I've said. But it is the whole truth.

'Are you aware of anything that was a source of conflict between them? Something so serious that Ben *would* walk out?'

'No,' I say. 'I'm sorry. I really have no idea.'

I think of Isaac. He probably knows more than I do about the state of their marriage. DS Cole is staring at me, as though she's hoping I might remember something.

'Did Vivien by any chance tell you about plans for an important dinner at her home on the night before she died?'

'No,' I say. 'Look, DS Cole, please, can you tell me

what this is all about? Quite frankly, you appear to know more than I do about the state of my daughter's marriage.'

She takes pity on me, and answers my question, at least in part. 'We understand,' she says, 'that there was supposed to be a catered dinner for thirty people at your daughter's home the night before she died. The dinner was related to a significant business transaction, a merger between Ben's company and another investment firm. But Ben cancelled at short notice, telling his clients that he had to leave the country on business. He has subsequently told us that he and Vivien had argued and she'd then refused to host the dinner. That was the real reason for the cancellation. He says that after they argued, he left your daughter at the jeweller's, had a few drinks at a pub and checked into a hotel near his office. He stayed there overnight. To cool down.'

'So Ben told you about the argument himself?'

'Yes. But only after a colleague came forward to tell us about the cancelled dinner plans and the fact that Ben had said he was out of the country when he wasn't.'

'I see. Did Ben say why they'd argued?'

'Apparently there was a disagreement over a piece of jewellery – an expensive piece your daughter wanted. Ben said he's been having a tougher time than usual with his cash flow, because he's invested most of his capital into his investment firm. Does that sound like something your daughter would do – push him to buy her something expensive?'

'I imagine my daughter could have played her part in this argument,' I say, 'in winding Ben up. Ben is much more easy-going than Vivien ever was.'

'Can you explain what you mean?'

'Vivien could be controlling. She liked everything to be just so – the way she looked, what she wore, what she ate. It could get . . .' I pause as I search for the right word. 'Well, it could get exhausting. Frustrating. She grew up in a council flat, with a mother who worked twelve-hour shifts and who was permanently anxious about money. That kind of life leaves its mark.'

'The thing is,' DS Cole says, 'the owner of the jewellery shop doesn't remember it the way Ben does. He remembers Ben encouraging Vivien to pick out any piece she wanted, as though money was no object.'

'Memory is a strange thing,' I say.

DS Cole picks up her pen. I think she might be going to write something down, at last, but all she does is draw a series of short black lines as she runs her pen back and forth in the corner of the page.

'May I ask why this argument between Vivien and Ben is of any significance?'

'It may not be,' she says, 'but your daughter's death is still unexplained. And it seems the earrings that Ben and Vivien eventually settled on buying are missing from the house.'

'I see.'

'So your daughter didn't contact you at all on that Thursday, perhaps later on in the evening, after the argument?'

I shake my head. 'No, she didn't.'

DS Cole closes her notebook, the pen still inside, making a bulge down the middle, and shoves it back into her large bag.

'Thank you for taking the time to talk to me,' she says. 'I apologize again for disturbing you at work.'

We stand and shake hands. I'm aware of how cold and dry my skin must feel. There is a strange tension between us.

I watch her walk away, waiting until she's disappeared through the wide glass doors of the main entrance.

Chapter 7

I see Vivien, as a newborn. Her skull is so perfectly formed, her fontanelle still soft and vulnerable. Her eyes are closed, her lashes long and black, her mouth a rosebud—

'Rose?'

A woman's voice, far away, disturbs my reverie.

'Rose?' The voice is louder, closer.

I look down and I see I'm holding a bottle of breast milk in my hand. I'm standing in front of a small fridge. I don't know what I'm supposed to do.

'Are you all right?'

Amanda, a young nurse from New Zealand, is standing beside me. She's one of the nurses I most enjoy working with. When I was managing the ward and she was on duty, I could relax. I didn't have to watch her, or stay alert for errors, the way I did with some of the others. Amanda is kind. There is a link, I believe: those nurses who are careless with the babies, who handle them a little roughly or laugh too loud over their cots, those are the ones that make careless mistakes. Amanda is not one of those.

'I drifted off,' I say. 'I don't know how long I've been standing here.'

This has never happened to me on the ward. Up until now, I've been in control here at work. Amanda is looking at the bottle in my hand. I can see she's worried.

'Do you need help with something?' I say.

The staff still come to me for advice, they're used to me being in charge. I've been here such a long time. Forever.

'Aren't you looking after the Jones baby today?' Amanda says.

I nod. She points at the milk bottle. 'I think you've grabbed the wrong bottle there.'

I look down. The handwriting on the bottle is blurred. I hold it further away from my face until I can make out the label, which says *James*. The two bottles of milk must have been side by side, and distracted by DS Cole's questions, I've picked up the wrong one.

'Let me help you out there,' Amanda says. She takes the bottle from me and places it back inside the fridge. She finds the one I need and hands it to me.

'Thank you.'

She's saved me. If I'd given the wrong milk to a baby and my mistake had been discovered, either by me or by the parents, there would have been drama. And panic and HIV testing and a vulnerable baby at risk. There would have been a complaint.

'I'm going home,' I say. 'Can you ask Wendy to get cover for me?'

'Of course. No worries. Go home and rest.'

Amanda is blonde and full of curves; it's like looking at the opposite of my daughter. I place the bottle of milk back in her competent hands and leave the room.

As I make my way down the corridor, I feel myself dipping and sinking, my head slipping underwater, as though there are waves beneath my shoes instead of blue linoleum. The chaos and the confusion and the breaking apart have found me here. I suppose it was only a matter of time.

Forty minutes later I step out of the side entrance to the hospital and into the wet and miserable afternoon. Isaac is waiting for me.

'Thank you for coming to get me,' I say.

'Is everything all right?'

'I'm not sure.'

My cashmere coat is wrapped tight around me but it cannot ward off the cold. The paving stones are slippery after the rain and I stumble slightly. Isaac reaches out, takes hold of my arm and steadies me for a brief moment. I look around, as though DS Cole might be lurking somewhere, following me, camouflaged between the grey skies and the grey pavement.

The car is parked a street away. I'm worn out, as though fatigue has burrowed right down inside my bones, and I'm grateful Isaac is beside me. I couldn't bear the bus, not today, couldn't bear to sit amongst all those poor and exhausted people. Stop. Start. Stop. An interminable journey ending at an empty flat. I am one of them. Poor. Exhausted. Alone.

When we reach Vivien's car, Isaac opens the passenger door for me and waits while I climb in. The car is spotless. I wonder if he has removed all traces of Vivien, or if there are still remnants, bits of her life secreted in the crevices between the seats, down the sides of the doors, tucked away inside the glove compartment.

As I fasten my seatbelt, I'm sure I catch her scent, the scent of flowers, though I'm not sure if this is real or in my imagination.

Isaac gets in, closes the door with a soft whump, and starts the engine. This car purrs. Cocooned in the plush interior with Isaac, I feel a little better. I begin to revive.

'DS Cole came to see me today,' I say. 'She turned up at the hospital, out of the blue.'

Isaac is checking his side mirror, pulling out into the traffic.

'She asked about an argument between Ben and Vivien, the day before Vivien died. She told me that Ben didn't spend the night at home.'

I turn in my seat, so my body is angled towards his. But Isaac looks straight ahead, and he gives nothing away. He stays silent, his profile inscrutable.

'Isaac, did you know Ben walked out on her the night before she died?'

'Yes,' he says. 'I knew. But it wasn't my place to pry, and I didn't ask questions.'

We're making slow progress, edging our way onto the flyover.

'Ben called me and told me where he was staying,' Isaac says. 'He asked me to go past the house, to check everything was all right. Vivien had really shafted him by calling off the dinner; those people were critical investors. He needed some time on his own, but he was planning to go home the next day.'

'Was everything all right, when you went past the house?'

'As far as I could tell. When Vivien came to the front door she was calmer than I expected, she didn't seem that upset.' Finally, he glances over at me. 'She didn't invite me in. She asked me not to press the buzzer again because she didn't want the noise to wake Alexandra. She said she'd just managed to get her to bed. In hindsight, I wish I'd stayed for a while. Or persuaded Ben to go home.'

'In hindsight we'd all do things differently,' I say. 'I didn't mean to accuse you of anything.'

'I have no idea what the argument was about,' he says. 'I'd dropped Vivien off at the jeweller's earlier that day and they seemed happy to see each other. They were holding hands.'

'Did he leave her alone like that often?'

'I don't know. I doubt it. That was the only time he's ever asked me to drive past to check on the house at night.'

He looks sideways at me again and his eyes linger on my face a moment before turning back to the road. His left hand rests on the handbrake, inches from my thigh. His fingernails are neatly trimmed and clean.

'They were married a long time, Rose. All married couples argue. And if it's any consolation, there was more affection between them than most other couples I've seen.'

'That's exactly what I told DS Cole.'

The smell of flowers has faded, now all I'm aware of is the subtle, masculine scent of Isaac's aftershave.

'Did you know Ben's ex-girlfriend has been visiting him? I bumped into her the other night outside the house. Her name is Cleo Baker.'

Isaac nods. 'I gathered.'

'Had you seen him with her, before Vivien died?'

'No.'

I stare at Isaac's profile. He doesn't show much of a reaction to what I've said. His calm demeanour, his inscrutability, which up until now I've found a comfort, is beginning to irritate me. I get the impression Isaac's first priority is his loyalty to Ben, and that he'd rather protect Ben than tell me the truth.

'I was wondering if Cleo might have been the cause of their argument.'

'Rose, I really have no idea. I wouldn't think so, but I really don't know.'

I keep my eyes straight ahead of me, on the road, on

the back of the black cab in front of us as we crawl down Wellington Road.

'Do you think the police are allowed to just turn up like DS Cole did this morning,' I say, 'whenever and wherever they like?'

'I suppose they are,' Isaac says.

'I don't want to say anything stupid. I don't want to give them any sort of ammunition if they've decided to dig into Vivien and Ben's relationship.'

'Ben doesn't need you to protect him,' Isaac says. His eyes are back on the road, both hands on the wheel. 'We were out in Surrey together that morning, on a site survey. He's not a focus of the investigation.'

'I know,' I say. 'But whenever I'm with DS Cole, I feel guilty. As though she's accusing me of something, even though she doesn't articulate it.'

'Everyone feels that way when they're being interviewed by a police officer. I had quite a grilling myself since I was the one who found her.'

Isaac clears his throat and then he falls silent. He looks across at me, only briefly. I sense he wants to say more. He is waiting for me to ask, to give him permission to continue. But I am not ready to know.

I turn to look out of my tinted window. London is so clogged up with traffic. I worry about Lexi growing up here; no fresh air, no respite.

'I didn't tell you the whole story at dinner the other night,' I say. 'When I said I brought up my daughter alone, perhaps I gave you the wrong impression, as though I was some kind of saintly, self-sacrificing single mother. I wasn't. That's part of my guilt.'

I hear myself sigh. I have such a strong urge to confess, for someone else to know my burden.

'I fell pregnant with Vivien by mistake. I was in the final year of my basic nursing training and the timing could not have been worse. I'd been offered a place on a specialist training course and I was desperate to take it up. The training would mean I could carry out many of the same procedures as a neonatal paediatrician does – inserting cannulas, intubating the babies, that sort of thing. But the course was in Southampton and it would have been impossible with a baby to look after. My mother said she would support me. I think she was quite excited, even, about having a baby in her house. My father died of a heart attack when he was in his thirties, and she was lonely. So I ended up sending Vivien to live with my mother when she was three months old, and I went to Southampton as planned. Vivien stayed with my mum until she was four. She was more of a mother than I was.'

It's a relief to say this out loud.

'I paid a price for those lost years. We both did. Vivien came back to live with me when she was starting school but even then she spent more time at the childminder's than she did with me. I was lucky because Jane – the childminder – was an amazing woman. I felt she was doing a better job than I was anyway, and she was happy to have Vivien to stay overnight if I was working a night shift. In the end, I didn't even have Vivien with me for that long. She was really gifted at ballet, and when she was sixteen, she asked if I'd send her to ballet school, as a boarder. And once again I was relieved. It wasn't easy running a neonatal unit and dealing with a teenage daughter.'

I roll down my window, I want to breathe in some fresh, cold air. Instead I taste the bitterness of this polluted city. Isaac is concentrating on the oncoming traffic as he pulls into the lay-by outside Cambridge Court. It's almost dark.

I close the window and look at my bruised hand as it rests on soft pink cashmere. Isaac turns off the engine, and we sit for a few moments without speaking. Then he reaches over and places his hand over mine.

'I was not a good mother,' I say. 'I was just going through the motions, and I never found it particularly rewarding. I had to bring up my daughter alone, in a damp-infested council flat. I gave up any social life I might have had. But more than that – I love my job and I always found being on the ward much more enjoyable than being at home. I often thought it would have been better for me not to have gone through with the pregnancy. And now that she's died, it feels like my fault. I feel so guilty. As though I'm responsible because I wished her away.'

Isaac squeezes my hand. He doesn't try to make me feel better, or to deny this horrible, irreversible truth.

'There's only one way I can redeem myself,' I say. 'And that's to watch over Lexi.'

I feel he understands me. His hand is warm over mine, his eyes are kind and wise. Or perhaps I'm imagining what I want to see; conjuring up the kind of friend I need.

I unlock the front door of Cambridge Court and Isaac follows me into the lobby and waits by my side for the lift to arrive. Once inside, under the bright light, we stand with our backs against the mirror, staring straight ahead.

I stop at the threshold of my flat, holding my keys. Isaac is next to me, his hands tucked into the pockets of his long coat. I wonder if he notices the smell that bothers me so. The sourness of Vivien's childhood.

'I had a word with Ben,' Isaac says. 'He's not comfortable with you fetching Alexandra from school. Not yet. He's trying to keep her routine as much the same as possible, and he thinks it will be too disruptive to have a different person pick her up.'

I turn and brace my back against my front door, stiffening my spine against the surge of disappointment. 'What if I come over to the house, to meet her when she gets home?'

'It's too soon, that's all.' Isaac looks embarrassed.

'I imagine Ben had a few choice words to say about me.'

Isaac says nothing. There is a scuffling from

underneath the door across the hall. We've disturbed Mrs Shenkar's two Pomeranians. My neighbour is morbidly obese and she is always home, usually in her dressing gown. Sometimes she'll open her door and peer out.

'I can help Lexi,' I say. 'I should be seeing her every day. This is cruel. Ben is punishing both of us. I know I've screwed up, but does it count for nothing that I've lost my daughter?'

A knife-sharp pain rips through my temple, and lodges behind my right eye. The dogs across the hall launch into a high-pitched yapping as they hear the distress in my raised voice.

I cover my face with my hands.

'Let me finish,' Isaac says. 'It's not all bad news.' Gently, he pulls my hands away from my face. He keeps hold of me.

'Ben wants to take Alexandra to the funfair on the South Bank on Saturday,' he says. 'He's asked me to drive them over there. I suggested we should ask you to come with us, and Ben said that would be fine.'

'So I have to wait until the weekend?'

I sound churlish and ungrateful, but I resent the fact that I'm reliant on this near stranger, benign as he may be, for access to my own granddaughter. Isaac knows nothing of the days, the weeks, I spent sitting next to Lexi's incubator. I was the one who stayed with her during the gruesome eye-testing, to make sure the ventilator hadn't damaged her vision. Ben and Vivien couldn't bear to see her suffer.

'I think it'll be a good place to start,' Isaac says. 'On neutral ground, so to speak.'

The pain in my head makes it difficult to think coherently. I remind myself that none of this is Isaac's fault. 'Thank you,' I say.

But I can't look at him. I pull my hands away and turn and fumble with my key; finally I manage to fit it into the lock. As I push open the door, Isaac places a hand on my back.

'It's early days,' he says. 'Everything will get better.'

Chapter 8

The last of the leaves turn to mush under my boots and the hems of my jeans are damp and flecked with mud as I make my way up the slope to the café in Regent's Park.

Cleo has arrived early. She's sitting at a table next to the window inside the round, glassed-in building. When she sees me approaching, she springs up and opens the door.

'I'm so glad you could come,' she says. She kisses my cheek with chapped lips.

She looks more herself today, with her hair pulled back in a rather severe ponytail, and no make-up except for her pencilled-in brows. She pulls out a chair for me and I sit down. The steel frame is cold and uncomfortable. On the round table between us there are two steaming paper cups and two plates, each with a slice of cake lying on its side.

'I ordered you an Earl Grey,' she says. 'Do you still drink Earl Grey? I remember it used to be your favourite.'

'I do,' I say. 'Thank you.'

Cleo talks nervously as she levers the lid off her drink. 'I hate these takeaway cups,' she says. 'You can never get the lid back on again, once you take it off.'

A cloud of steam rises in the air between us. I reach for my drink, leaving the lid on. The side of the cup is scalding hot against my palm.

'Do you remember,' Cleo says, 'how I would bring you your tea in bed sometimes, on weekend mornings, when you had a lie-in?'

I smile as though I do, but the truth is I have no memory of this at all.

'I can't tell you how much I've missed having you in my life,' she says.

I take a sip of my boiling-hot tea through the plastic slit and my eyes well up as my tongue burns. Cleo is watching me closely, as though I am some sort of invalid.

'I wanted to make sure everything is okay between us,' she says. 'I thought I picked up some tension the other night. I take it Ben hadn't told you that I'd been over to the house?'

'No,' I say. 'I had no idea.'

I still can't put my finger on what it is about Cleo that bothers me, but I feel uneasy. Perhaps it's the sense of disquiet she carries with her.

'Did you and Vivien ever make up?' I say.

She shakes her head. 'No. But when I read about what happened, I wanted to offer Ben some support.'

I begin to shred my serviette into tiny fragments. 'How often do you see him?'

'I try to go over there every evening,' she says.

Now I think she looks somewhat uncomfortable, or embarrassed, but I can't be sure because Cleo often looks this way. She has never been comfortable in her own skin. She runs her fingertips along her forehead, back and forth along her hairline.

'You were so kind to me, Rose,' she says. 'I'll never forget how many meals I ate at your place, how many hours I spent at your flat. You were so strong and you worked so hard. You were my role model growing up. I used to pretend that you and Vivien were my real family.'

'That's generous of you, Cleo. But I'm sure I could have done more for you. You were always such a timid little thing. You didn't talk much, but whenever you did say something it was always very thoughtful and very grown up. And you were so often wandering around the estate or up and down the high street, with no one watching over you. Maybe I should have contacted someone – the school or social services. But I didn't know if it would end up making things worse for you, getting them involved.'

'No, you shouldn't have,' Cleo says. 'And I wasn't the only one with no one to watch over me. You had to work such long hours. Viv and I looked out for each other.'

In that moment, I wonder if she's merely insensitive,

or if she's deliberately trying to rub salt in my wounds. Then I realize she's simply being honest. It's not Cleo I'm angry with so much as myself.

'I've never met anyone like Vivien,' Cleo says. 'You never knew what she'd do or say next. Did you ever find out what she'd been doing with the money you gave her to buy food, on the days when you were working late?'

Again the sense of unease returns. It hurts, to be confronted with the reality that Cleo knew my daughter better than I did.

'No, I had no idea she was doing anything other than buying food.' My tone is sharp, but Cleo doesn't notice.

'You always gave Vivien more than she needed. She'd give me half and I'd buy myself a pizza. I always used to order the same thing, Margherita with extra chicken. I can still remember the smell of the melted cheese and the wood-fired stove. I was so starving after school, and she must have been too. But Vivien never ate a thing. Even in the pizza place, with that smell, she'd never change her mind. And then I'd offer her half of whatever I had, and she'd refuse to take it.'

I don't look her in the eyes. I stare out of the window at the failing light. The colours in the park are muted, everything blends into one grey palette.

'So what did she do with the money?' I say.

'She'd save up and then buy herself something she knew you wouldn't let her have. I remember one time she bought this leopard-print jumper.' Cleo laughs. 'She was very secretive when she was a teenager. I don't think you had any idea what she got up to.'

I don't want to hear about the way Vivien deprived herself, about her loneliness, or her propensity for deception. There are things I don't want to know, knowledge I would prefer to be spared. But this is no less than I deserve.

'I got you a piece of lemon drizzle cake,' Cleo says, pointing at my plate. 'Or do you have Vivien's iron will when it comes to boycotting white flour and sugar?'

Again, this feels like a dig. I don't respond. I break off a small corner of the cake with my teaspoon and taste it. It's bland and dry. I cut off a few more small pieces but I end up leaving them scattered around the paper plate. Cleo has nearly finished hers, but I have no appetite.

'Do you remember how Vivien let me tag along with her to the eisteddfods? I was her personal valet.'

I smile now, an easier smile. 'Yes, I do.'

Cleo and I share many of my daughter's childhood memories and this one brings with it a rush of pride. I see Vivien, standing on stage, smiling from ear to ear, her hair scraped back into a bun, with a winner's sash draped across her leotard and flowers in her arms. And poor Cleo, in her tracksuit, content to bask in the glow of Vivien's reflected glory and not needing to be centre stage.

'I felt so important,' she says, 'when I was allowed to go backstage to help her get dressed. It was all so magical to me, the way Vivien would sleep in ringlets, or you would tease her hair and spray in ten tons of hairspray and then arrange it into a bun. Her tutus were so beautiful and so pink, with all that tulle. I remember you would put glitter on her cheeks, and make it stay on with Vaseline.'

I'm grateful to her, for reminding me I was there for Vivien, sometimes. Sometimes I was present, even if it wasn't often enough.

'You had your talents too, Cleo. You were top of your class, right the way through school. I don't think Vivien would have made it through as far as she did without your help.'

'I loved school. It was so much better than being at home. My parents couldn't stand the sight of me.'

'What did you do,' I say, 'afterwards?'

'A degree in languages. It was my dream to work as a translator for the UN. But instead, there was Ben.'

We both fall silent. I can't help but feel sorry for her.

A gust of cold air from the door blows all the little white pieces of serviette to the floor. I try to gather the remaining shreds from the steel table top and, not knowing what else to do with them, I shove the scraps into my pockets. I leave my ice-cold hands deep down inside my coat.

Cleo's fingers dance restlessly across her forehead as she pulls strands of her hair loose from her ponytail.

I've never known what happened, between the three of them. All I know is that Cleo and Vivien stopped speaking. I always suspected that Vivien had interfered in Ben and Cleo's relationship and that she was the cause of their break-up. I didn't want to know the details. I didn't want to see that my daughter might be capable of hurting someone weaker than she was.

We both reach for our paper cups. The tea has cooled down and I take a few more sips. I do still like Earl Grey.

So far we've had the café to ourselves, but now a group of teenage girls bursts in through the glass doors. They're all black-rimmed eyes, long hair and short skirts.

Cleo bites down on the rim of her paper cup. She leaves teeth marks all around the edges. Her fingers creep up to her hairline again and she scratches at the skin of her forehead. I remember now, how she used to have a nervous habit of pulling at her eyebrows. There was barely anything left of them by the time she was in secondary school.

As I watch her, awkward and fidgeting, I find it hard to believe she had anything to do with the argument between Vivien and Ben. I simply cannot imagine Ben choosing Cleo over Vivien.

'Cleo,' I say, 'we've known each other a very long time and I hope you don't mind if I'm direct.'

'Of course not.'

'What exactly is the nature of your relationship with Ben?'

'He's in shock and he's lonely,' she says. 'I keep him company. He doesn't want to be alone.'

'Do you understand how vulnerable he is?'

I can see by the blankness in her eyes that she doesn't want to hear what I've got to say.

'Ben doesn't talk about you very much,' she says. 'I thought I'd see more of you at the house.'

The teenage girls arrange themselves across three tables, with their feet propped up on chairs. They're becoming louder and louder, laughing and screeching. A paper cup lies on its side, the straw fallen to the floor and vanilla milkshake leaking across the table top. Cleo is staring at them.

'What sort of relationship do you have with Ben?' she asks.

'It's complicated,' I say. 'Things aren't great, between us.'

'Maybe I can help,' she says. 'I could talk to him.'

If what Cleo says is true, that she's fond of me and always has been, then she might be able to help, in my quest to win Ben over.

'It's worth a try,' I say. 'I'd like to convince him to trust me more, with Lexi.'

'I can tell him how wonderful you were to me when I was her age.'

Cleo is staring at me, watching the way I rub the side of my head. 'Would you like another cup of tea?' she says.

'No, thank you.'

I glance over at the counter. Behind it, there are two women, both young, both attractive with fair skin and dark hair. They laugh as they share a joke. I think they are speaking a foreign language. I wonder if one of these women was the one who saw Vivien on the morning of her death.

'Are you all right?' Cleo says.

'I get these headaches on and off,' I say. 'I think I need to walk for a bit, to get some air.'

Cleo holds the door open and I walk out ahead of her as we leave the café and head down the slope. In front of us, the BT tower rears up in the midst of the fading London skyline.

A wooden jaguar is poised above an empty bench, as though he's waiting to pounce. I hear a lion roar.

As we walk, the fog creeps down around us, lower and lower, until I can hardly see anything but white mist. I don't know if we're alone on this path, or if there are people nearby. My daughter used to run this route, day in and day out.

'It was like this on the day she died,' Cleo says. 'You could hardly see two feet in front of your face.'

Chapter 9

We arrive at the funfair early on Saturday morning, before it gets too crowded. Giant teacups swirl pink and yellow against the dull sky. Lexi is pulling us towards the twisted tracks of the rollercoaster which snake high above the river. Her ginger curls blow into her eyes and her already pale skin grows ever more pale as the wind coming off the river whips against her face. *Ghost-like*, Vivien used to say.

The grey coat she wears is so dour; I don't understand why Vivien never dressed her daughter in anything bright, or why she kept Lexi's hair so short when the colour is so lovely.

Maybe I'm holding her hand too tight. I ease my grip a little.

'Thank you for inviting me today,' I say to Ben. He's holding on to Lexi's other hand. Like the other night, he looks terrible, his eyes bleak.

'You can thank Isaac,' he says. 'He seems to agree with you that Lexi needs her grandmother in her life.'

'I'm glad.'

Whatever Ben may think, his daughter does need me. And I need her too. With her hand in mine, I feel a little stronger.

Isaac, as usual in his mackintosh, walks a few paces behind us. I feel reassured by his presence.

'Have you been on a rollercoaster before?' I ask Lexi. I have to raise my voice, because the wind drowns my words.

She shakes her head.

'You're sure you want to do this?' Ben says.

Lexi nods, but her eyes widen as she looks at the tracks looming in front of us. But in the end, it's Ben and I who are most nervous, and Isaac steps forward. He claims he's not afraid of heights or speed, he took his stepdaughters on these rides often, he says. Ben gives him a grateful pat on the back.

Lexi lets go of our hands and she and Isaac take their places in the short queue. Ben and I lean against the railings and keep watch over them. As they inch closer to the front, Lexi grows more subdued. She tucks her hands into the pockets of her coat and her head droops down. I wonder if she's going to be sick all over Isaac. I feel a little better when I see that children even smaller than she is have joined the queue. They all cling to their mothers' hands.

My hair blows across my face as I smile and wave at my granddaughter. I take out my phone and ready the camera. When their turn comes, Lexi shuffles in to the small carriage first and Isaac follows close behind her. The attendant has a downy black moustache and his hair is tied back in a ponytail. He looks much too young and too careless to be in charge of safety issues. Disinterestedly, he clicks the harness bar into place. Lexi feels for it and pulls it back and forth several times, checking it's secure. I take a photograph, but she's not smiling and the shot is blurred. Isaac whispers something in her ear.

I wave as the little cart trundles away but they don't see me. Slowly, they climb. Higher and higher. Lexi's body is pressed up right against Isaac's side. Their cart stops for a second or two at the highest point on the track. It sways in the wind and I hold my breath, then it pitches forward and down, as though flying straight off the edge of a cliff.

'I had tea with Cleo yesterday,' I say. 'In Regent's Park.'

Ben is looking up at the rollercoaster as it begins the next climb.

'She's been a great support,' he says. 'Vivien and I made a few friends in the area, through the school, but it's not the same. In a weird way, having Cleo around is like having a piece of Vivien back with me. She knew Vivien inside and out, I don't have to explain anything. I suppose that sounds odd.'

'I'm glad for you,' I say. And I am, truly.

Ben's vulnerability does not come as a surprise. I see this every day at work; the way trauma opens a person up, and pulls down their defences. I only hope Cleo doesn't take advantage.

The ride is mercifully brief. And a rip-off, considering the price. Isaac and Lexi pull in to the start position in their little cart and the disinterested employee unlocks the bar and sets them free. Lexi runs over to Ben and pulls at his arm, she's insistent, jumping up and down and pointing at the ticket booth. Ben is laughing and it is a pleasure to see them happy, free of their pain for even a short time. He goes to buy them another set of tickets.

The cart sets off again, Lexi gripping the safety bar and grinning as Ben and I wave goodbye. I feel my heart contract. She looks like any other normal child, I tell myself. She can recover. Once again, the rollercoaster begins its slow, suspense-filled ascent as Ben and I stand side by side at the railings. Lexi is already a seasoned rollercoaster fan, and this time her screams are more for show. She pitches down towards us, her arms in the air. Isaac, on the other hand, looks a little greyer and less enthusiastic.

'Has DS Cole been in touch with you again?' Ben says.

'Yes. She was at the hospital.'

He turns to face me. 'What did she want?'

I hesitate. Things are tentatively good between us. Here I am, a normal grandmother on a normal family outing. I don't want to talk about Vivien and Ben's argument or the night he spent in a hotel. I don't even want to think about it. But I have no choice, because I'm not about to lie to him.

'She asked if I knew about an argument, between you and Vivien, the day before she died. I told her I didn't know anything about it. Which I didn't.'

Ben nods. His jaw clenches. I reach out and give his shoulder a gentle squeeze. 'I'm sorry, Ben. I can imagine how you feel.'

I'm desperate not to say the wrong thing, not to make his guilt worse, and so I say nothing more. I feel as though I'm walking a tightrope, trying not to make things worse for Ben, and between us. Though he doesn't look at me, he reaches up and pats my hand, which still rests on his shoulder.

'I worry about the press,' Ben says. 'You need to be careful what you say, I don't want any gossip being leaked. Our story is a lucrative one and Met officers are only human. Isaac said he had several police contacts who used to feed him information.'

I'm shocked by what Ben has said. I had assumed he would be consumed with regret, not concerned about gossip. Because the last time he ever saw Vivien, he was angry at her. He abandoned her.

My hand slips from his shoulder. My skin is mottled from the cold. 'I answer her questions, that's all. I don't embellish.'

'Good,' he says.

The Lizard Man is coming closer, he's bare-chested, covered in green scales from head to toe. His forked tongue flickers as he calls out, offering us tickets to the freak show. I can't look at him, at the grotesque damage he's inflicted on himself, the tattoos, the spliced tongue, the protuberances along his eyebrows.

When Ben speaks, his tone is bitter, even as he smiles and waves at his daughter as the little cart trundles back to the starting point. 'Don't forget,' he says, 'that anything reported in the press will be all over the internet. It will stay there, in perpetuity. And it will hurt Lexi when she's old enough to search for information about her mother's death.'

'Ben, I understand.'

There hasn't been as much in the papers about Vivien's death as I had expected. Perhaps this reflects the extent of Ben's influence, or the rarefied community they live in where their neighbours and friends are wary of gossip and the impact of such reports on house prices. In any event, my daughter remains as private in death as she was in life.

Isaac helps Lexi to step down from the rollercoaster and they walk through the barriers and back towards us, hand in hand. They are both smiling, at ease in each other's company.

'I haven't said anything to anyone,' I say. 'There's nothing to say. I knew nothing about the argument, and Vivien never talked to me about your marriage, if that's what you're worried about. I have no intention of ever compromising my daughter's privacy. I was surprised to hear you walked out on her, because that's so unlike you. But my only concern is Lexi's well-being, and yours, too.'

Ben has turned his back on me and I'm not sure if he's heard me. He holds out his arms and Lexi runs towards him. He swings her up into the air and then clasps her close to his chest.

The wind doesn't let up, and silver-blonde strands blow around my face as I try in vain to pat them down into some kind of order.

I notice that as Isaac draws closer, he pats Ben on the back. It is a gesture of warmth and of familiarity. It makes me think of a father's touch.

At around eight thirty that night, my mobile rings. I can barely hear what Ben is saying because of the noise in the background. Lexi is screaming.

I can hear he is desperate and even before the brief call is over, I am grabbing my coat and pulling on my boots. The door of my flat slams shut behind me and I run down the stairs. I flag down a passing cab and I tell him to hurry.

I know it's wrong to feel this way but I am pleased. Pleased that Ben called me; pleased to be needed.

When he opens the front door, Lexi is in his arms, barely, and he's trying to restrain her. She twists her body back and forth, her fists pound at him and her legs thrash. She is red in the face.

She is shouting *No*. Over and over again. *No. No. No.*

I push open the gate and rush up the stairs towards them, and I hold out my arms for her. Ben stumbles, as she slips from his grasp and I am there to grab hold of her. She pushes me away at first, but I manage to catch both of her wrists. She's a solid little thing, but I'm much stronger. I kick the front door shut behind me.

Ben takes a few steps away, looking shell shocked.

My surprise appearance seems to have done the trick, because Lexi has stopped shouting and she's no longer struggling. I loosen my grip on her wrists and wrap my arms around her middle. I sit down on the floor, pulling her onto my lap, and I hold her tight.

Ben stands over us. His T-shirt is damp and creased and there are sweat stains under his arms. He's barefoot and unshaven and I think I catch a whiff of alcohol. There is an angry red mark on his left cheek, under his eye.

I don't say anything. I sit on the floor of the hall, my arms wrapped around Lexi, and I simply hold on. Gradually she settles. I notice the unusual coldness of her skin. Mine is the same, as though, since Vivien died, our bones have turned to ice, freezing us from the inside out.

Ben walks away, into the living room. I can see him through the doorway and I watch as he pours himself a glass of whisky.

'What's the matter, Lexi?' I whisper, my mouth against her damp curls. Her hair smells sour, as though she's been ill. Her eyes are red and puffy and snot streams from her nose. She looks wretched.

I keep hold of her with one hand as I reach into the pocket of my coat with the other, and take out a tissue. I wipe her cheeks, her nose, her mouth.

'*Mummy,*' she says.

I think that's what she says.

She lays her head back against my chest. Ben is watching us again, from the doorway of the living room, a glass in his hand. Father and daughter are the same shade of ashen.

I carry Lexi up to her bedroom. It takes all my effort, but I manage. Her head lies heavy on my shoulder. When I lay her down on her bed, she turns away, onto her side. Her eyelids droop as I lean over her to smooth her wild curls away from her face. I pull her duvet around her, and tuck the quilt down under the edges of the mattress.

I sit on the edge of the bed and hold her hand and watch her as she drifts away. I hope my touch might give her some sense of comfort in a world that has become so unsafe. I feel helpless, looking at her.

Ben has not come up to check on her.

Lexi seems to be fast asleep, and so I walk back downstairs. I pull my boots off, leaving them under the round mahogany table. I drape my coat over the banister. I could do with a whisky myself.

'Ben?'

I peer inside but the living room is empty. The drinks cabinet stands wide open and the whisky bottle is gone. I return to the entrance hall and peer down over the banister, into the basement, where there is only a thick and silent darkness. I walk up again, to the first floor, and pop my head round Lexi's door. She's sound asleep.

The lights on the landing seem too bright. It's eerie, standing here, surrounded by these photographs, by the ghosts of a happy family.

'Ben?'

There is no answer.

I climb up to the second floor, gripping the banister for support. By the time I reach the top of the staircase, I feel drained and my legs have grown weak, as though they no longer have the strength to hold me upright. I stop.

My favourite portrait of Vivien hangs here, on the landing. Her wedding veil covers her face, softening her features as she gazes out at me. Her eyes still burn, intense and alive. She is my exotic princess, my sleek, dark-eyed panther.

My daughter always stood out. Not quite Asian, not quite Caucasian, her features shifting and blending. There was something arresting about her, something that made people want to stare; the almond shape of her eyes, perhaps, or the way she held herself.

I reach out and place my hand against the cool glass that covers her skin. Then I turn away and I step into the master bedroom.

On my left is a dressing room lined with tall oak wardrobes. The lights are on in here and I catch sight of myself in the standing mirror placed at the far end of the room. I look as haggard as I expected, my face is crumpled, my hair lank. There is something eerie about my reflection. I am drained of colour, as though I'm looking at myself in black and white, as though I'm looking at my own ghost.

I see Vivien, as a toddler, staring at herself in the mirror, pouting and smiling and pleased with what she saw.

I walk deeper into the room, and I open each of the cupboards in turn. The first two are filled with suits, shirts and ties. They smell of leather and vetiver, of Ben. But when I open the third one, Vivien's scent floats out, her sweet, floral perfume. Her clothes still hang in neat rows, as though she might return. My fingers close around a soft crêpe dress. I pull it out and hold it against my face. I breathe her in.

When I open my eyes, Ben is standing in the doorway. Embarrassed, I push the dress back into place, and close the cupboard.

'I'm sorry,' I say. 'I didn't mean to intrude. I came up here to look for you.'

He gestures towards the cupboard behind me. 'Did you want to take something of hers?'

'No. Thank you. But I'm sure Lexi will want to have her things, when she's older. You won't throw them away, will you?'

'No. Of course I won't throw them away,' he says.

'Lexi's fast asleep.'

Ben seems disoriented. 'I meant to lie down for a few moments and I passed out.'

'I'm glad you called me. I'm glad I could help.'

'Thank you. You were a lifesaver tonight. I think all the excitement this morning must have been too much for her. She fell asleep at around five, in front of the television, and I carried her up to bed. Then a couple of hours later she woke up, and she was in a state. I couldn't get her to calm down. She'd been hysterical for half an hour before I phoned you. I thought I was going to lose it.'

'But you didn't. You did the right thing in calling me.'

'She's always been a terrible sleeper,' he says. 'She's always had nightmares and tantrums. And Vivien had to deal with all of it on her own. I was never home for bed-time, for any of it. And since Viv died, she wakes almost every night. Sometimes I hear her crying in her bed, other times I find her wandering around the house. It's never been as bad as it was tonight.'

There is a sheen of sweat on his face, and the smell of body odour and alcohol is strong in the small dressing room.

'She was calmer with you,' he says.

'She was worn out by the time I got here.'

'No,' he says. 'You've always had a way with her, ever since she was a baby. I've noticed it before, the bond between you. That's why I've never understood why you stayed away.'

This is not the time to tell him. He's exhausted and his words are a little slurred.

'I was so angry,' he says. 'It frightened me, how angry I was with her. I could have hit her.'

'You're under extreme stress. And you didn't hit her.'

I look at the red mark underneath his eye, and I wonder what did happen. I hope he didn't hurt her. 'Ben, alcohol isn't going to help with the stress you're under. I think you need to be careful about how much you're drinking.'

He nods, but I'm not reassured. He is deteriorating in front of me, losing control. He isn't coping.

'Go to bed and get some rest,' I say. 'I'll stay. I'll go to her if she wakes up again.'

Ben sways, then braces himself against the doorframe.

'Please, go back to bed. I'll stay another couple of hours and then I'll let myself out. That way you'll get a few hours of uninterrupted sleep and you'll feel better.'

I sound more like myself. Authoritative and in control. I'm comfortable in this role.

Ben turns away from me. He opens the door behind him, the one that has been closed all this time. The door that leads to their bathroom. My blood turns cold as he disappears inside and I hear the click of the lock. I imagine Vivien, lying on the floor. She is waiting for me, desperate, hoping her mother will come and save her.

I have to get out of here. I lurch down the short passageway and out onto the landing. I can't bear to look at her wedding portrait. I can feel her, staring at me. Begging for help. No wonder Ben drinks.

The basement kitchen is a long and narrow space, with stainless-steel worktops and stone floors. I flick on the lights, glad to be as far away as possible from Vivien's bathroom, though this room is not much of a comfort. Even with the lights on, it's a gloomy space, and full of shadows.

Outside, rain drums down onto the square patch of lawn.

One end of the kitchen is dominated by a cast-iron Victorian fireplace; the other has narrow windows looking out onto the back garden. In front of these there is a row of potted herbs in ceramic containers: basil, sage, mint and coriander. The plants are wilting.

I had intended to make myself a cup of tea, but I decide I don't have the energy. Tall grey cabinets loom over me on each side, and I don't know where to start looking. Instead, I lift a coffee-stained mug out of the sink and I give the plants a little water.

When I hear the sound of the buzzer, I am not surprised. I was expecting her. Cleo is waiting outside in the rain.

Chapter 10

Cleo rushes inside. Water drips onto Vivien's tiles as she takes off her long, hooded coat. She opens the cupboard next to the front door, helps herself to a hanger and hangs it up. Then she unzips her knee-high boots and pulls them off, leaving them lying next to mine, under Vivien's mahogany table.

I'm taken aback by the ease with which she moves around my daughter's home.

'Ben's upstairs, asleep,' I say. 'He's exhausted. Lexi's having a really bad night.'

My somewhat impatient tone implies this is not the right time for a visit, but Cleo doesn't seem to notice. She pats her cheeks, wiping away the last of the rain. She looks elegant tonight, in a navy polo-neck and tapered jeans. Her hair is tied back again, this time loosely knotted into a bun at the base of her neck. Large hoop earrings dangle from her ears.

'Let's have a glass of wine together,' she says.

'Cleo, I think . . .' I say. 'Forgive me for being blunt

but I think it's best if you go home. Ben really needs to get some rest, Lexi has been in a terrible state.'

'I've struggled across London in this awful weather,' she says. 'Have one drink with me before I head out into the rain again.'

She smiles at me as she goes through into the living room and makes her way to the open drinks cabinet. 'I see the whisky bottle is missing,' she says.

Cleo's noticed the drinking too.

'Ben must have taken it upstairs with him. Is he drinking every night?'

She nods. 'I'd drink too, if I was alone in this house, thinking about what happened upstairs in that bathroom.'

Her cavalier tone disturbs me. She peruses the wine rack, pulls a few bottles out and scrutinizes the labels before choosing a Merlot. She locates the bottle opener with ease, in a small drawer next to the mirrored cabinet. Then she chooses two large wine glasses and pours.

'You look like you need this,' she says.

The adrenalin rush of earlier this evening has dissipated. I'm on edge, unsettled after my journey upstairs, into Vivien's bedroom. It doesn't take much for me to relent.

'You're right, I do need a drink.' I take a sip from the glass that Cleo gives to me. My mouth fills with a soft, plummy taste; the Merlot goes down so smoothly, soothing my throat and my aching head.

'If Ben's having trouble coping, he should see his GP,'

I say. 'Maybe he needs an antidepressant. That would be better for him than alcohol. Maybe you can have a word with him? I've mentioned he should be careful but I don't think I'm having much impact.'

'Sure,' she says.

We stand and sip our wine at the back window as we look out at the garden, at the rows of tiny lights and the sad concrete lion. Before I know it, my glass is almost empty and I feel myself unwinding, like a rope that's been twisted tight.

'Do you remember how Vivien and I first met Ben?'

'I do,' I say. 'You met him because of me. Ben's father was a patient on the stroke ward, and the entrance is directly opposite the Weissman Unit.'

Cleo nods. 'It was in the December holidays, Vivien was back from performing-arts school and we were hanging around the vending machine, waiting for you to finish your shift and take us Christmas shopping. Ben came out of his father's ward to get a coffee. He was smitten with Vivien the moment he laid eyes on her.'

'Vivien was already seeing Sebastian at that stage, wasn't she?' I say.

Sebastian was as tall, chiselled and blond as Vivien was petite, Eurasian and dark. He was from old money; she was from a council estate. He was in our lives for five long, fraught years and all Vivien wanted for those five impressionable years was a ring on her finger.

'That's right,' Cleo says. 'Vivien wasn't interested in Ben at all. He asked her out and she said no. I, on the other hand, knew the moment I met him that there was something special about him.'

Cleo refills my glass. I'm feeling calmer. I'm pleased she stayed, pleased to be standing next to her, reminiscing about my daughter. I understand what Ben means, how it helps to be with someone who knows Vivien's history; all of our history. It seems so sad, that Cleo and I – for different reasons – both lost contact with Vivien these past years.

'I was desperate to see Ben again,' Cleo goes on. 'I made sure we went back to the ward the next day and I asked him out myself. It was the first time I'd ever done anything like that and I don't think Ben was even remotely interested, but he humoured me by agreeing to go out to dinner. We became friends and we kept in contact by email while he was at Cambridge. At first I was pretty sure he was only friendly with me because I could feed him information about Vivien. But then she and Sebastian got engaged, and Ben got a job in London, and we ended up moving in together.'

'Vivien and Sebastian were so unhappy,' I say. This sounds as though I'm making excuses for my daughter, but I feel as though I need to explain, to stick up for her. 'Vivien always worried about where Sebastian was, when he wasn't with her, she thought he prioritized his friends over their relationship, and she was devastated when she wasn't included in a family holiday to some or other island or Scottish castle. She idolized him. She tried so hard to make herself part of his family and to ingratiate herself with his sisters, but she was out of place, out of their league. Sebastian moved in a world she could never be a part of. So no one was more surprised than I was when he asked Vivien to marry him.'

I find that the second glass of Merlot is now empty and I'm feeling a little light-headed. I lean against the back of the sofa. I want to keep looking out at the pretty lights in the garden. Vivien made everything around her so beautiful.

'The engagement didn't last long, did it?' Cleo says.

'I suspect Vivien pressured Sebastian into it somehow or other,' I say, 'and he soon regretted it.'

'Vivien knew you wanted the relationship to work,' Cleo says. 'She thought you'd be devastated about the break-up.'

'That's not true.' I'm surprised to hear this; something else I did not know. 'I was relieved when they broke up. I worried that Vivien was with him for the wrong reasons. I always felt that Sebastian's money and status were more attractive to her than Sebastian himself. Not that I would have blamed her if that was the case. You remember what things were like, growing up?'

'Of course I do.'

'While Vivien was growing up I was always afraid,' I say. 'Money frightened me, or rather, not having enough of it to survive.'

Up until Vivien came back to live with me, I sent most of my salary home to my mother. In those years, I had enough money for one bus fare per day: I could travel either to or from the hospital by public transport, I had to walk the other journey. I had to choose and I'll never forget how that felt.

And I told Vivien how hard it was. I shouldn't have, but I did. She knew what it was like to worry about money, all the time; I put my fear and my exhaustion inside her. She saw how the years of struggle as a single parent on a nurse's salary had eaten away at me. I didn't hide it from her and I didn't protect her.

'Vivien told me she was the one who broke off the engagement,' Cleo says, 'but reading between the lines, I knew Sebastian must have been sleeping around again. I think the humiliation was so bad that even Vivien couldn't keep up the pretence any more.'

Cleo's words have become sharp objects, striking at the side of my already tender head. I feel my shoulders tense up and I have the same sensation I had in the park, where I can't help feeling that, even if she isn't consciously aware of it herself, she has a desire to hurt me.

She was always this way, she has a tendency to say exactly what she is thinking. I can't help but rise to the bait.

'It was different when she got together with Ben,' I say. 'They were good for each other.'

The wine was probably a mistake; I'm bound to say something I regret. I feel woozy, but I don't want to lie down in case I fall asleep and I don't hear Lexi calling out. I put my glass down and I stretch my arms, interlacing my fingers and pushing them out in front of me, straightening my spine, setting my shoulders back. I should go upstairs and check on Lexi, but I'm still too light-headed.

Cleo walks slowly around Vivien's living room. She trails her hand along the edge of the leather-topped desk. She lifts the large silver frame, with the photograph of Vivien, and then she places it back down again. But it's not quite right now; the angle is wrong. Vivien no longer faces into the room, she's been turned a fraction towards the wall.

'The strange thing is,' Cleo says, 'that it wasn't Ben I thought about for all these years so much as Vivien. She was my closest friend and I missed her like crazy.'

She looks at me, as though expecting me to say something, but I don't. And each time Cleo touches something that belongs to my daughter, I want to yell at her to stop.

'I've typed the words *Vivien Kaye* into the search bar more often than I like to admit,' she says. 'There are lots of women with that name: business people, even an art historian. But none of the profiles or photographs belonged to your Vivien, to Ben's wife. She had no Facebook page, no Twitter account, there was no trace of her at all across social media. She was always so private.'

'Yes,' I say. 'Yes she was.'

Perhaps with good reason, I think.

'I had better luck with Ben,' Cleo says. 'There are hundreds of photographs and articles about him; he's all over the internet. Did you know his firm's just led a five-hundred-million-pound investment in the Central European broadband industry?'

'I didn't.'

'I only ever found one photograph of Ben and Vivien together,' Cleo says. 'They were at a charity fundraiser. Vivien looked so beautiful. She had her hair swept back, away from her face, and she was wearing a white, sleeveless dress. I can still see the muscles in her arms. And she looked so happy, like the cat that got the cream. As though she had everything she'd ever wanted.'

I'm not sure what to make of what she's told me. After all, we all Google each other. I've looked up Isaac's name, read some of his articles online. I've searched for pictures of Andrew Lissauer and his wife. But I wouldn't admit this to anyone.

'It's surprisingly easy,' Cleo says, 'to find people and to see how they live. I found bits and pieces of information and I put it all together, like a jigsaw. I knew where Ben and Vivien lived; I knew the events they attended, the charities they supported. There's really no such thing as privacy any more, is there?'

'No,' I say, 'there isn't. But it doesn't mean you should go intruding into people's lives, Cleo.'

She blinks and looks around the room. 'Vivien's house is quite breathtaking,' she says. 'Isn't it?'

She takes a sip of her wine and the colour is a deep red, like blood, and it stains her lips so they're almost black.

'I feel like I'm being seduced every time I step through the front door,' she says. 'I almost can't bear to leave.'

She turns to me and smiles, as though we're chatting at a cocktail party, not standing inside the house where my daughter died. 'I don't want to go back outside into the real world,' she says. 'I want to stay here, inside Vivien's fantasy.'

Her expression darkens as she drifts further away from me, to a place inside herself. 'I think we're very alike,' she says, 'you and me. You of all people know what it's like to be alone. We've been on the outside, looking in at Ben and Vivien and their gilded life. We've been standing out there in the cold, peering in through the shutters. But now it's our turn, we're inside. Admit it, Rose, don't you like it better, being on the inside?'

'That's a very odd thing to say, Cleo.'

She smiles at me again, as though she hasn't heard the implied criticism.

'Rose, you look so tired. You should go home and get some sleep.'

'I told you, Cleo, I'm going to stay in case Lexi wakes up again.'

She walks round the sofa and puts her glass down on Vivien's Perspex coffee table. She rubs at her eyebrow. It's not that Cleo is unattractive. It's only that, next to Vivien, her features always seemed rounded and plain. Her hair is mouse-brown, while Vivien's was a dramatic, raven black.

I steady myself against the back of the sofa.

I don't have the patience to mince my words. The blasted throbbing in my head makes tact impossible and the wine makes it even easier than usual for me to be blunt. I no longer hold back for fear of hurting her feelings.

'Look, Cleo,' I say, 'you're visiting Ben every night and I don't think it's a good idea. You're basically foisting yourself onto this family. We haven't even had a chance to give Vivien a proper funeral yet, and Ben is struggling. I understand you still have feelings for him, but I would ask you to do the right thing and give us some space. Ben and Lexi are extremely vulnerable.'

Her cheeks flush, but Cleo doesn't say a thing. I'm not sure she's even letting my words reach her. I suspect she doesn't want to hear what I have to say. I carry on, hoping to have some impact.

'I think your relationship with Ben might get in the way of his grief. Your presence in this house is a distraction, like putting a plaster over a deep wound. It may make him feel better in the short term, but in the long term it could lead to problems for both of you if you start a relationship so soon.'

'What sort of problems?' she says.

Her response is bizarre, as though she's chosen not to hear half of what I've just said.

'If you really have Ben's best interests at heart,' I say, 'then wait a while. If it's meant to be, it will happen. But not now, not while he's still traumatized. You don't want to be a temporary solution to his pain, do you?'

I'm trying to find something that will appeal to her rational side, something that will make her understand that it might be in her own interests to give Ben some space.

'Vivien wouldn't have waited,' Cleo says. 'Vivien always understood that if you want something, then it's up to you to grab it by the throat.'

I'm angry now, because she has no respect for the loss this family has suffered. All I want is for her to leave. Right now, right this second.

Tonight, standing in front of me in my daughter's home, Cleo no longer seems awkward or uneasy in her own skin. She is coming into her own. Like some sort of vulture, feeding off the corpse of my daughter.

Though I haven't spoken, she has noticed the expression on my face.

'Rose,' she says, 'please don't be offended. You know me, I'm just being practical. I know Ben better than anyone, and he isn't good at being alone. He's a family man. And he is rich, attractive and still young. Think about it. He *will* marry again, it's inevitable. I'm not going to stand aside and take the chance of losing him a second time. It's in your interests to have me around too. I adore you. I'll make sure you're always an important part of Lexi's life.'

I see now she wants it all. It's not only Ben she's interested in. She wants this house, she wants his child and perhaps she even wants me, too. A mother.

'Cleo,' I say, with what I think is admirable restraint,

'it has been a difficult day. For now, what I want is for you to go home and leave us in peace. Please. If you respect me, as you say you do, then you will do as I ask.'

'I didn't mean to upset you,' Cleo says. 'That's the last thing I'd ever want.'

'Then put on your coat and your boots and go home.'

'All right.'

I'm both relieved and surprised that she's backed down so easily. She swigs the last of her wine, and clatters the glass back down. She brushes past me, grazing my shoulder as she leaves the room. She sits on the bottom step while she pulls on her boots, then she stands up and retrieves her still-damp coat from the cupboard.

'I'm sorry if I've intruded tonight,' she says. 'I know my suffering is nothing compared to yours. And Ben's and Lexi's. Please forgive me.'

Before I have a chance to respond, she rushes towards me, takes me by the shoulders and kisses my cheek. I back away, and walk around her, towards the front door.

The combination of the wine and the pain in the right side of my head makes my stomach churn. It's a relief when I pull open the front door and a rush of cold air engulfs me.

Cleo does not make eye contact as she leaves. She does not say goodbye. I watch as she walks slowly down the stairs and along the short pathway. As I press the buzzer to release the front gate, I already know she will not be able to stay away for long.

Chapter 11

'There you are,' Wendy says.

Small and immaculate and always so light on her feet, she walks over to the window of Special Care where I am standing with Yusuf in my arms. He's on my hip, facing outwards and sucking his fist, and we're having a look at the cars down on Praed Street below.

Wendy pats Yusuf's head, then she reaches into her pocket and pulls out my phone. 'You left this in my office,' she says, 'and it's been buzzing away. I thought it might be something important.'

She smiles and tries to look nonchalant, but she fails. My own heart plummets down into my gut as I see Ben's name on the screen. I have five missed calls from my son-in-law. I was with Wendy the last time I missed his calls, too.

My arms shake as I pass Yusuf over to Wendy. She rocks him as she watches me. She's scared too. I try to hit the right buttons, but I miss, my fingers seem to have swollen. Finally, I manage to dial Ben's number.

'Please pick up,' I say out loud. 'Please pick up.'

Yusuf senses our tension and he begins to grizzle in Wendy's arms.

I don't want to think about what might have happened to Lexi. I should never have left the house in the early hours of this morning. I should have stayed. But she had stayed asleep, all through the night, and I had to go home to pick up my uniform before my shift.

When Ben answers, he's out of breath.

'What's happened?' I say.

'I have a situation here,' he says, 'and I wondered if you were free this afternoon to help out with Lexi.'

'Of course. But is everything all right?'

'The police have asked if they can come over to the house this afternoon, and I don't want Lexi to be here when they arrive. I don't want her to sense there's anything to be afraid of. Could you pick her up from school?'

'Yes. That's no problem. So Lexi's all right?'

'Yes, I'm sorry, I should have let you know. She was absolutely fine this morning. I don't think she remembers anything about last night. Thank you again for your help.'

I start to breathe normally again. I'm light-headed with relief.

'There's no need to thank me,' I say.

'So if you pick her up from school, then Isaac will fetch her from your flat later, around six.'

I hold the phone away from my ear, staring at the

screen of logged calls, shocked. This all seems much too easy. I notice then that Ben's wasn't the only call I'd missed. Mrs Murad's office has called me. Again.

'Wendy, I'm so sorry,' I say. 'I have to leave early again today. Ben needs me to pick Alexandra up from school.'

'Don't worry about the ward,' she says. 'I'll get cover for you.'

I feel a rush of gratitude. Cleo is wrong, I have not been alone all these years.

Wendy settles Yusuf in his cot. She lies him on his back and then she winds up the mobile that hangs over his head. Sounds of Bach fill the ward as the coloured animals begin to spin. On impulse I put my arms around her and I hug her, taking her by surprise.

Finishing time at the Endsleigh School is twenty past three and I make sure I arrive early. The red-brick Edwardian building is a cheerful place with a front door the colour of sunshine and children's paintings strung up like bunting along the sash windows on the first floor. At my feet, the lines of a football pitch have been painted onto the asphalt.

Before long, the playground begins to fill up with mothers, nannies and au pairs; younger siblings hurtle down the slide and swing from the monkey bars on the climbing frame. I shove my rough hands deep inside the pockets of my coat, relieved to be behind oversized sunglasses which I don't really need on this cloying and cloud-filled afternoon.

I imagine people are staring at me. The imposter. My granddaughter is eight years old and I've never set foot on the grounds of her school before. I haven't been inside her classroom to admire her drawings and her projects. I haven't attended a soggy sports day to watch as the other children win medals.

I smooth down my hair. Vivien was always so elegant, so petite in her signature fitted shirt and skinny jeans and her pale-pink lipstick. My daughter understood the need to present a certain image to the outside world. I don't know who her friends are here. But I have already decided that if anyone does approach me, I am not going to answer any questions. There may be some people who cared about her and who mean well, but there will also be those who revel in the sordid details.

At long last, the doors of the school swing open and the children swarm out. It's easy to pick my grand-daughter out from the crowd because her bright curls shine and bounce even on this dull, dull day. She drags her Spiderman rucksack behind her as she scans the faces of the mothers, the nannies and the handful of fathers. She is a solid and slow-moving child, dazed in the middle of a sea of fast-moving bodies. She's not expecting to see me and she walks right past, plodding on as though her bag is filled with lead.

I rush forwards and place a hand on her shoulder, holding her back.

'Hello, Lexi,' I say. My voice sounds unnaturally cheery.

She turns to look up at me with eyes that are gentle and mournful, eyes that remind me of Ben. Vivien's eyes were always mischievous, even a little cunning.

'Your dad asked me to fetch you today,' I say.

Lexi blinks, with her almost-blonde lashes. I reach out my hand and although she hesitates at first, she reaches back and takes hold. I take her schoolbag and swing it onto my shoulder and walk on, grasping her hand with a smile fixed to my face. I imagine my every move under scrutiny and I try to focus only on her small hand, warming up inside mine. I ask about her day at school; I don't think she answers. I guide her across the playground and towards the exit.

'Do you feel like a hot chocolate?' I say. 'It feels like a hot chocolate sort of a day today, don't you think? With marshmallows on top?'

I look down to find she's staring at me with eager eyes and an almost-smile. Her smile is hesitant, the smile of a child who sees her grandmother as a benign stranger, rather than as the closest thing she now has to a mother.

I wonder if she remembers anything at all about last night.

We've made it; we're outside the school gates. I feel better, more relaxed now there's distance between us and them. Even so, I hold on to Lexi's hand as firmly as I dare without hurting her.

She sits at my dining table in her school blazer and her pleated skirt. Her legs, in thick tights, kick back and forth under the table. Back and forth. Back and forth.

I am performing my special grandmother's trick. Using a paring knife, I peel the orange in one smooth movement, so the skin comes away in a long spiral. Lexi is transfixed, she doesn't say a word. When I have finished, I hand her the orange peel and then a Sharpie pen. With great care and concentration, she draws eyes and a forked tongue onto the skin of the orange. As she does, my eyes focus on the tiny needle-prick scars all over the back of her hands, the legacy of her time with us as a baby on the Weissman Unit.

Together, we have made a snake.

'My granny used to make these for me,' I say.

'Did you make one for my mummy?' She's holding it carefully, cupped in her hands.

'I did,' I say.

I'm trying to remember. I must have done, surely, because this is the way I always peel oranges. Vivien and I must have sat at this table, next to each other, just like Lexi and I are now. Only, I can't picture the way my daughter looked at eight years old.

I have these gaps in my memory and I don't attribute them to age, but rather to distraction. I was always torn in different directions, between work and home; it was hard to simply focus on one thing. On sitting, as I am with Lexi, and being fully present.

Her expression still serious, Lexi lays the orange peel down carefully on the table. Her mug of hot chocolate is empty and only a faint chocolate moustache is left on her upper lip. I lean over and gently wipe away the brown marks with my fingertips.

Her legs still kick under the table, making a dull thudding sound against the table leg. She's restless, but she's so reserved, she won't ask to leave the table until I invite her to. She's compliant, as though the fire inside her has been extinguished. Or perhaps, she was always this way, a quiet girl.

I'm on high alert around her, watching for signs of anything different, anything wrong. So far, there is nothing obvious. Only, she does not smile since she lost her mother. And she doesn't talk much at all.

'Would you like to look at some photographs, of your mummy,' I say, 'when she was a little girl like you?'

Lexi nods.

The photograph albums stand in a row on the bottom shelf of my bookcase. They are older ones, with red covers and gold borders, and inside there are sticky-backed cardboard pages filled with colour photographs. Some of them have begun to fade.

Lexi and I sit together on the sofa. She draws her knees up and huddles next to me; she presses her body against mine. I choose the album with the photographs of Vivien in her ballet costumes: in class, before her exams, in recitals, with full stage make-up. The photograph Lexi looks at the longest, the one she likes best, is the one where Vivien is made up to look like a mouse, with pink ears and a long tail. Lexi traces the shape of her mother beneath the plastic covering.

There are also several photographs of Vivien in one of her dance classes, after school. She's at the barre, in the community hall. Vivien is in sharp focus, but everything in the background, including the other girls, is blurred. Vivien is captured in different poses, in pliés, jetés, turning. She was so graceful, such a slender girl, and solemn, with large eyes and hollow cheeks, her head slightly too big for her small body.

I know I did not take these photographs. I don't remember this class; I remember Vivien dressed as a mouse, and in a purple leotard as the Sugar Plum Fairy, but not like this. It must have been Cleo who made this tribute to her friend.

I hug Lexi closer to me. I feel at peace, with this child curled into my side. I want to ask her if she is in pain, but I cannot find the words. I tell myself she's going to recover. That she can bear this. That although her mother is gone, I am here. I stroke her hair and I think how easy it is to love her.

By the time Isaac arrives to fetch her at six, we are both on the floor, kneeling beside the coffee table, drawing with felt-tips. Lexi has drawn a house – a fairly standard one with a square for the body of it and a triangle for the roof. But she takes great care over the garden, drawing several large pink flowers and then a black cat with whiskers. My job is to colour in the petals of the flowers with a light-pink colour. Lexi gives the cat two large and startled green eyes. So far, there are no people in her world.

At the sound of the doorbell, Lexi drops her pen and stands up, her face full of hope. I feel certain she has forgotten, and in that moment she thinks her mother has come for her. Then, the fleeting hope is replaced by a certain blankness, as though she is retreating from this world where she has to face the fact that her mother is never coming back.

When I open the door, Isaac is standing on my doorstep holding a bouquet of ivory roses. After a moment's hesitation, I reach out and accept the flowers. I close my eyes as I bring the silky petals to my face and breathe in deep. The delicate smell makes me feel horribly sad.

I keep my eyes closed for a few seconds, and I remind myself that babies die on my ward all the time; I am by no means the only parent to suffer. Then I look at Isaac. As he smiles at me, I feel the skin on my face become hot, flushed.

'Will you come in for a while?' I say.

'I'm sorry,' he says, 'Ben is expecting us home.'

'Lexi's eaten some pasta,' I say. 'I doubt she'll want much dinner.'

'I'll let him know.'

He waits in the doorway of my small kitchen, arms crossed in front of him in the way he does, while I search for something to put the flowers in. I find an old green glass vase under the sink and fill it with water. Carefully, I cut away the paper and the elastic band and I arrange the roses. When I've finished I turn around, holding the flowers in front me.

'What was the police interview about?' I say. I keep my voice low.

From the living room I hear the clatter of felt-tip pens falling to the wooden floor.

'Let's talk later,' Isaac says.

He turns to look behind him, at the glass door, through which we can see Lexi's silhouette as she kneels at the coffee table.

Isaac stands aside to let me pass, then follows me down the passage. Lexi barely glances up as we come into the room. Her head is bent over her page and she's frowning in concentration, biting her upper lip, as she puts the finishing touches on the flowers in her garden. She has outlined each of the pink petals in electric blue.

'What a lovely picture,' I say.

She nods, ever serious.

I place the flowers in the centre of the dining-room table, where they look quite lovely.

'Lexi,' I say, 'it's time to go home.'

She is careful to place the lid back on to her felt-tip pen before she stands up. Once again, I find it unsettling, how obedient she is. Vivien was so defiant, always ready with an argument. That, I do remember.

'Would you like to take your drawing home with you?' I say.

'You can keep it,' Lexi says. She leaves it lying on the low table.

She doesn't fuss as I help her on with her grey coat and her school shoes in the entrance hall. I place our orange-peel snake carefully inside a plastic bag and hand it to her.

'Will you put him on the radiator in your bedroom when you get home?' I ask.

'Why?'

'Because then your room will smell of oranges and you will remember how much I love you.'

'Okay.' Lexi gives me a small and shy smile, though it's so fleeting I think I might have imagined it.

There is a look of pity on Isaac's face. He puts an arm around her shoulders and guides her out of the open front door and into the stale-smelling corridor.

'I'll see you soon,' I say. I keep my voice casual as I bend down to kiss Lexi's cool cheek. I hug her, my closed eyes against her tangled curls. She smells of chocolate. My eyes burn but I don't cry. Lexi has enough to deal with.

I wave and smile as the lift doors open but she doesn't look back. It's hard to say whether or not she minds leaving me. I suppose the truth is she doesn't.

Chapter 12

At around nine o'clock that night, when I know Ben will have put Lexi to bed, I arrive at Blackthorn Road. I'm carrying a tray of roast chicken, bought from a deli on the high street, one Vivien often used for catering. There is an elderly Greek lady behind the counter, who is always dressed head-to-toe in black, and today I could empathize with her dour expression.

The driveway is well lit. The matching Range Rovers, with their BKAYE and VKAYE plates, are parked side by side. The lights are on in the basement, and on the ground floor, but the first and second floors of the house are in darkness. I hope Lexi has found peace in her sleep tonight. And I hope Ben isn't too far into his bottle of whisky.

I press the buzzer with my elbow as I balance the tray in my arms. I think about what I'm going to say to Ben. I could say I wanted to drop off some food, to make sure they're eating properly. I could say I want to find out how Lexi is, how she responded after her visit to my flat.

And then, if the atmosphere between us is still cordial, I will ask Ben about the visit from the police.

I wait. I look into the round glass eye of the camera. Under the tinfoil covering, the chicken is succulent and spicy and swims in oil. The smell grows stronger by the minute.

When the front door opens, a woman appears at the top of the steps, a dark silhouette against the bright lights of the entrance hall. My heart stops dead, then lurches against my ribs. I feel a surge of joy that defies rational thought. *My daughter is alive.*

And then, as she moves, I see it isn't Vivien at all. Her gait is not as graceful as she walks down the few steps towards me. Vivien never lost her ballerina's posture, she walked with her neck long and her chin lifted; this woman's shoulders are a little rounded and her footsteps heavier than those of my daughter.

My heart still thrashes in my chest. The surge of hope was so powerful.

It's Cleo, of course. She could have released the catch on the gate from where she stood at the front door, but instead she walks down towards me at an irritatingly slow pace, until we are standing face to face on opposite sides of the locked gate.

She seems surprised to see me. 'Rose,' she says, 'what are you doing here?'

'The release catch for the gate is just inside the

front door.' I balance the tray of chicken in one arm and gesture up towards the house and the open door behind her.

'This really isn't a good time,' Cleo says. 'Lexi's had another one of her nightmares and Ben's upstairs trying to calm her down.'

'Open the gate. I need to see her.'

Cleo does not move. I could swear I recognize the scent of her perfume. The sweet scent of gardenias.

'Cleo, would you please open the gate. Now.'

She looks back towards the open front door, then she takes a step backwards.

'Cleo, is Ben all right? Has he been drinking?'

I wonder if Ben knows I'm standing outside the house. I wonder if he's asked Cleo to keep me out. I wonder what exactly the police had to say to him this afternoon.

I'm anxious at being shut out, at being kept apart from Lexi. I dump the tray of chicken down on the pavement and grab hold of the cold metal bars.

Cleo has turned her back on me; she's halfway up the stairs. I reach out and hit the buzzer. I slam it over and over again.

She stops, whipping her head round. 'Stop it!' she says. 'Lexi's had such a difficult night. Rose, please.'

My palms burn where I clutch at the icy bars. I shake them though they do not budge. Cleo comes back down, she stands very close.

'Rose,' she says, 'it's better if you call first, before

visiting.' Her smile is patronizing and it infuriates me. I am powerless.

'Go home, Rose.' She says the words calmly. Gently, even. Then she turns her back on me once again and I watch as she climbs the shallow stairs, steps through the door and shuts it behind her.

White hot with anger, I bend down and pick up the tinfoil tray. The lid has come off and oil leaks all over the concrete. The smell makes me sick.

As I look around for a dustbin, a movement catches my eye from inside the house. Down to the right, in the basement kitchen, the shutters are tilted slightly open. Inside, the figure of a man is walking across the room. I recognize Ben, his shape and the determined set of his shoulders.

I return to my flat, deflated and defeated. I am frozen out of Vivien's house and out of Lexi's life. I cannot watch over my granddaughter as I know I must. I am frantic but I don't know what to do.

The pain strikes behind my right eye, it's as though an anvil smashes at my temple. In the kitchen I grab a couple of codeine tablets. I wash them down with water.

The pain in the right side of my skull won't let go of me and I begin to feel nauseous. I start down the passage, bracing my hand against the stippled walls for support, but I don't make it further than the bathroom. I press myself into the hard-tiled corner, I fold into the small space on the floor between the sink and the toilet while

I wait for the painkillers to work. I'm clutching at my head with both hands, with claws for fingers.

I drag myself forwards, hold on to the white enamel rim of the toilet bowl and retch. The bitter yellow bile keeps coming, in waves of nausea. I only hope some of the codeine stayed inside me.

My mobile vibrates as it lies on the side of the bath. I don't reach for it.

I'm walking down the staircase at number sixty-three Blackthorn Road. Vivien is standing at the bottom, looking up at me. Her hair is clean and glossy, she's just come back from the salon. She looks beautiful, in a fitted shirt and skinny jeans. She's well rested.

I've been up all night. I did all of Lexi's night feeds. Early this morning I collected up the empty bottles from Lexi's room and took them down to the kitchen to sterilize them.

And then, instead of going back to bed, I packed my suitcase.

I've reached the bottom step and I set my suitcase down on the tiles.

'It's time for me to go,' I say.

For a moment, Vivien is still, confused. Then she steps forward and she embraces me. Her hair smells so fresh, so lovely. I stand stiff as a board and then I push her away.

'It really is time,' I say. 'Lexi is bigger now, she's off the oxygen and I have to go back to work. They won't

136

hold my post for me any longer.'

'You don't need to work,' Vivien says. 'You never need to work again.'

'Yes, I do.'

She trembles. 'So let me get this clear,' she says. 'We have all the money in the world, more than we know what to do with, and you're choosing to stay in that disgusting flat of yours and go back to work with other people's sick children instead of helping me to take care of your own grandchild?'

'She's well, Viv. She's a perfect little girl. You don't need me.'

'I can't do this,' she says.

'Yes, you can. You're her mother.'

'I'm not her mother.'

'I don't want to hear you say that ever again.'

I tell myself she's afraid, that's all, that's why she says these things.

'Don't leave me,' she says. *Tears spill over and trickle down her cheeks.*

I look right past her and not into her eyes. I lift my suitcase and I walk across the chequerboard floor, in a straight line, towards the front door.

I feel myself growing calmer as the codeine kicks in, dampening my pain. I reach over and pick up my phone. I have a text message from Wendy, confirming my shift tomorrow. And a voicemail, from Isaac. He wants to come over. He needs to talk to me.

At the sound of his voice I feel comforted. I do not want to be alone tonight. I need someone to talk to about what's happened, and I need his advice. I need an ally.

Chapter 13

Isaac shrugs off his mackintosh and I hang it up on the coat rack next to the front door. It must be raining again because his coat is soaking wet. Underneath it, he's wearing a white shirt over a pair of black jeans. His sleeves are rolled up to his elbows.

He follows me through to the living room, where there are two cold bottles of beer on the coffee table. They are Peroni, the same brand we drank at the Italian place; the label caught my eye at Waitrose the day afterwards.

Isaac tilts my glass as he pours. I am next to him on the sofa, my knees folded underneath me. My hair is still damp from the shower and the headache has lifted. The codeine makes my body light and weightless, and, next to Isaac, with a glass of Peroni in my hand, I feel I am hiding from the black guilt that dogs me day and night.

'I was over at Blackthorn Road earlier,' I say. 'Cleo answered the door and she refused to let me inside. I've always thought she was timid as a mouse, but it appears I was wrong.'

Isaac raises his eyebrows, but he doesn't yet give a view.

'Isaac, does she stay there overnight?'

'I don't think so. I'm usually at the house by six, and there's no sign of her. But I can't be sure. I clean up a bit,' he says, 'to help Ben out, and most mornings there are two glasses out in the living room.'

'Cleo said some very odd things,' I say. 'She talked about searching for photographs of Vivien and Ben on the internet.'

We're face to face, up close. I dread to think how haggard I look. I know Vivien's death is etched into the lines on my face.

'I'm frightened for Lexi. Do you understand, Isaac? I'm responsible for her now. I'm the closest she's going to get to a mother. I'm furious that Cleo thinks she has the right to keep me from my granddaughter.'

Isaac reaches out. He puts his hand over mine as it rests on the sofa between us. I look down, and it is a strange sensation, as though these two weather-beaten hands belong to other people.

'I need to talk to Ben,' I say. 'I'm going to ask him about that damn argument. I want to know why he walked out on Vivien. And then I'm going to ask him exactly what's going on between him and Cleo. I'm going to tell him I don't trust her.'

Isaac clears his throat. 'That's actually why I wanted

to talk to you,' he says. 'I thought you should know what Ben and the police discussed this afternoon.'

His hand clasps mine.

'Did you know that Ben owns a property in Bermondsey?' he says. 'A flat in a block called Cinnamon Wharf.'

'I know the flat. But I wasn't aware he still owned it. He and Vivien lived there together, before they were married.'

'And did you know that the current resident of the property is one Cleo Baker?'

I pull away from him as I swing my legs onto the floor. 'I had no idea Cleo still lived there.'

'But you did know that the three of them lived in Cinnamon Wharf together? Ben, Vivien and Cleo?' Isaac sounds incredulous. I prickle.

'Yes. For a brief time they were all there together. A few weeks, maybe. But this was years and years ago. I suppose it sounds bizarre.'

'I have to say it does.'

'Cleo and Ben were a couple before he and Vivien got together. I think Vivien asked if she could move in with them for a while, after a bad break-up. And I guess she and Ben were attracted to each other. Cleo was pushed out.'

'So would it surprise you to know,' Isaac says, 'that Cleo Baker continues to live in this flat without paying any rent?'

'Yes,' I say. 'That would surprise me.' I take a swig of my beer. Isaac does the same.

'Ben is obviously a wealthy man,' Isaac says, 'but I'm wondering why he would subsidize an ex-girlfriend for all these years?'

I look down. The veins on the back of my hands protrude and bruises have spread where I dig my nails into my skin.

'You're saying you think they have been having an affair?'

'I'm saying,' Isaac says, 'you might wait a while before confronting Ben. His loyalty to Cleo might run a lot deeper than you think.'

I reach for my beer bottle and I drink from it until it's half-empty. Isaac sits forward on the couch and he's right up close. My hand rests on my thigh, and he runs his fingertips over the angry half-moon bruises.

'What happened to you?' he says.

'Nothing.'

Isaac has the good sense not to ask again.

'Has Ben ever told you that there was a time when I lived with them in the house on Blackthorn Road?' I ask him.

He shakes his head. 'No.'

'Lexi was an IVF baby, a twin actually, the only one of the babies to survive a disastrous pregnancy. But she was born very premature, and she was in the Weissman Unit for three months. When she was discharged, she was still on oxygen, and Ben and Vivien were really anxious around her. They needed a lot of support. So I took leave and I moved in with them for six weeks.'

I cover my eyes with my hands, as I remember. I see myself walking out, walking across those black-and-white tiles. I should never have left them alone.

For a few moments we sit in silence. Isaac's hands are wrapped around his beer bottle again.

I turn my body towards his. 'You were the one that found her?' I ask.

I didn't mean to say this, but I do. He doesn't seem surprised by my question. I think he's been waiting for me to ask him.

'Yes,' he says. He looks at me with compassion and sadness and I think he may be going to apologize to me again, and if he does, I am going to scream. But he doesn't.

'I tried everything,' he says. 'CPR. Mouth to mouth. There was nothing I could do for her.'

'I understand.'

'She looked so tiny,' he says, 'like a child.'

'She would have hated people to see her that way. She hated being vulnerable.'

'I covered her with a blanket from her bed,' he says. 'I suppose I shouldn't have touched anything, but I had to cover her. I put a pillow underneath her head, as though she was asleep. I couldn't bear to leave her on that cold floor. I stayed with her, until the ambulance came. I didn't leave her alone.'

I have tears in my eyes, but they don't spill over.

'I've seen my share of dead bodies,' I say. 'I bathe the babies and I dress them, and then I hand them back to their parents for one last cuddle. They are small and at peace. Not like my daughter.'

I shudder as I take a deep breath. 'I don't understand how Ben can live in that house. I don't understand how he can bear to set foot in that bathroom.'

Isaac reaches out and takes hold of my hand with both of his. His skin is so warm.

'That house is their home,' he says. 'Everything the child knows is in that house. Her mother is in that house.'

The throbbing in my head has quietened down. I have a few precious hours before I wake tomorrow morning and it all comes back again. I consider that my every waking moment is consumed with thoughts of Vivien and of Lexi. Perhaps even I deserve a few moments of peace. I feel the pressure of his thumb through the cotton of my jeans, against my thigh. I lean against him.

'Will you stay, tonight?' I ask him. 'I don't want to be alone.'

He feels so sturdy, so compelling as he holds me, and I feel so very alive and then so very guilty.

Chapter 14

I am woken by a series of loud bangs. Three aggressive bursts of sound. Someone is knocking on my front door.

I turn onto my back and open my eyes. My room is dark; there is blackout lining on the curtains, so I can sleep through the day when I'm working night shifts.

I reach out with my right hand and feel the empty space beside me. Isaac left early this morning, while I was still hazy with sleep. I lift my head to look at my clock, my vision still a little blurred from sleep. It's mid-morning.

I lay my head down on the pillow where he slept, where I can still smell him.

The banging starts up again.

I stand slowly and walk, heavy-limbed, to the front door where I grab my coat from its hook and throw it on over my nightgown. I peer through the peephole, then remove the chain from the door and open up to the familiar, acrid air of the passageway.

DS Cole is standing in front of me, and this time she is not alone. A tall, thin man lurks behind her. My eyes are back in focus, and I see he's older than she is, somewhere in his early forties. His high forehead, sharp blue eyes and Roman nose combine to give him an intense, predatory appearance.

'DS Cole,' I say. 'This is a surprise.'

'I apologize,' she says. 'I did try to call you earlier but I think your phone's turned off.'

'I was just about to leave for work.'

DS Cole takes in my hastily slung-on coat and my bare feet and looks unconvinced.

The man behind her introduces himself as DI Hawkins. He keeps his hands in his pockets as he talks to me, which I think somehow disrespectful. His eyes flicker as he peers over my shoulder and down the passage. I stand there stubbornly, one arm on the door handle, the other on the door frame, and I don't invite them in.

'We won't disturb you for long,' DS Cole says. 'But we've had some toxicology tests back and we wanted to talk to you about these.'

She shifts her canvas bag, adjusting the strap so it sits more comfortably across her body. She's in a tailored grey suit today and her hair is a fresh, pale blonde. The dark roots I noticed at the hospital are gone.

DI Hawkins takes his hands out of his pockets and folds his arms. I remain planted in the doorway, frozen still. I can hear the Pomeranians across the hall snuffling at the gap between the door and the floor.

'The results show unexpected levels of amphetamines in your daughter's body,' DS Cole says.

'Amphetamines?'

'We believe Vivien had taken diet pills before she died,' she says.

DI Hawkins is looking at me, expecting me to say something. I picture him kneeling down and turning over rocks. All kinds of ugly insects swarm out from underneath. I dislike him.

'Did you know Vivien was using these pills?' DS Cole says.

'No. I didn't. Vivien was always conscious of her weight, but she was careful about her diet. I had no idea she was taking pills to control her appetite.'

I cough. The lump in my throat is back again.

DI Hawkins speaks for the first time, and his voice is harsh and too loud. 'We've looked at Vivien's GP notes, and there's no record of any such prescription. In fact, her GP had no idea she was taking these pills.'

'I see.' I sound cold, detached.

'Do you find any of this a cause for concern?' DI Hawkins says. He sounds impatient, irritated with me. It seems the dislike is mutual.

'Of course I'm concerned. I'm shocked. I'm trying to digest all of this. Are you saying these pills are linked to her death?'

'Yes, I am,' he says.

There is something about his tone I don't like. Something accusatory. DS Cole fidgets. She adjusts her bag again and runs her fingers through her peroxided hair. I want to believe she doesn't like the way DI Hawkins talks to me, that she's on my side.

I don't know why they have come to see me at my home, or what they're looking for. I feel as though I'm taking a test I haven't prepared for. DI Hawkins is staring at me with those shrewd eyes of his.

'You're a medical professional,' he says.

'I'm a nurse.'

'A senior nurse.'

'Yes.'

'And you work in a large hospital?'

'Yes. On a neonatal unit.'

'So as a senior staff member of a large hospital, you'd have access to all kinds of controlled substances?'

I laugh. A nervous laugh. An incredulous one. 'That's ridiculous,' I say.

'Did you ever provide your daughter with diet pills?' DI Hawkins says.

DS Cole definitely looks uncomfortable. She smiles at me, in an attempt at reassurance, but the look on her face only increases my sense of impending doom.

'Of course I didn't provide my daughter with drugs.'

A high-pitched yapping starts across the hall. I feel sure Mrs Shenkar is going to open her front door and peer out, to check what's going on. Then the barking stops, abruptly. I imagine her in her muumuu, bending down and scooping up the two fluffy dogs and whisking them off for their breakfast.

The two officers don't budge from my doorway.

'Look,' I say, 'are you accusing me of something?'

'We're trying to understand Vivien's state of mind when she died,' DS Cole says. 'She didn't leave a note. No one who had contact with her has reported any changes in mood. She didn't talk about being suicidal or having plans to harm herself. But now we know she took substances before she died. So it's important that we understand where she got this medication from.'

I hear myself exhale. They're both watching me.

'And not only that,' DI Hawkins says, 'but there was no sign of any empty packaging in the home.'

'I'm sorry, I can't help you,' I say.

'Thank you,' DS Cole says. 'I'm sorry if we've delayed you.'

She smiles at me again, but DI Hawkins remains grim. 'You know,' he says, 'relatives of the deceased usually have a lot of questions for us. They're usually desperate to know all the details, to find out every last bit of information we might have.'

I see a millisecond of anger cross DS Cole's face as she looks at her colleague.

'Well,' I say, 'in my experience, all families grieve differently. I don't like to be a drain on your resources, and I know there's no point asking questions if you haven't had time to find the answers yet. I'm sure you'll let me know when you have something concrete to report.'

I won't rise to the bait. If he wants to accuse me of something, he'll have to be more explicit.

'Oh, we will most certainly let you know,' DI Hawkins says rather acerbically.

DS Cole touches my arm, just for a brief moment. 'You can contact me any time,' she says. 'If there's anything you want to ask me or tell me. Please don't hesitate.'

I step back and shut the door on them. Then I lean against it for support and I close my eyes.

Chapter 15

I arrive early for my shift. But instead of going up to the Weissman Unit, I walk around the side of the building until I reach the entrance to the private wing. I take the lift up to the third floor, to Mrs Murad's rooms.

Her reception area resembles the plush lobby of an upmarket hotel. There is a Louis XV silk-upholstered sofa, sage-green curtains and a sage-green carpet dotted with little white diamonds. These rooms could not be more different from the Weissman Unit with its chipped Formica reception desk and blue linoleum floors.

I explain to the receptionist that Mrs Murad has left several messages for me, and I ask if she might have a few minutes to see me, in between patients. The young woman, with glasses too large for her face, looks at me with pitying eyes, a look with which I am now all too familiar. A look I myself have given many other bereaved parents. She offers me a cup of tea, which I decline, and she tells me there might be quite a wait. I sit rigid-backed on the sofa.

I run my fingers over my hair, tucking loose strands behind my ears. I hope I look presentable, and not as though I'm caving in under the burden of guilt and grief. I tuck myself inside my protective carapace, formed during many long years of self-reliance. I think I might look almost normal.

In the end the wait is not long at all. A couple leaves her office, a woman with the laboured gait of late pregnancy, her husband with his hand on the small of her back. Moments later, Mrs Murad herself appears in the doorway of her office. She's a petite woman in a black suit, and her hair, like mine, is mostly a silver-grey.

She ushers me into her office, gesturing to a wingback armchair as she closes the door. In keeping with the waiting room, her consulting room is replete with soft furnishings and thick curtains. She sits opposite me, behind a large desk. In front of her there is a wafer-thin laptop.

'I was so sorry to hear about Vivien,' she says. 'I wanted to tell you in person.'

The seconds pass. I look down at my fidgeting hands, my nails pressing into my own soft skin.

'Thank you,' I say. 'I'm sorry I haven't returned your calls.'

'I thought you might want to talk to me,' she says. 'I thought you might have questions.'

'Have the police been to see you?'

'Yes, they have.'

'They're trying to understand her state of mind before she—' I clear my throat as my words disappear.

Mrs Murad nods.

'You treated Vivien for several years,' I say, 'you must have known her very well.'

'Almost ten years, on and off.'

'I've often wondered why you called me the day she died,' I say. 'When she missed her appointment, I mean. Because, surely, people miss appointments all the time? I'm guessing something was worrying you.'

'Yes, you're right,' she says. 'I don't know if Vivien told you, but we had a very difficult consultation some weeks ago. She was unhappy and angry with me when she left my office because I had advised against another round of IVF. So I suppose, when she missed her next appointment, I was more concerned than I ordinarily would have been, because she'd left our last appointment so distressed.'

I've known Mrs Murad for several years, and I know she can be a little brusque, somewhat blunt with her patients. She is not known for having the most comforting of bedside manners. But she is brilliant at what she does.

'Maybe I should have contacted her earlier,' Mrs Murad says, 'in between appointments. But I thought it was better to let her cool down and reflect on what I'd said. I assumed we'd talk again in a few weeks.

I took it as a positive sign she'd made another appointment.'

'I think we all feel guilty,' I say. 'With hindsight everyone can think of something they should have said or done.'

'That's generous of you to say.'

I understand that she too must keep her distance: she deals every day with infertility, with the deepest of longings and the most painful of disappointments. We both know it would not do to cave in to the sadness or to absorb the emotions of our patients. If we did that, we could not go on.

'May I ask why you'd advised Vivien against another round of IVF?'

Mrs Murad puts on her reading glasses, which hang from a beaded red cord around her neck, and she peers at the screen of her laptop. Then she closes the lid, takes off her glasses, and begins to speak.

'The last time I saw Vivien was around eight weeks ago,' she says. 'She came back to see me, over the years, for more investigations of the fertility difficulties she was facing. We looked at different treatment options, and new treatments that became available. But we didn't have as much success as I would have hoped after her first pregnancy.'

She pauses, and deliberates for a few moments, choosing her words carefully.

'Vivien was young when we first started to look into her difficulties becoming pregnant. She was still in her twenties. She had polycystic ovaries, which I didn't see as the main barrier to falling pregnant. But as time went on, my main concern wasn't her fertility per se, but her weight.'

'Her weight?'

'Yes. It fluctuated. There were times when it dropped below levels of what was normal.'

She smiles regretfully at me, the smile of a professional about to deliver bad news. 'Quite early on I suspected your daughter might have an eating disorder. Perhaps she didn't fulfil all the criteria for a diagnosis, but she certainly had several of the features of anorexia.'

I feel her words as a blow to my stomach and I have to catch my breath. I had always admired my daughter's self-control. I'd seen her ability to deny herself the pleasure of food as a virtue, not an illness. I saw her iron will as a strength. Now I have to wonder: exactly how blind have I been?

I am stunned. Then I feel a fool. And then I am angry.

'But you're not a psychiatrist,' I say.

I regret this immediately. I hadn't intended my words to come out sounding like an accusation, because the last thing I want is to put her on the offensive. My stomach tenses up. I expect she might clam up and ask me to leave; I know a bit about consultants' egos. But Mrs Murad is confident enough, or perhaps pities me enough, that she doesn't take offence.

'No,' she says patiently, 'I'm not a psychiatrist. But my impression was that Vivien had become quite skilled at concealing the extent to which she controlled her food intake. As I said, her weight fluctuated, and there were times when it was so low it interrupted her menstrual cycle. There was a point at which I had to confront her with the fact that what she needed treatment for, first and foremost, was not her fertility problems, but her eating disorder. Unfortunately, as far as I know, Vivien never took up my recommendation that she see a psychiatrist. I don't think she ever accepted she had an eating disorder.'

A voice in my head is demanding to know how I could have been so neglectful.

Mrs Murad weighs her words. 'So,' she says, 'in answer to your question about why I advised against further fertility treatment – I thought a combination of factors made it unwise to go ahead. Unethical, even.'

I change the cross of my legs and run my hands along the creases in my trousers. 'A combination of factors?'

'As I'm sure you know,' she says, 'parents of IVF babies can carry a lot of anxiety. For some parents this can be very intense. In my experience, symptoms of eating disorders and anxiety and depression often go together. I thought it would have been the wrong decision to go ahead with fertility treatment under the circumstances. Given Vivien's emotional state.'

'I've been told,' I say, 'by the police, that Vivien was taking both antidepressants and slimming tablets when she died. But the slimming pills weren't prescribed by her GP. Did you know she'd started taking these?'

I imagine a note of caution enters her voice. 'Vivien never disclosed to me that she was taking slimming tablets.'

'But did she tell you that she'd got hold of some of these tablets, or where she got them from?'

She shakes her head.

'Did you ever tell Ben that you believed Vivien had an eating disorder, or that she should see a psychiatrist?'

'I did.'

'When?'

'It was after she last came to see me.'

'A few weeks before she died?'

'Yes, Vivien had stopped bringing Ben to the consultations with her, and that worried me too. But I do believe I acted in her best interests – by referring her for psychiatric help.'

She is on the defensive now, I can see it in the pursing of her lips and I can hear it in her clipped sentences.

'I did break confidentiality,' she says. 'I told Vivien I was going to talk to Ben and she wasn't happy about it.'

'If you broke confidentiality,' I say, 'then you must have been extremely worried. Did you believe Vivien was a danger to herself?'

'No,' she says, 'I didn't. I really had no reason to believe Vivien was suicidal.'

'I don't understand. In that case, why would you break patient confidentiality and talk to Ben?'

'Because it wasn't only Vivien I was worried about,' she says. 'It was her daughter. That's partly why I wanted to talk to you.'

I don't want her to see how fearful I am. I grip my hands together, clench them in my lap. 'Why would you be worried about Lexi?'

'I was concerned that Vivien was not only fixated on her own weight, but had developed distorted perceptions about her daughter's weight. I suppose it was a displacement, or an extension of her own body-image problems. Of course, as you rightly say, I'm not a psychiatrist.'

She looks at me pointedly.

'I apologize,' I say. 'I do understand that you acted in Vivien's best interests. Please go on.'

'Vivien told me her daughter was being bullied at school because she was overweight. She said she'd tried to encourage Lexi to eat more healthily but it wasn't working. She asked me if there was any link between obesity and IVF, which I said was unlikely. And then Vivien told me she was thinking of medicating her daughter. She asked me a question about dosage. Of course I'm not a paediatrician and I told her I wasn't the right person to advise her. But I was really concerned, because Alexandra is so young. I advised her to see a paediatric dietician about diet and so on, but Vivien had certain fixed ideas that worried me. I had the impression she wasn't going to listen to proper medical advice. I must stress this was just an impression, but I've learnt to trust my gut instinct. The infertility treatment can be psychologically traumatic in itself – both the procedures and the repeated failure. In combination with her weight problems and some of her ideas around her child, I was worried about her mental state and I believed I needed to let Ben know about my concerns.'

I sit quietly while I try to digest everything she's just told me. 'So you told Ben about all of this?'

'Yes. I telephoned him after our consultation. He said he would convince Vivien to see a psychiatrist. I'm only sorry I didn't have a chance to talk to her myself, after that last appointment. And of course I've wondered about the timing, and why this happened right before she was due to see me. I'm only human. I'll always wonder if there's something more I could have done. But I like to think Vivien understood I had her best interests at heart. I hope so.'

'I think she did,' I say. 'She was coming back to see you. She trusted you.'

Mrs Murad moves her laptop to the side of her desk. She gives me a rueful smile and I understand my time is up. There are patients lining up outside, I'm sure, anxious and expectant couples perched on the expensive sofa.

'Come back and talk to me any time,' she says. 'If you let me know in advance, I'll make more time for you.'

'Thank you,' I say. I stand up, and we shake hands across her desk.

As I reach the door, Mrs Murad calls out: 'How is Alexandra doing?'

I place my hand on the doorknob but I don't turn it and I don't turn around to face her.

'I'm keeping a close eye on her,' I say.

This is not entirely a lie, I tell myself.

'Ben loved your daughter very much,' Mrs Murad says. Her voice is clear and strong. 'Sometimes we can love people too much. So much that we don't want to see what's wrong. But your granddaughter is in safe hands.'

Vivien

Seven years ago

Alexandra is crying again. I lie still, as though I'm asleep, but my eyes are wide open. The cot is on Ben's side of the bed. She has passed her one-year milestone, yet still sleeps in our bedroom.

Ben sits up, swings his legs over the side of the bed and scoops her up into his arms. He takes her out of the room, so as not to disturb me. Ben doesn't mind getting up in the middle of the night, who knows how often. I've lost count of the times Alexandra wakes us. I hear him whispering to her, soothing her as he leaves our bedroom. *Lexi*, he calls her.

Ben never complains about these disturbances in the night. I've begun to suspect he might even welcome them; he says he doesn't get to see his daughter enough during the day. I don't understand how he manages the night-wakings and then the early-morning start and yet is more contented than I've ever known him to be. Ben really is a family man.

I pull the duvet up around my face. I'm cold, now that he's left me.

Alexandra is no trouble during the day. She's a quiet, contented sort of baby, and doesn't cry much. She takes the bottle when I offer it to her, and she looks up at me, trying to fix on my eyes as she drinks. I try hard not to look away, but it's a strange sensation, holding her and being stared at. I always feel as though my daughter is accusing me of something. I sometimes feel angry with her, for no reason. And sometimes, I have to force myself to pick her up. I have to remind myself to smile at her. Babies need those things: physical affection and smiley faces.

She is so needy and so small, and yet so powerful and all-consuming. Ben barely looks at me when he comes through the door. He wants me less often; what he really craves is the feel of his daughter against his chest. I don't know any more whether the child is my saviour or my undoing. And yet I am Alexandra's mother and that makes me queen of Ben's kingdom. He will never leave me now.

My thoughts are always dark, paranoid and irrational in the early hours of the morning. I can't get back to sleep. There is no sign of Ben or of the baby. I get up and walk, silently, out of the bedroom and down the stairs, towards the light in the nursery. Ben has his back to me as he stands at the changing table. Bare-chested and barefoot, he leans over her. Alexandra never cries when her father changes her.

'That's a wet nappy,' he says. 'What have you been drinking today?' Alexandra gurgles.

'What strong legs you have!' Ben says. He holds her with one hand, slides the nappy out from under her, unfolds a new one, and parcels her up again. He and the baby don't take their eyes off each other. It's a love affair.

Ben picks Alexandra up and walks over to the window. He slides open the shutters, so she can see the lights of the street below. When she begins to niggle, Ben rocks her, placing his little finger to her lips.

I stay in the doorway, watching them. Alexandra, I'm sure, is asleep, but Ben does not put her down. He sways, rocking her. I have never seen him so contented. Or so compelling.

I creep back to our cold bed and I trace the contours of the empty space where Ben should be lying beside me.

Chapter 16

We have three new admissions and all of the babies are on ventilators. The agency nurses on duty don't have as much experience as they should, and so I have to keep an eye on them. The portable X-ray machine is perpetually in operation, as we clear the room and then return, over and over again.

By the end of the night shift I am worn out. My arms and legs ache and I'm ready to go back home and face my empty flat and my thoughts about what Mrs Murad has told me.

Instead of heading home, though, after handover, I find myself visiting little Yusuf. He's awake in his cot, the yellow feeding tube still taped to his bulging cheek. As I reach over him to wind the mobile, he smiles up at me. He reminds me of Lexi sometimes, his temperament so settled and quiet. He is so uncomplaining in his solitude. I lift him up and carry him to the window, where I show him the same old sights.

There is a rustling behind us, a tentative sound, and I

turn to find a young woman standing beside Yusuf's empty cot. She is slight, with a magenta sari drawn up to cover her hair. In all the months Yusuf has been on the ward, I've glimpsed his mother only once before. On that visit she was trailing, submissive and head down, behind her husband, a loud and corpulent man.

She smiles at me but does not try to approach me, or to reach out to claim her son. She's very young and she doesn't speak English. She doesn't understand any of it: the hospital, the incubators, the feeding tube, any of what's happened to her and to her baby.

Amanda sticks her head round the door. 'We're just waiting for the translator,' she says, smiling.

Yusuf's mother nods as though she understands. She stands next to his cot and waits. I tighten my grip on her baby. Yusuf is floppy in my arms, his muscle tone is low and he will need specialist care going forward. He'll need to come back to outpatients for follow-ups with the paediatrician, for appointments with the physio-therapist and the speech and language therapist. It's so important he comes back, or all of his suffering will have been for nothing.

I know Yusuf will never make it back here. She will not bring him to see the specialists, she's overwhelmed already. I glance down and I see her belly is rounded and the shock of it makes me furious.

'You don't visit Yusuf often enough,' I say. 'Your baby is very sick. How are you going to look after him at home if you don't watch how the nurses are feeding him? How will you help him with the exercises for his neck?'

Her face falls because my tone has worried her. She looks at me, doe-eyed and confused.

Amanda is back in the doorway with Andrew Lissauer beside her and they're both looking at me with Yusuf in my arms, like I'm some sort of unguided missile. Amanda comes forwards and holds out her arms, but I don't want to let him go. I hold him tighter, closer.

'How can you send him home with her?' I say. 'She's a stranger to him. She has no idea how to operate his feeding tube. He'll starve if you let her take him.'

Amanda looks at Andrew. He takes a few steps towards me.

'Rose,' he says, 'put Yusuf down. You know we have a great home-visiting team, we'll make sure he gets the care he needs.'

I don't budge. There's so much we're not allowed to say, but I hear myself saying it anyway. I'm so tired of pretending that everything is all right.

'We provide twenty-four-hour care, day and night, for months, and then we send these babies home.' I cradle Yusuf's head because he's begun to squirm as my voice rises. 'We send them home to irresponsible, useless teenagers, or drug abusers, and we pretend we don't know it. We send them home to people who can't afford to have all the children they do. We pretend it's all right when people insist on multiple IVF pregnancies when they know how high the risks are and then the babies are born early with all kinds of complications. I'm so tired of cleaning up other people's messes.'

Yusuf's mother looks between me and Amanda and Andrew. She is silent and frightened. I'm shouting at them and I don't seem to be able to stop.

'I'm sick of seeing these babies suffer. They grow up with detached retinas and brain damage and chronic lung fucking disease. And in all of that, she can't even be bothered to visit. What are we doing this for?'

I retreat from them, my back up against the window. Yusuf is fighting me now, uttering small half-strangled cries.

His mother is so terribly young, her features so delicate. Her large, dark eyes stare out from under the bright-pink headscarf. She has a tiny gold stud in her nose. She doesn't understand why I'm yelling at her. Her husband never comes. She has a three-year-old and an eighteen-month-old at home. I'm squeezing Yusuf and rocking him and he's crying, a rough, gulping sound.

Andrew and Amanda rush forwards together, Amanda puts her hands under Yusuf's arms as though she's afraid I might fling open the window and hurl both of us through.

I loosen my grasp, I let Amanda take him from me.

Yusuf's mother is crying now. Amanda goes over to her and shows her Yusuf is all right; she makes reassuring murmurings. Andrew grips my elbow and marches me out of the ward and down the corridor.

He's still holding on to my arm as he shuts the door of Wendy's office behind us.

Wendy is behind her desk. My old desk. Her in-tray is overflowing, her workspace messy. I used to be so organized, so competent.

When Andrew lets go of me, I clasp my hands together, digging my nails as deep as I can into the back of my left hand. I am trembling. I try but I cannot control the shaking. I shut out Andrew's words, as he explains to Wendy what I've just done.

'I don't think Yusuf's mother will file a complaint,' he's saying. 'But she would certainly be entitled to do so.'

'That child is neglected,' I say. 'We can't just turn a blind eye.'

'It's the parents' prerogative to leave him in our care,' Andrew says. 'We have round-the-clock nursing staff and you know there are older siblings at home. You know full well the difficulties some of our parents face. This is ridiculous, Rose. You don't need me to lecture you about this. We all know this isn't the real issue.'

He adjusts his glasses.

'Yusuf has been on this ward his whole life,' I say. 'He's in Special Care now, he's fully conscious, he needs to be held and talked to and played with. He needs constant attention from his mother.'

'Rose, that's not for us to say. If you've got concerns, make a referral to the psychologist on the ward. But failure to visit is not considered child neglect. And whatever the situation with his parents, your outburst was completely unacceptable.'

'Fine. Duly noted.'

Andrew is fidgeting, adjusting his tie, which is covered in pictures of Mickey Mouse. He pushes his wire-rimmed glasses higher up his nose. As I watch this familiar gesture, I am filled with so much fondness and so much regret.

I stand in front of Wendy's desk, my head down, a criminal waiting for sentencing. 'I'm sorry,' I say. 'I don't know where all that came from.'

'It's my fault,' Wendy says. 'I should never have let you come back to work so soon. And if I let you stay on, you're going to do something you regret.'

Wendy and Andrew exchange a loaded glance and I understand they've been talking about me behind my back.

'We've had concerns,' Wendy goes on, 'ever since you came back to work, so soon after—'

'What concerns?' My stomach lurches. I know I'm not myself but I don't remember doing anything to cause harm.

'There have been problems with your handover notes,' Wendy says.

'What about my notes?'

'The language you've used,' she says, 'to describe Yusuf's parents, and a couple of others. It's inappropriate.'

I breathe out, relieved. 'Is that it?' I say.

'Well, it is a concern. The language you used is clearly

derogatory. I'm not sure if you're aware of it, Rose, but you're carrying a lot of anger.'

'You're reviewing my case notes?'

She doesn't trust me any more. I suppose her instincts are right, I barely trust myself.

'Did you hear what I said, Rose?'

'Is there anything else?'

I'm not going to talk about the anger. Not here.

'Amanda reported the incident with the breast milk,' Wendy says.

'I see.'

'It's completely understandable,' Wendy goes on. She jumps up and rushes around the desk. She puts her arms around me. I hug her back, with my weak, heavy arms.

'Rose, you've worked here longer than I have,' Andrew says. 'You're an incredibly devoted and talented nurse. We all understand what you're going through.'

I know they hate what they are doing. I know they are on my side. Still, it hurts. 'Being on this ward is saving my sanity,' I say. 'Please.'

'You know how much we care about you,' Wendy says. 'We would like you to take indefinite leave. If you don't, we will have to suspend you.'

'Is that a threat?'

'I'm so sorry,' Wendy says. There are tears in her eyes.

'No,' I say. 'I'm sorry, I should be the one apologizing.

I'm so sorry I've put you in this position. I'll go.'

Wendy leans across her desk and picks up a business card. She hands it to me. 'This psychologist works with staff members in the Trust when they're under severe stress. Please contact her.'

I push the card into the pocket of my uniform without looking at it.

I've been so proud of the work I have done in this unit. At the end of every shift, I believe the baby I've been looking after feels better, because of my care. And now Andrew is looking at me as though I am a danger to our babies, as though he has to keep them safe from me.

Wendy takes my hand in hers. Her touch is soft and tender. 'We're worried, Rose. We hardly see you any more. You don't talk to us, you don't return phone calls.'

'I spend all my spare time with Ben and Lexi.' I pull my hand away from hers.

'Please don't shut us out,' she says.

For some reason I haven't told Wendy about the time I spend with Isaac. She wants to care for me and I understand; I'd feel the same way. But at the moment all I can focus on is my need to be close to Lexi, and the closer I am to Isaac, the better my chances.

I can't look at the two of them any longer. I don't want to break down here. I walk over to the door and I try to open it, but my hands are shaking too much and my fingers slip from the handle. Andrew comes over to help me, and the look on his face is awful when he sees the half-moon bruises that run across the back of my hand.

'I'll phone you later,' Wendy says. 'As soon as I finish my shift.'

I nod but I don't turn around.

Andrew follows me all the way to the door of the unit. I suppose he wants to make sure I actually leave.

'We'll be in touch,' he says. 'Go home and rest.'

'Don't worry,' I say. 'I won't try to come back.'

With my back to him and with unsteady hands, I pull on my coat. I don't bother to change my shoes. I haul my bag over my shoulder and walk, like an old woman, slowly down the linoleum-lined passage and past the parents' suite.

Wearing a uniform changes a person. It gives me authority and it makes me brave. When I put on my uniform, when I'm at work, I am competent and confident; I lose myself. My uniform holds me together; the moment I take it off, I feel myself falling apart. I don't know how I will manage without this hospital, without the smell of disinfectant, so sharp and strong and clean it wipes everything else from my mind.

I don't have the energy for the stairs and so I wait for the lift. I can feel Andrew's eyes burning a pity-shaped hole in my back.

Chapter 17

I wake at five thirty the next morning and I follow my familiar routine, as though it is any other working day. I wash, dress and make a cup of tea. I cut up an orange and a banana and sprinkle oats across the top. I sit in front of the television while I eat my breakfast. I pack my uniform into my holdall.

My legs carry me to the bus stop, where I wait for the bus that takes me to the hospital. I get off at my usual stop. It's only then that I stop and think.

Across the road is the greying, pockmarked building, which I regard with so much fondness and so much pride. This hospital has been my true home. My daughter was born here, my granddaughter, too. I don't know how to fill my days now I cannot return to the Weissman Unit.

I don't want to go home.

I turn back on myself and walk towards Paddington Station. The Underground is subdued after the morning rush hour, I make my way through the turnstiles, down the escalators and through the maze of passages leading to the Bakerloo Line.

I know where I am going now and I feel energized at the thought of an overdue confrontation.

I get off the train at Baker Street and I change to the Jubilee Line. I travel all the way across London, to the east, to Bermondsey. When I emerge from the station, the day is mild and dry, and there's even a little sunshine. I lose myself in movement, in my brisk walk. I have visited Cinnamon Wharf only once before, more than a decade ago, but it's easy enough to find, only a ten-minute walk from the station.

I don't press the buzzer at the green-painted front gate because I don't want to give Cleo another opportunity to shut me out. Instead, I slip through behind a delivery man in brown overalls who is carrying a large cardboard box. I'm in luck, he walks across the courtyard, past the rows of mailboxes and makes his way inside the front door of the building. I catch the door before it closes and walk through right behind him. We travel up in the lift together. He gets out on the third floor, but I carry on up to the seventh. When I step out of the lift, the long corridor is familiar; it looks just the same, with the jute carpet and the apricot walls. The lights are on a timer switch, they come on as I step out of the lift, but by the time I reach the end of the passage, by the time I'm standing in front of Cleo's front door, they have gone out, leaving me in darkness.

I knock. I brace myself and stand staring squarely at the peephole.

When Cleo opens the door, she has a large and welcoming smile on her face. I was ready for a confrontation, but now I'm thrown. She steps forward, rests her hands lightly on my shoulders, and kisses me on the cheek.

'I'm so glad you're here,' she says. 'Come in.'

I follow her into a small hallway. It's as though the incident at Blackthorn Road never happened.

The flat is exactly as I remember it from all those years ago when Vivien lived here with Ben. The walls are painted the same pale apricot shade as the passage; the floor is a beech laminate. Cleo leads me through to the right, where living room, dining room and kitchen are combined in a compact space.

Even the sofa is the same; the fabric is a distinctive red and gold brocade.

I've never forgotten this view. From the large windows I can see out across the yellow-tiled rooftops and, in some cases, through into other people's apartments. The river is only a few streets away, though the view is obstructed by all the buildings.

'Look, I'm sorry about what happened,' Cleo says. 'I felt terrible afterwards.'

She does a good job of looking sincere.

'But not terrible enough to open the gate.'

Cleo's drawn-in eyebrows stand out against her face. Her hair is covered by a charcoal-grey headscarf and she's wearing an oversized sweatshirt with the words 'Cambridge University' printed across the front. I have no doubt that shirt once belonged to Ben.

'I had to make a judgement call,' she says. 'Ben was in a state and I knew it would only make things worse if you came inside.'

'What do you mean, he was in a state?'

'Lexi was being really, really difficult. He couldn't get her up to bed until eight thirty, and then she was up again within half an hour, wanting to come downstairs. Ben was at the end of his tether.'

'Was he drinking?'

She nods.

I remember what Ben said, about being afraid he would lose control. I feel a deep sense of unease. I am more convinced than ever that I need to be in that house, watching over my granddaughter.

'When the buzzer went,' Cleo says, 'he asked me to go to the front door.'

'Did he know it was me?'

She nods. 'I'm sorry. We could see you on the cameras.'

I'm not sure I believe her. The last time Lexi was in distress, Ben had begged me to come over to help him. I think last night was payback, and that Cleo has been holding a grudge ever since I'd asked her to leave the house. We seem to be in some sort of ridiculous power struggle. A struggle for territory.

'Ben finds the nights in that house unbearable,' she says.

'Lucky you were there to comfort him.'

'It's better if you phone first, when you want to go over there.'

'Is that what you do, Cleo?'

Wendy was spot on, as usual. There is an anger inside me, a bitterness fermenting in my core. And the more I'm kept apart from my granddaughter, the more it grows. I don't want to think about what I did to poor Yusuf's mother.

'I was just making myself a cup of tea,' Cleo says. She walks away from me and busies herself in the kitchen, which is tucked into an alcove at the back of the room. 'Would you like a cup?'

She doesn't respond to my sarcasm, she ignores it. Once again, I realize I am powerless. Ben has decided he trusts her and he values her company. This visit was a waste of time because Cleo is never going to agree to stop going to the house on Blackthorn Road.

I have to find another way to handle the situation.

'So Ben bought this place when he first started working in London?' I say. I force myself to adopt a less hostile tone.

'Yes. And you wouldn't believe what these flats sell for now.'

She has her back to me. The kettle screeches as it boils.

'When we first moved in here,' she says, 'this flat was full of sunshine. I swear to you, when we lived together, the sun shone every single day. Or that's the way I remember it, anyway.'

Cleo returns to my side in the living area, carrying a large red mug. She brings the tea to her lips and blows into it. 'Are you sure you won't have a cup?' she says. 'I've got Earl Grey.'

'I'm fine.' I try again. 'So Ben lets you live here rent free?'

'He doesn't need the money. And things have always been perfectly amicable between us.'

'I thought you'd said the two of you weren't in contact?'

'Have you seen my little terrace?' she says.

She has an infuriating way of ignoring questions she doesn't like.

She unlocks the door on the opposite end of the room, and throws it open. There is a balcony, a tiny space that clings to the edge of the building, with just enough room for a small wrought-iron bench.

Cleo steps outside and beckons to me to join her. I walk over, and take a look down over the railings. Below me is the roof of the fire station.

'It's lovely,' I say. My words come out sounding rather acidic.

'Ben and I used to sit out here and drink coffee and read the papers on weekends. It was our perfect little nest.' Her smile is sad. 'For the first time in my life, I wasn't lonely. My life was just unfolding, in a way that was beyond anything I had hoped for. Ben was kind and smart and destined for big things. I should have known it was too good to be true, shouldn't I?'

The day is an iron grey and it's cold out here.

'Ben and I have not been having an affair,' Cleo says. 'If that's what you want to know.'

We stand only inches apart out on the small balcony. Cleo looks me straight in the eyes and I can see no sign that she's lying or hiding anything from me.

'Then why?' I say. 'Why would Ben hold on to this property? Why does he let you live here? What's the connection between you?'

'Ben feels guilty.'

'About what? I understand he broke off your relationship, but that was so long ago. You weren't married. Relationships end all the time.'

'I've always wanted a chance to tell you my side of the story,' Cleo says. 'I don't know what Vivien may have told you.'

'Vivien didn't say anything. She never talked about what happened between the three of you.'

I've always known my daughter had done something she wasn't proud of. In a way, I was relieved she spared me the details.

'The night Vivien broke up with Sebastian, she called me,' Cleo says. 'I was the first person she told, even though we'd barely seen each other in ages.'

We are side by side, looking out at the rooftops below. The sound of traffic is a distant hum. Cleo stands very close to me, closer than she needs to be, and

I feel her breath on my face as she talks softly and urgently.

'She asked me to meet her, at Browns, the one on the Thames next to the Design Museum. It's only a few blocks away from here. It sounds ridiculous now, but I remember I felt so happy that I was the first person she turned to. It was like some kind of honour. I was glad to have my friend back. And I remember the bar was full of people and the windows were all misted up so you couldn't see out, you couldn't see the river at all. And I remember exactly what she was wearing. A really low-cut vest, with sequins along the neckline, and tight white jeans. She didn't usually dress that provocatively. Every man in the place was salivating over her. Every single one of them.'

Salivating. I don't like the way Cleo speaks about my daughter. I shiver as I feel the cold cut through my coat.

'I did wonder if Vivien was using me, to fill the gap left by Sebastian and his disposable income and their over-the-top wedding plans. But I actually didn't care. I thought, even if she was using me, a bit, we were such old friends. Vivien reached out to me when she needed help, and I knew I could do the same, I knew she'd step up if I was in trouble. Or that's what I thought, anyway.'

Cleo grimaces as she sips her tea, as though she's tasted something bitter.

'Vivien could have had any man she wanted,' she

says. 'I had no doubt new candidates would soon be lining up. I just didn't expect her to be interested in Ben. He wasn't good-looking enough and he wasn't nearly rich enough. So when she asked me if she could stay with us for a couple of weeks while she got herself sorted out, I said yes.'

I have to force myself to look at her, because I don't want to see the pain that's still fresh. I don't want to hear that my daughter was a thief, that she stole from a friend.

'There were moments when Vivien first moved in with us,' she says, 'when I was so happy. Being together with Vivien again was like coming home. I was with my two favourite people in the world, the two people I loved most, and I so wanted them to like each other. As usual, I was desperate for Vivien's approval. I wanted her to tell me I'd done well, with Ben and with our new home. And I suppose I got it, though not in the way I expected.' Her laugh is dry and cynical. 'Vivien saw something in Ben. She knew where he was headed.'

'It's cold out here, Cleo, let's go back inside.'

I turn away from her and go back in to the living room, and she follows. I watch as she shuts the door to the balcony and locks it. I sit down on the red and gold brocade sofa that's really much too big for this small room. The fabric is rough under my fingertips as I run my hand up and down the cushion.

Cleo sits down next to me.

'I remember thinking that Ben was so patient,' Cleo says. 'He never complained about Vivien camping out on this sofa, even though you can see how tiny this place is and there was barely space for the two of us let alone a house guest. He was always friendly to her. He acted as though he'd forgotten all about the time she refused to go out with him.'

Cleo leans forwards, her elbows on her knees. She's facing the windows, talking more to herself than to me, I think.

'Vivien was a practical woman,' Cleo says. 'She wasn't getting any younger, and she needed a new source of adoration and of financial security. And by that stage, Ben was on his way up in the world. Vivien quickly put two and two together. She might not have been an academic, but in some areas – like self-preservation – she was an expert.'

The acrimony in her voice is ugly now.

'You may wish that was true,' I say. 'You may wish it was about money, but it wasn't. Ben and Vivien loved each other.'

There is a loud crash that startles us both and I nearly jump out of my skin.

Cleo has left her red mug on the balcony, and the wind has blown it to the floor. The shards are scattered across the bench. Cleo doesn't move from my side.

'The weekend after Vivien first arrived, I began to feel afraid,' she says. 'It started with such a small thing. It was a Saturday morning and Ben got up to make us coffee. Usually he'd bring me my cup in bed, but that day he didn't come back to me. I heard their voices in the kitchen. Eventually, I got up to see what was going on.'

Cleo stands up.

'I remember I was so angry when I walked in here. Vivien was always so messy – her bedding and her clothes were spread out everywhere over the sofa, and there were dirty plates and cups all over the coffee table and on the floor.'

She points at the kitchen tucked into the alcove.

'That's where they were standing,' she says. 'I'll never forget the scene. It plays like a film, on a loop inside my head. Vivien is leaning back against the kitchen counter, one foot curled up behind the other shin. She's wearing a short lacy nightgown, and one of the straps falls down her shoulder. She keeps pushing it back up again, but it falls right back down. Her hair is so black, so shiny. She's laughing, tilting her head to one side. She's asking him about his job.'

'I get the picture,' I say.

'I felt like an intruder,' she says. 'Like some kind of voyeur as I stood in the doorway and watched them.'

Cleo is looking at the kitchen now, as though Ben and Vivien are right there in front of her. 'They didn't notice me. I was so pathetic, such a fool, standing there in an old T-shirt of Ben's and tracksuit bottoms. I had no idea how high the stakes were. And even if I did, I couldn't compete with her, anyway.'

It's creepy, and also desperately sad, the way Cleo

is still living this fifteen-year-old story as if it had happened yesterday.

'She was a snake,' Cleo says. 'Hypnotizing him with her big brown eyes and that husky voice of hers.'

She falls silent. We both do. The expression on her face is odd, as though she's confused, or disoriented.

'Cleo?' I say.

She snaps back. She looks at me, then she sits down again.

'I knew it was only a matter of time,' she says. 'I knew they both wanted me out of the way, even if Ben hadn't admitted it to himself yet. He would never make a move on Vivien until he'd broken it off with me, because he's not that kind of person. So I made it easy for them.'

'What do you mean, you made it easy for them?'

'I mean, there was no point delaying the inevitable. So I packed my stuff into a couple of boxes and left one day while Ben was at work and Vivien was out.'

'So you were the one that walked out on him?'

'I could always read Ben like a book. I knew he was so desperate to have her and I also knew he wouldn't admit it. He'd wanted her first; it was always Vivien he wanted. I was a poor second choice. So really, Vivien only came back to claim what was hers in the first place. Neither of them were to blame.'

'But are you saying you didn't even talk to Ben about your decision to leave?'

I don't say so out loud, but I wonder what kind of

relationship Ben and Cleo really ever had, if she couldn't talk to him about her jealousy of my daughter, about her insecurities. But then, perhaps I'm trying to excuse Vivien, by putting the blame on Cleo.

'At first, when I moved out and I left them alone together,' she says, 'I hadn't really given up. I still had hope. I thought there was a chance they would tire of each other and realize they weren't truly a good match. Once lust had run its course.'

I can't help but feel for her. I sense the emptiness of her life, the regret, the loneliness. Because I've known all of these things too. I reach out and squeeze her hand. But only briefly. Because something about her touch sets me on edge.

I find it difficult to understand how Ben can find Cleo's company a comfort. Perhaps she is different with him. Less bitter, less fixated on the past. But that, too, I find difficult to imagine.

'I got a letter from Ben's solicitor when they moved out,' she says, 'confirming that half the flat was in my name, and saying that Ben would continue to pay the entire mortgage.'

Cleo manages a wretched smile, but tears are so close to the surface. 'Neither of them ever tried to contact me. When Vivien wanted Ben, it suited her for me to disappear. It suited both of them. I lost all of you.'

'I'm sorry,' I say. 'We should all have been kinder.'

'I never understood,' she says, 'how it could be so easy for all of you to erase me from your lives.'

The horrible truth is that we have meant much more to Cleo than she has to us.

'I turned a blind eye,' I say. 'I was so happy that Vivien was going to have a different life to the one I'd had. A life with financial security and a loving husband. I suppose I didn't want to know that she'd hurt you. Even though I suspected. I didn't ask and she didn't tell me.'

My daughter caused harm. And there have been times when I have stood aside and watched her as she has damaged other people. I never did take a stand for right and wrong when it came to Vivien. I think Cleo knows this. She sees through me. I am neglectful. I am a silent witness. I am guilty by association, by omission. I accept my own culpability.

'But after all this time,' I say, 'after all these years, surely you must have moved on?'

'In some ways,' she says, 'yes, I have. I carry on. But in other ways, my life stopped the day I walked out on Ben and Vivien.'

She's dead serious..

'But now everything has changed,' Cleo says. 'She's gone. And everything has begun all over again.'

Her words are chilling.

I cannot bring myself to respond. Whatever I say will make no difference, anyway. Cleo has made up her mind and she's not open to reason.

I stand up. I cannot wait to leave. This flat is a tomb full of old and unhappy memories.

As I walk out of the living area, I find myself looking

into a small room, a study, which I didn't notice when I came in. I stop when I see the photographs on the wall. There are nine of them, all in black and white, all framed in simple black wooden frames. They hang in rows of three.

Cleo stands silently beside me. 'They're beautiful, aren't they?' she says.

And in some ways, they are. But they are also sinister.

I step into the room to get a closer look, examining each of the portraits in turn. The photographs have been taken over several years and they are a record of my daughter's life. A testament to her, a twisted love story. On the top row there are two close-ups of Vivien's face, taken when she was a teenager. In the first, she is wearing a pair of sunglasses I remember well, pointed cat's-eyes with a gold frame. She is laughing, pleased, it seems, to be the subject of the picture. In the second photograph, Vivien is at a ballet recital, she wears a black leotard and a thin film of a skirt that brushes the tops of her thighs. Her hair is slicked back into a bun and she looks back over her shoulder at the camera, intense and unsmiling.

'Did you take all of these?' I say.

Cleo nods. 'I've become something of a keen amateur photographer. I've invested in some amazing equipment, and I've been on quite a few courses. Sometimes I think about trying to make a career out of it. I love portraits. I work only in black and white.'

Cleo is talented. The photographs are quite stunning,

artful and full of feeling, and they cut right to the heart of my daughter's sensuality, her vulnerability. But, with the exception of the first two early portraits, I don't think Vivien knew she was being photographed.

'Most of these were taken after Vivien and Ben were married,' I say.

'Yes.'

'But you said you had no contact with her?'

'You don't need to have contact with someone to take their photograph.'

I cannot read her expression. She's solemn as she answers my questions, but also rather detached. I would expect her to be embarrassed at the fact that I've been witness to her preoccupation with my daughter.

'So Vivien didn't know you were taking these photographs?'

'No, I don't think so.'

The next photograph is of the house on Blackthorn Road. It was taken at night. The shutters in the basement are tilted open and Vivien is standing with her back to the window. Next, she emerges from a restaurant, in a cream evening dress and a dark cape; she is laughing, looking at the person beside her, though they are cropped from the picture. She is holding hands with someone, with Ben I imagine, but only his hand appears at the side of the frame.

'I understood why Ben chose Vivien,' Cleo says. 'Because I loved her too. You can tell, can't you?'

'Yes,' I say. 'I can. I had no idea.'

In the final row, Vivien bends forward to kiss Lexi's cheek. They are standing in front of the school gates and Lexi looks to be about four years old.

In the penultimate shot, Vivien is in a vest, Lycra leggings and trainers and she is running in what I imagine is Regent's Park. The shot captures her in motion, while the background is a blur.

I'm not sure what scares me more as I look at Cleo's shrine to my daughter: the extent of her obsession with Vivien or how emaciated Vivien looks in these photographs.

I don't understand how I didn't see what was in front of me all these years. I didn't see she was ill.

'Cleo,' I say, 'if you'd known I was coming over, would you have closed this door?'

'I'm not sure,' she says. 'I don't really feel I have any-thing to hide.'

'You're not embarrassed?'

'No, I'm not embarrassed. How is it embarrassing to celebrate beauty?'

'Cleo, this isn't celebration. This is stalking.'

She doesn't seem to take offence. In fact, she doesn't seem to take this seriously at all. Or perhaps she's relieved, to share this with me.

'There came a point,' she says, 'where a computer screen wasn't enough for me. I needed to see Vivien again. To really see her. In the flesh. I tried for so long *not* to go to their house, but in the end, I did.'

'So it was Vivien you wanted to see?' I say. 'Not Ben?'

'Both of them, really,' she says. 'All three of them. But it was always Vivien who fascinated me.'

'When did you start watching her?'

'Soon after they moved in to Blackthorn Road. I saw an article in a magazine about the renovations, about the way Vivien and the architect had worked together to redesign the house. The first time, all I did was stand outside for a few minutes. That was all.'

'And then?'

'I wanted to see Vivien with her baby.'

I have no idea whether Cleo understands how disturbed I am by what she's telling me. She is quite calm, quite casual about it all, as though this is normal behaviour.

'I started going to Blackthorn Road really early in the mornings,' she says. 'Ben always left for work at the crack of dawn; it was the same when he and I lived together. So once he'd gone, I'd walk up and down the street, until Vivien came out of the house, with the little princess in her carriage.'

Cleo is so earnest, her eyes narrow and her forehead creases with concentration, with the intensity of memory. 'I remember when Lexi started walking on her own,' she says. 'It was winter, and she was still so tiny and she had on the most beautiful little tailored coat. It was a bright emerald-green colour, and it looked so pretty against her ginger hair. And she had a little knitted hat on too, with a crocheted white rose on the side. That outfit was so typical of Vivien, so perfect.'

Cleo is so sad and so lonely. She's still wrapped up in her relationship with Vivien and with Ben, with relationships that ended more than a decade before.

'They would wear matching gloves,' she says. 'Vivien's were beige leather, but Lexi's were softer, the same colour, but woollen. And they used to hold hands. Vivien would point at things, showing Lexi everything, all the way to school. Whenever I used to read about something – like Mother's Day – or if I'd pass a beauty salon and see a mother-and-daughter special offer, I'd think about Vivien and her daughter and I'd want to know what they might be doing together, to celebrate. I was envious.'

When Cleo speaks about Vivien and Lexi, it is with a terrible sense of loss. I don't understand how Ben has been oblivious to the danger here. Cleo's need is so strong, it emanates from her with an intensity that's palpable.

'Does Ben know about these photographs?'

'No. I loved Vivien and I missed her,' she says. 'I would have liked to have had all three of them back in my life. These photographs are something – not much, but something.'

I turn back to the wall, to the last photograph, which scares me most of all.

She has captured Lexi. Close up, the shades of grey caress the contours of her small face, her sad eyes, her wild curls. She is standing just inside the open school gates, gazing at something beyond the lens. I am quite sure it is her mother she sees, because there is a longing in her expression. She is watching as Vivien walks away from her.

I want to snatch the photograph of Lexi off the wall, to take it away with me.

'Cleo, I think you need to talk to someone about all this.' I gesture at the wall. 'Now that I've seen this, I'm not comfortable with you having contact with my granddaughter.'

'That's not your decision to make,' she says.

'I need to tell Ben.'

'That's up to you,' she says. She doesn't seem alarmed. She's quite calm.

I curse myself for telling her my intentions. By the time I see Ben, she could easily have disposed of this display.

I don't know what to make of her, or what exactly she is capable of. Perhaps she's harmless, a shy social misfit who was manipulated by my daughter, and who now wants another chance at happiness. Or she might be someone entirely different, someone I don't know at all. A stalker who's been fixated on Vivien for all these years.

Either way, I will not allow her anywhere near Lexi.

Chapter 18

I approach the wide-open gates of the Endsleigh School with some apprehension, because I know I'm breaking the rules by turning up here without warning. But I can't wait, I need to talk to Ben about what I saw at the flat in Cinnamon Wharf.

He's arrived early too; his Range Rover is parked alongside the pavement. I hope Isaac is driving him – I could do with some support. I walk up to the car and tap against the driver's window. As it rolls down, I see that Ben is in the driver's seat. He's alone in the car.

'I need to talk to you,' I say. 'It's important.'

He does not look pleased to see me.

'What about?' He frowns and his tone is strangely cutting, but I pretend I don't notice.

'It's about Cleo,' I say.

Ben rolls up the window again. He opens the door and I move back, out of the way. As he steps out onto the pavement, he looks towards the school playground, which is filling up fast, though the doors of the school are still firmly shut. Parents and children pass us by on their way in through the gates, talking, laughing, pushing buggies.

'Ben?'

He looks at me, with some reluctance.

'Look, I'm worried about Cleo and I don't think it's a good idea for you to be having her over to the house.'

He gives me a look that could turn water to ice, but I don't stop.

'I don't know if you realize it, but you're getting her hopes up. She thinks she can go back in time and pick up where you left off, and I think this situation could become very complicated if you decide you don't need or want to be with her at some point in the future.'

Ben rubs his hands over his eyes. Then he begins fiddling with his wedding ring.

'Ben, I've just been to Cleo's flat and I'm extremely worried. I think she's unstable. She has a wall full of photographs that were taken without Vivien's knowledge. I don't want her spending time with Lexi.'

'You don't get to decide who spends time with Lexi,' he says. He spits out the words, like barbs. This rudeness, the cold aggression, is so unlike him.

'Look, is something wrong?' I say.

'Do you have a problem with me, Rose? Do you not think I'm capable of caring for my own daughter?'

A young Filipino woman turns to look at us, worried perhaps at the way he is talking to me.

'Ben, what on earth are you talking about?'

'Cleo called me, to tell me you were at her flat this morning. She says you keep asking her if I've been drinking.'

'What?'

'She said you think I have a drinking problem. Have you told the police, Rose, about my supposed alcohol abuse?'

'No, Ben—'

'Next thing you'll be reporting me to social services.'

Ben notices the woman, who is still staring at us, and he tries to pull himself together. His hand stills, as he stops twisting his wedding ring.

'Ben, listen to me. My comments have been taken out of context. Ben, please.'

'Did you or did you not ask Cleo if I'd been drinking?'

I try to remember exactly what I did say to Cleo. All I can see are those photographs.

'I might have asked her,' I say. 'And yes, I do think you should be careful about how much you drink at night when you're alone with Lexi. But I said it because I care about you. It would be better to see your GP, to get antidepressants or a short course of sleeping tablets if you're having problems—'

His expression unnerves me as he raises his eyebrows, mocking me, the interfering mother-in-law. 'I'm sure you're right,' he says.

'Ben, you need to go to Cleo's flat and have a look for yourself.'

But he's so livid that he's not listening to anything I'm saying. I'm so furious I didn't take a photograph of that wall.

'It seems to be my day for taking phone calls about you,' he says. 'Andrew Lissauer also gave me a call this morning.'

It takes me a moment to get over my surprise at hearing this, but my main concern is that Ben isn't listening to what I'm trying to tell him about Cleo.

'Ben, did you hear what I said? I have serious concerns about Cleo's mental state.'

'I heard you,' he says. His voice is even colder now. 'But according to Andrew, it's your mental state that's the real problem.'

I clear my throat, but the lump I struggle with has grown larger, more dense. I cannot dislodge it. 'Why have you been talking to Andrew about me?'

'I've known Andrew for years. As you know, he was Alexandra's paediatrician. We're on the board of the fundraising committee for the Weissman Unit.'

Ben is looking at me strangely, and he's talking slowly, as though he thinks I've lost my mind. 'Andrew called me because he's concerned about you. I gather you won't be going back to work, that you had some sort of outburst?'

I'm sure Andrew meant well but I could throttle him. He's just undermined any credibility I might have had. I exhale. 'I'm sure he didn't put it like that,' I say.

'What exactly did happen at the hospital, Rose?

Andrew wouldn't tell me the details. He's very protective of you.'

'I've been distracted lately, as I'm sure you can appreciate. It was nothing serious and no one was hurt. Nothing like that.'

Am I telling the truth? Because Yusuf's mother was hurt. I hurt her.

'It wasn't serious,' I say again. My voice lacks any conviction.

'And yet Andrew Lissauer, who adores you, doesn't think you're in any fit state to be around patients? And he was concerned enough to alert me to the fact that he thinks you're in crisis.'

'I would never do anything to hurt Lexi. Please.'

Ben looks confused. 'What are you talking about?'

'I don't know.' I'm struggling, and my thoughts are scrambled. I can't get my words out in a straight sentence.

'Look, Rose.' Ben's calmer now, he has his emotions under control. 'I know you're having a terrible time of it. I think your guilt about the way you treated Vivien colours everything you see and everything you do. But you cannot make up for neglecting her by trying to take over as Lexi's mother. I'm her father and I'm perfectly capable of looking after her. I won't have you undermining me.'

'Ben, my comments were made in confidence, out of concern. Cleo has twisted what I said.'

'I'm furious, Rose. How dare you go around telling

people I have a drinking problem, implying I'm not fit to look after my daughter?' He's standing close to me, talking in harsh whispers, so the people passing us don't overhear what he's saying. He doesn't wait for me to answer his question. 'I have enough on my plate, I won't tolerate your outbursts and your acting out. I'm warning you, don't pull another stunt like this, or you will be sorry.'

'I would never do anything to hurt you.'

'And yet you have.'

'I'm sorry.'

'You're unreliable and you think only of yourself and your own needs. I see now why Vivien struggled so much, why she had the issues she did.'

'That's a low blow.'

'Is it? I think you need to take a look at your sudden urge to be part of Lexi's life after all these years, before you do something that hurts her even more than she's hurting already.'

'Does it really matter, Ben? My reasons for wanting to be in Lexi's life? Doesn't it count for something that I am Vivien's mother? That I lost her too?'

He shoves his hands in the pockets of his coat.

I'm sick of being the villain. Sick of his accusations.

'If one day you are unlucky enough to have to look at the dead body of your daughter, then you may judge me.'

'I think it's best if you go now,' he says, 'before Lexi comes out. I don't want her to witness some kind of scene. I need you to stay away from my daughter until you sort yourself out. We have enough to deal with and you seem determined to make everything worse.'

He strides off towards the school gates. A blonde in skinny jeans and high-heeled boots approaches him, puts a hand on his arm and inclines her head in sympathy.

Chapter 19

I do not go home. I phone DS Cole on her mobile and I ask if I can see her. I tell her it's urgent.

The police station is inside a two-storey golden-brick building, with a pair of antique lamp-posts flanking the front door. The building is charming, and it holds the promise of comfort and security. But the quaint exterior is deceptive and once I'm on the inside I find myself back in the dismal surrounds of Interview Room One, in the bleak, small space I remember.

Almost immediately, I feel that coming here was a mistake. I hope I'm wrong.

'Thank you for seeing me so quickly,' I say.

DS Cole and I sit next to each other, this time, instead of on opposite sides of the table. She is wearing her tailored white shirt and her tan brogues. Her hair seems to have turned a paler shade of blonde.

'No problem,' she says. 'Has Ben told you about the toxicology results?'

I hesitate. I have the same sensation I always have

200

when I'm talking to DS Cole, as though I'm treading on eggshells, and I must weigh each word with care. As though each sentence I utter might incriminate me and then she will see right through me, right inside to the rotten core. I'm relieved when she carries on talking.

'We've had a look at your daughter's laptop and we've managed to trace the source of the pills she'd taken. The drugs were prescribed by a private GP, a weight-loss specialist. I thought you might like to know.'

'I see. Yes. Thank you.'

'The thing is,' she says, 'this medication wasn't actually prescribed for your daughter. The prescription was for Alexandra.'

My hands are folded in my lap, left under right, so she doesn't see the bruises. Other than the bags under my eyes, I hope I appear my usual calm and controlled self.

'Does that come as a surprise?' she says.

'I – it would have. But I had a conversation with Mrs Murad the other day, and she told me Vivien had developed some kind of preoccupation with Lexi's weight. So now it makes sense. I really had no idea. I would never have let her give that kind of medication to a child; I don't care if it was prescribed by a doctor. If I'd known, I would have done something.'

'Ben didn't know either.'

'I see.'

'And there's still the question of what happened to the empty packaging.'

'Yes.'

There is a pause, we fall silent, each waiting for the other to speak. I came here intending to tell DS Cole about Cleo's photographs, about the fact that she's admitted to watching my daughter. But now, sitting here in this windowless room, I'm having second thoughts. I wonder if more police interference is really what this family needs.

'Was there something else you wanted to talk to me about?' DS Cole asks.

I decide to tell her. I have to, because Ben won't listen to me. And I trust DS Cole.

'I'm concerned about someone named Cleo Baker,' I say. 'She's an old friend of my daughter's and she and Ben were in a relationship, many years ago. I understand you've already talked to Ben about her?'

DS Cole nods. 'Have you also had contact with Ms Baker recently?'

'Yes. I bumped into her the other night, on Blackthorn Road. She was on her way to see Ben. And then we spent an afternoon together in Regent's Park.'

'Do you mind if I ask what you talked about?'

'We were reminiscing, about Vivien.'

'And what is it that concerns you?' DS Cole says. She leans forward in the way she does, when she's concentrating.

'I'm worried that Cleo is unstable.'

I tell her about the way Cleo refused to let me in to the house, and then I tell her about the photographs. DS Cole doesn't say much.

'My concern is that Cleo was watching my daughter. And now my granddaughter. Without their knowledge. Stalking them.'

'Right.' She is thoughtful. She doesn't seem alarmed.

'Do you think Cleo might have threatened Vivien in some way?'

I think back, to the bizarrely calm conversation I had with Cleo as we stood in front of her shrine to my daughter.

'No, I don't think she had any contact with Vivien. My impression is she wouldn't have approached or spoken to her. She was honest about taking the photographs in secret. She didn't try to cover up at all.'

'Do you think your daughter might have known she was being followed?'

'I couldn't say.'

'It might go to her state of mind, when she took the overdose.'

'It's Lexi I'm worried about,' I say. 'Cleo's been fixated on the family for a long time. I'm afraid she has some sort of designs on my granddaughter. I keep seeing that photograph of Lexi on her wall. Is there anything you can do?'

'I think I need to consult with my Senior Investigating Officer,' she says. 'You did the right thing, coming to talk to me.'

'Will you go to Cleo's flat, and see if the photographs are still there?'

'What do you mean, still there?'

'I mean, she may take them down. I took her by surprise. I would imagine she wouldn't want anyone to see them.'

I regret my stupid statement. Now I suspect DS Cole thinks the entire thing was in my imagination. And I put the idea into her head.

'Did she seem like she wanted to hide them?'

'No. In fact, she seemed proud of the pictures. She said something about going on photography courses.'

Is it my imagination, or is DS Cole looking at me like she thinks I'm an unreliable witness? A doddering, grieving grandmother. Again, I curse the fact that I didn't think to take a photograph.

'I'll see what I can do,' she says. 'I'll talk to my SIO.'

'Thank you.'

DS Cole is still looking at me, waiting to see if I'm going to say something more, but I've clammed up. I'm afraid of what I've just done. I'm afraid of stirring up a hornet's nest. I am afraid of Ben's anger and Isaac's disapproval. Isaac warned me to take this slowly, to be patient, but I've gone and done the opposite. I've reacted out of anger and fear. I wanted to get back at Cleo for keeping me away from Alexandra; and at Ben, too, for speaking to me the way he did this morning. And now I might just have sealed my own fate.

Ben is going to be furious when he finds out I've been here, casting suspicion on Cleo and laying him open to further scrutiny. This brief interview may well be the end of any relationship Ben and I might have had.

'Do you have to tell my son-in-law about this interview?' I say.

'Is there a reason you don't want me to?'

'I think he'll be angry. Ben doesn't want to hear anything negative about Cleo; he's become dependent on her since Vivien died. He doesn't like me interfering.'

And he'll take it out on me by keeping me away from my granddaughter.

'I'll do my best to keep your name out of it.'

'Thank you.'

And then I think, to hell with Ben. I've done the right thing. I'm finished with keeping silent. Keeping my mouth shut, not noticing. I tried to warn Ben but he wouldn't listen.

'DI Hawkins is wrong about me,' I say. 'I do have a lot of questions. But I'm also afraid of the answers. Sometimes it's better not to know, less painful. Do you know what I mean?'

'I'm not sure. I suppose I don't agree, or I wouldn't be a detective.'

We smile together, the tension broken.

I have come to like DS Cole. Sitting in this bleak room with her, I find myself wanting to confess. I want to have her pardon all my sins as a mother.

'How old are you, DS Cole?'

'Twenty-eight.'

'How long have you been a police officer?'

She smiles. 'Seven years.'

I'm surprised. Seven years seems a long time and she looks so young, so fresh-faced.

'I know what it's like to lose someone, the way you did,' she says.

'What happened?' This is the first time she has shared something personal with me. I'm surprised and also moved.

'My sister was murdered. She was a couple of years older than me, and she was away at college. One night she'd been out drinking and she had a fight with her boyfriend outside the pub. He let her walk home alone.'

She stops. I can see she doesn't want to say any more.

'I'm so sorry,' I say. Then, 'It's odd, isn't it, how people apologize to you all the time?'

'You get used to it.'

I stand up. 'I won't take up any more of your time,' I say.

She stands too, and opens the door for me. 'I'm sorry we still haven't been able to give you any clear answers,' she says. 'I know it's difficult to move on with your life while an investigation is ongoing. I know how important it is to have closure.'

Vivien

Three months ago

My daughter is avoiding me.

I'm standing outside her bedroom door, holding a tray with a glass of skimmed milk and a banana-and-oat muffin. The door is shut.

'Alexandra?' I call out. 'Open the door please.'

I hear a thud as she jumps off her bed and then her plodding footsteps, like a little elephant. When she finally opens up, she looks at me with that defiant expression that gets right under my skin. I try not to be angry. I try to smile.

'Are you hungry?' I say.

Alexandra shakes her head. She rubs her nose. She does this a lot when I speak to her, she's fidgety around me.

And sometimes I find it hard to look at her. The double chin she's developing, the way her belly pushes against the waistband of her skirt, the bracelets of fat bunched around her wrists. I have no control over what she eats at school or over what Ben feeds her when I'm not around. And she has no self-control, either.

I practically have to push past her to get inside her bedroom. Her clothes are strewn all over the floor, and there are felt-tip pens and little plastic creatures piled up on every surface, on the chest of drawers and bedside tables, and around her computer. I decide tidiness is a battle best left to another time since I am losing so many others.

I know she's always starving when she gets home. The school feeds them lunch early, at twelve fifteen. I hate to think about the junk they serve up: pizza, breaded chicken, and cake or ice cream for dessert. It's mind-boggling, given the levels of obesity in England. Alexandra promises me she'll choose a baked potato with tuna and that she won't take a dessert except on Fridays, but by the looks of her, she's choosing no such thing and depriving herself of nothing.

On the surface, she complies with me. Underneath, she defies me. My daughter is becoming a practised liar.

I place the tray down on the desk, next to a photograph of Alexandra and her father. Ben is standing behind her, with his arms around her, and both of them have the same serious expressions on their faces, the same vulnerable eyes. It's so easy for Ben, I envy him. He accepts the girl the way she is: pudgy and socially inept. It's left to me to try to mould my daughter into someone who might have even the remotest chance of finding a place in the outside world. Alexandra is my only one, after all. And already, she has become a target for bullies.

She sits on the edge of her bed, staring at me with those apprehensive eyes of hers, as though she's afraid of her own mother.

I don't like to encourage Alexandra to eat in her bedroom, but this is the best chance I have of getting this stuff down her. I lift the glass of milk and balance the plate with the muffin on my lap as I sit next to her on the bed.

'I've made you muffins,' I say.

'I'm not eating them.' Her small jaw is set.

She moves away from me. She goes to stand next to her desk and her beloved computer. And her photograph of her father. She seldom comes downstairs when we're alone in the house together. She waits until she hears Ben come through the front door, or until I call her down for a lesson with her tutor.

If I allowed her to, she'd stay holed up in her bedroom, sitting like a zombie, inert in front of the computer screen. If I tell her she's had enough screen time, she'll curl up on her bed and read. The child barely moves. When I was her age, I was at dance classes practically every day; I was exercising all the time, and even then my weight was an ongoing battle.

Her eyes fix on the muffin.

'Come on, Alexandra, I know you're hungry. Drink

this milk and then you can have the muffin. It's delicious. It's still warm.'

I smile at her again, but I have to force my mouth into the right position and I know the warmth does not reach my eyes and the girl sees right through me.

'Why does everything have to be such a battle?' I say.

Of course, she doesn't know the answer.

Being a mother is not what I'd hoped. I had hoped it would be different between me and Alexandra, different because of Ben and because we are a family, but really, it's just the same. It's the same pain and frustration I felt with my own mother, all over again.

'I don't want it,' she says.

I sigh, a deep, impatient exhalation, more like a hiss, really. My daughter is strong and smart and I love that about her. But she is also constantly undermining my authority, and this makes me afraid of what is to come in the teenage years. I have to get this right. She has to learn to listen to me. Alexandra, with her unkempt curls, in her white school shirt stained with brown dirt and blue ink and her thick waist straining against the waist-band of her skirt, does not yet understand that appearances matter. Already, she is becoming an out-cast. I see the way the other mothers look at her. I notice how she is never invited over to play at the other girls' houses. We are all out of place here, in the world of private schools, skiing holidays and dinner parties. We are out of our depth. And my daughter is different:

quirky and large. I'm doing my best to help her fit in.

Perhaps I am also trying to help myself, because I'm ashamed of her. I hate myself for feeling this way.

She is looking at the muffin. She's hungry.

I don't try to approach my daughter. I know better. She will only resist and wind herself up into a state. I have to be patient. I hold out the glass of milk, it's cold and slippery in my fingers. Alexandra shakes her head and purses her lips. She retreats behind the computer chair, as though she's cowering.

'Look, Alexandra,' I say, 'we can do this the easy way or we can do it the hard way. You have to drink this milk. The doctor said so. Drink it and that's the end of it. Or I can punish you and take your computer away. You choose. The easy way or the hard way.'

'I don't want to.'

There is pain in her eyes that I do not want to see.

'Whether you want to or not isn't the point. You know your medicine is in this milk and you know you're overweight. You have to do something about it unless you want to get sick with diabetes or heart disease or cancer. And none of the clothes in the shops for an eight-year-old even fit you any more. Aren't you embarrassed in front of your friends?'

I watch my daughter's face crumple and the life and joy go out of her eyes. I promised myself I wouldn't say these things. Not again. But Alexandra pushes me. If she tells Ben the things I have said to her, he will never forgive me.

'Come on, Alexandra,' I say. 'One glass of milk. And then everything will be fine.'

She takes two reluctant steps forward. She stops, then takes another few slow steps towards me, approaching as though I'm a predator about to pounce. I resent her for this too, for the way she makes me feel like I'm hurting her when I am desperately trying to help. I won't neglect her. She doesn't always know what she needs.

She takes the glass of milk from me, and drinks, a tiny sip. Barely any of it passes her lips. She makes a face.

'It tastes funny.'

'No it doesn't.'

'It does. The medicine makes it taste funny.'

'Nonsense, there's only a tiny bit of medicine in there.'

God, this is so simple and yet it takes forever each time. I can feel my anger swelling, and I have the urge to slap her pasty, pudgy little face. Of course I never would, not in a million years. But my daughter has a way of pushing me right to my limit, to the edge in this battle of wills between us. She saps my energy so there is nothing left of me by the time Ben comes home.

'Please, Mummy,' she says. 'Don't make me. It makes me feel sick. My heart goes all funny when I take it, it beats too fast.'

'It's good for you. And when you've lost some weight, we can stop. Don't make this difficult. Don't make me take the computer away. Don't make me tell Daddy you have to cancel the camping trip.'

She takes another drink, a longer one this time. There's still three-quarters of the glass to go.

'Good girl,' I say. 'And we can go shopping for a present, too. Once you've taken it for a whole week.'

Alexandra sits down next to me on the bed. From the look on her face, anyone would have thought she was being tortured. She tips the glass up, gulps the whole thing down, then puts on a big act, as though she's about to gag.

She reaches for the muffin. Eats it as though she's chewing through sawdust. Crumbs fall all over her bed and I try not to mind. It takes her ten minutes to eat one lousy muffin. By the end of it, her face is a mess of tears and snot.

I put my arm around her. She rests her head against my chest and tries to snuggle into me, to find somewhere soft. She puts her arms around me and clings on tight.

Chapter 20

My phone rings just as I close my front door behind me. I struggle to find it, because it's sunk right to the bottom of my handbag. I hate this bag; it's like a black hole.

DS Cole is on the line. 'Rose, I'm sorry to disturb you,' she says, 'do you have a minute?'

'Of course.'

DS Cole does not yet know I'm no longer working. I have several minutes; I have nothing else but empty minutes. I balance on one leg as I pull off each of my boots and arrange them neatly beside the door.

'You've known Cleo Baker a long time, since she was a child. So I wondered if you've ever known her to show any aggressive behaviour?'

'No,' I say, 'she's always been quiet and reserved. Although – maybe there was some aggression towards herself.'

'I'm not sure what you mean?'

I walk over to my fridge. Now I have two of Lexi's drawings on display. The one where she's standing next to her mother, and the newer one, of her house with the pretty pink flowers in the garden. When I look at the earlier picture, I see something I've never noticed before. Vivien is drawn as a stick figure with a large round head. But Alexandra has given herself a large, round middle.

'Rose?'

'I'm sorry, I'm still here. I mean, Cleo used to pull out her hair as a child. Her eyebrows and her eyelashes. At one point when they were in secondary school, I thought I saw a bald spot forming, on her head, but she usually kept it covered up. So I suppose, that's some kind of violence, isn't it, against herself? A sign that something wasn't right, at home.'

'I don't want to worry you too much,' she says, 'but I think it's in your interests to know that Cleo has previously been charged with assault. A woman in Bermondsey laid a charge against her several years ago, around the time she was living with Ben in Cinnamon Wharf. I can reassure you that this was an isolated incident.'

I'm shocked by what she's said. I wonder if DS Cole is supposed to be giving out this kind of information, and whether this call is really in the line of duty, or whether she's taken a personal interest. She sounds worried about me. Detectives are human beings, after all.

'Was she convicted?' I say.

'The charges were dropped,' DS Cole says.

I adjust Lexi's drawings, straightening them, and

making sure there's a magnet in each of the four corners to keep them secure.

'Could there have been some sort of mistake, if the charges were dropped?'

'No,' DS Cole says. 'There was no mistake. The woman dropped the charges but Cleo admitted the assault.'

The implications of what DS Cole is saying are gradually sinking in.

'Are you saying you think Cleo might have hurt Vivien? The injury, on Vivien's head, are you saying—'

'Rose, I don't think it's helpful to speculate. But I do want to ask you to be cautious, until we finish our investigation. I strongly recommend you don't visit her again until we've had a chance to look into this and to interview her. As I said, I really was reluctant to worry you because I suspect there's nothing in this. But I decided you should know. I'd rather you kept your distance from Cleo.'

I'm standing in front of my fridge, looking at Lexi's drawings. At the way she has drawn herself and her mother, both so small, as though they are cowering together in the corner of the page.

'Rose, is that okay?'

'Yes,' I say. 'Thank you. I understand.'

'You know I'm always here if anything concerns you.'

'Will you tell Ben, about this?' I say. 'He won't listen to me.'

'We're trying to reach him.'

I am afraid. Not for myself, but for my granddaughter. I can keep my distance from Cleo, but Lexi does not have a choice. Ben will let her in.

Chapter 21

The tables outside the pub on the corner of Blackthorn Road are empty, not even the patio heaters can lure drinkers. My steps are brisk and my limbs feel lighter than they have for weeks as I rush towards Vivien's house in the icy darkness. My outrage gives me a purpose, it energizes me. After DS Cole's call, Ben has to take my concerns seriously.

When I reach number sixty-three, I stand still for a few moments, watching the house. There is only one Range Rover on the driveway, Vivien's. The lights are on inside, on all four floors. The shutters are closed.

I've been trying to reach Ben on both the home number and his mobile, but he doesn't pick up. I need to talk to him, tonight. I have to tell him my side of the story, the whole story. I've already left it much too long.

I do not press the buzzer on the gate because I'm not taking a chance on being shut out. This time, I have come prepared: I have the spare set of keys that Vivien left with me at Cambridge Court. The key turns easily, the lock is well oiled.

I slip through and pull the gate shut behind me, then I make my way up the steps. I knock on the front door a few times, grasping the lion's head door knocker. Nothing happens. I knock again, harder. Still, nothing.

The next key turns easily too, and the front door opens without a sound. Now I am nervous. A dry-mouthed intruder.

'Ben?' I call out.

The heavy door bangs as I shut it behind me. My voice echoes across the hushed entrance hall.

'Ben?' There is no answer.

Letting myself into this house at nine o'clock at night, unannounced, now seems a stupid and even dangerous thing to do. The last thing I want is to alarm him.

I walk across to the doorway of the living room. The drinks cabinet is closed. Only the large black stone bird stares at me malevolently from her corner.

I turn back and move slowly across the chequered entrance-hall tiles, calling out Ben's name. Vivien always kept this house well heated, a hothouse for a tropical gardenia. I can feel I've begun to sweat. I shrug off my coat and drape it over the hall table.

Holding onto the banister, I walk down the staircase and peer into the basement. Once again, the lights are on but the room is empty. The grey cabinets and stainless-steel surfaces glint, cold and clinical. I can no longer find my voice to call out as I return to the ground floor, to the still and silent entrance hall.

I climb up to the first floor. I'm aware of my heart beating faster than usual, aware of feeling much too hot.

Lexi's room is in darkness. Her door creaks as I push it open. Light from the landing falls across the floor in a wide stripe.

'Ben?' My voice is a whisper.

There's no response. I walk over to Lexi's bedside and I almost trip over her quilt, it's fallen to the floor. I sit down on the edge of the bed and place my hand on her back, feeling for the rise and fall of her breath.

The door creaks. My breath catches in my throat as I look up.

The apparition is back. She is silhouetted in the doorway, dark hair falling poker straight to her shoulders.

'Did you not hear me knocking at the door?' I say.

'I'm sorry, I didn't,' Cleo says.

She doesn't look at all surprised to see me in Lexi's bedroom. I'm sure she heard me knock, and I'm sure she heard me calling out.

'Where's Ben?' I say.

'He had to go back to the office. He had a conference call with some investor in the US. He asked me to watch over Lexi.'

'What about Isaac?'

'I've no idea.'

Cleo walks across Lexi's room and goes over to the window. She opens the shutters and looks out at the street. Orange light filters through into the room. My hand stays still on Lexi's back. Rise. Fall. Rise. Her breathing is slow and easy.

'Sometimes I see Isaac,' Cleo says, 'just sitting out there in the car, reading his newspaper. For hours on end. He gives me the creeps.'

She talks in a loud voice, with no heed to the fact that Lexi is asleep.

'Ben says you and Isaac have been spending time together,' Cleo says.

'Is that so?'

'He's in desperate need of money. Did you know?'

'He's been quite open about his job situation.'

'Do you think Isaac is manipulating Ben?' Cleo says. She closes the shutters and stands with her back to the window.

'Ben is no fool. If he trusts Isaac, I think that says something.'

'Of course Vivien had both of them wrapped around her little finger.'

'Meaning what, exactly?'

'Vivien was always insecure. She needed male attention, she thrived on it.'

I feel a twinge of something. An uneasy, nasty suspicion. My daughter was beautiful, she was controlling, and she was unhappy. I remember Isaac telling me about the late nights when he'd visit, when she'd be alone in the house. He too was lonely, in crisis and in need of a boost to his self-esteem. I remember the look on his face as he spoke about Vivien.

I remember DS Cole's question, the one that took me by surprise. About whether Vivien might have been seeing someone.

This is ludicrous. Isaac is old enough to be her father. I try to bury my doubts. I won't allow Cleo to confuse me, to get to me. I won't allow her to corrupt my feelings for Isaac. I want to believe that the night he spent at my flat meant something, to both of us. I don't want to see myself as pathetic, over the hill, easily manipulated.

'It's cruel of you, to talk about Vivien that way,' I say. 'She's no longer a threat to you, Cleo. Perhaps you can let go of a little of your bitterness. Out of respect for me, if nothing else.'

'I don't think of myself as bitter,' she says. 'I try to be honest. You always wanted to see Vivien in a certain light. Because you're a good person. But there were things about her you didn't want to see. I don't blame you, you're her mother. I don't know what it feels like, to have a child. But you're right, maybe I should keep my mouth shut. It's only – I don't want you to be taken advantage of.'

Cleo is playing games. She is the manipulative one. The one with a wall full of incriminating photographs. I'm furious that Ben would leave Lexi alone with her. But then he doesn't have all the facts. About either of us.

I stay close to Lexi, unsure what to do. I sense I need to be cautious, so as not to upset Cleo.

'When will Ben be home?' I say, in an attempt to change the subject.

'I've no idea. I can stay as long as he needs me to.'

'I don't want to wake Lexi,' I say. 'Why don't we talk downstairs?'

Slowly, I stand up. Lexi murmurs and turns onto her back, but her eyes stay closed. 'I could do with a cup of tea,' I say.

Cleo leaves the window and begins to walk towards the doorway, but then she stops, at Lexi's bedside. She kisses her fingertips and places them against Lexi's forehead.

I swallow. I stay very still. I pretend not to mind and I quash the urge to grab hold of her and drag her away from my granddaughter. To my relief, she follows me out of the bedroom. I close the door behind us.

I head to the staircase, but Cleo stops dead in the middle of the landing. Under the recessed ceiling lights, I notice the black eyeliner, drawn in a sweeping line along her eyelids. The same way Vivien used to wear her eye make-up. And her hair – I don't remember Cleo's hair ever being this dark. Her natural colour is a soft brown. For the first time, it's not tied back or covered, and I can see she's dyed it almost black and had it cut so it hangs straight to her shoulders. It looks just like Vivien's, in the photograph in the living room. Her lips are painted a delicate pink.

'Cleo, let's go down to the kitchen,' I say again.

She doesn't answer me. When I look into her damaged eyes, and at her sad imitation of my daughter's beauty, I wonder what Cleo is capable of doing to get what she wants.

All I want is to put as much distance between her and my granddaughter as possible. As quickly as I can. I glance at Lexi's room, at the closed door, and now I worry that if she wakes up I won't hear her calling out.

'I talked to a detective working on Vivien's case today,' I say, 'and she told me about the assault charges laid against you.'

Cleo takes a few slow steps forwards. She leans against the banister and looks over the side. I follow her gaze, I can see all the way down the curved staircase to the chequered tiles on the ground floor.

'Cleo, do you understand that when Ben finds out, he won't want you anywhere near his daughter? And he will find out. They're going to tell him.'

She's staring down at that black-and-white floor. I have the horrible vision of her throwing herself over this railing, of a second death in this house.

But she does not throw herself down. She laughs.

I'm stunned by her reaction and I wonder if she's completely out of her mind. But she turns to look at me and when she speaks, she sounds quite sane.

'Ben knows,' she says. 'He's always known.'

'I don't believe you.'

'It's true. Ben was the one who hired the lawyer who managed to get the charges dropped. I was going through a difficult time,' she says. 'I wasn't myself.'

'What do you mean, a difficult time?'

'When I left Ben, it wasn't easy to find somewhere to live. I looked at so many places, but London is so expensive, and student accommodation was impossible to come by in the middle of term. In the end, I managed to find a place not too far away from Cinnamon Wharf, sharing with an elderly lady, Mrs Beezley, a school music teacher. And her cat. I got the room because she was only prepared to let it to a single female. She didn't want any men around.'

'Was she the woman you assaulted? An elderly music teacher?'

She nods. 'It wasn't about her. I had a breakdown of sorts, you could say. The shock of the change was the hard part, thinking my life was going to be one way, and then finding out it was going to be something else entirely. I went from living in a flat I loved, with my soulmate, to being completely alone in a strange bedroom with just enough space for a single bed and a falling-apart MDF wardrobe. I didn't make it back to any of my classes. I failed the year.'

I'm still at the top of the staircase, my hand on the smooth banister. Cleo shows no sign of budging. I suspect she wants to stay up here, near Lexi.

'You wanted to know why Ben let me live in that flat all these years,' she says, 'and why he doesn't ask me to pay rent or to buy him out?'

'Yes.'

'I didn't tell you the whole truth before,' she goes on. 'About why he feels so guilty. But I don't want there to

225

be anything hidden between us. You're like family to me, Rose.'

'I'm listening,' I say. 'But please, keep your voice down. I don't want to wake Lexi.'

Cleo leaves the railing and comes right up close, so her face is inches from mine. I'm at the edge of the stairs which suddenly seem rather steep. I don't move a muscle. I can feel my entire body heating up again, I'm sweating. But I don't move.

'I was pregnant when Vivien took Ben away from me,' Cleo says. She says this so softly. I can see the extent of the pain in her eyes.

'Let's go downstairs,' I say. 'We can sit down together and talk properly. I know how important this is. Please.'

I'm not sure she's heard me. She stays frozen in front of me, imprisoned in her own past. My legs feel shaky, as though I might fall. I could pass out, from the heat in this place.

'Because I want you to know everything,' she says, 'I should also tell you that I fell pregnant on purpose. You see, when I realized that Ben still wanted Vivien, I was really scared. So I stopped taking the pill, because that was the only weapon I had. For once, I wanted something Vivien didn't have. I wanted Ben; I wanted to tie him to me for ever. For once, I wanted to win.'

She begins pulling at her hairline with restless fingertips.

'What happened?' I say.

'I only found out I was pregnant a few weeks after I'd left Cinnamon Wharf,' she says. 'By that stage, I was barely leaving my room. I'd stopped getting dressed, stopped going to college. I kept my door closed, so Mrs Beezley couldn't see inside. I had a kettle in there and I'd fill it from the bathroom tap and make tea in my room, so I didn't have to make conversation with her in the kitchen. I remember lying on my back for hours and hours, rubbing my hand across my belly, trying to feel Ben's baby.'

Cleo stops. She looks at me with such intensity, seeking some sort of affirmation, begging me to understand her or to pardon her, I can't tell. I'm unsure what to say or do, but increasingly certain that Cleo is volatile, and that the potent mix of emotions inside her is ready to ignite.

Though, of course, I am hardly one to judge.

'Did you tell Ben?'

'I waited one month,' Cleo says. 'Exactly four weeks. I was hoping that Ben or Vivien would contact me. But they didn't. Not once, not a single phone call. I lay in bed watching my phone and willing it to ring. I wanted them to come and find me and ask me to go back, but neither of them did. And I understood then that it suited them for me to disappear. When I started to feel nauseous in the mornings, I knew I couldn't wait any longer, I had to make a decision. So I dragged myself up and I went back to our old building. I went to see the caretaker and I asked him about Ben. He told me they were still there, still living together in our apartment.'

Cleo is staring past me, towards the ground floor. I don't feel as though she's really present, or having a conversation with me. She's somewhere else, in some distant terrible place.

'I finally accepted that Ben was relieved I was gone. I understood he was never going to leave Vivien. It was as though I came back to my senses and I knew that, rationally, I couldn't go through with the pregnancy. I was in a state, I had no money, I knew I'd never cope on my own with a baby. It had all been a pathetic fantasy. I'd had a terrible mother and I knew I would be a terrible mother. I was still sane enough to know I had to pull myself together and leave Ben and Vivien behind and live my own life. So I went to a clinic and I filled in the forms and I swallowed the pills they gave me.'

Her eyes soften with tears. I should reach out to her. But I can't bring myself to touch her.

'There was a moment,' she says, 'when I still felt hopeful. I thought I could pull myself together and I could still have a career and a life. I kept telling myself it was only temporary, the feeling that I'd lost everything and that I was no one.'

'I'm sorry,' I say.

Ben and Vivien had been cruel, to someone who was vulnerable. They betrayed her. I force myself to reach out and put my arms around her, as I know I should. She puts her arms around me. Her jumper is soft against my cheek. A pale-pink cashmere. Something Vivien would choose.

I pull away from her. There's something uneasy in her touch, something about Cleo, an invisible force that makes me wary of her and makes me want to keep my distance. I feel a combination of pity and unease. The dyed-black hair, the drawn-on brows, the thick eyeliner. All of this disturbs me. I see the wall of photographs. Cleo has lived in a fantasy world all these years, and as much as I pity her, I fear her too.

I wonder how far gone Ben is in his grief, that he would let this woman anywhere near his child. I wonder whom it is Ben sees when he lets Cleo into his home. Whether he really sees her at all, or whether, with the help of his Bell's Special Reserve, he conjures up the ghost of his dead wife.

Cleo has fallen silent and I think her confession might have come to an end. She steps back, away from the top of the stairs, and I feel the tension in my shoulders and my chest ease up a little.

But then she heads for the other set of stairs. She begins to climb, up towards the main suite. And I have no choice but to follow her, because I can't let her out of my sight.

Cleo walks past Vivien's portrait, without looking at her, and she enters the passageway that leads to Vivien and Ben's bedroom. She passes the dressing room and then she pushes open the bathroom door. This door does not creak, it opens smoothly, silently. Cleo steps onto the grey marble tiles and stands with her back to me.

I hold my breath. I do not move.

I know I'm imagining things and this is not rational. But still, I feel it, a sudden drop in temperature, as though the cold outside cannot be kept at bay, as though the marble floor has turned to ice. I'm freezing cold.

'After I took the pills they gave me,' Cleo says, 'I went back to my dark bedroom and I locked myself in. I thought it would all be over with quickly. But I started to feel sick, and then I couldn't stop shaking. I had these terrible cramps. And there was blood. So much blood.'

I don't know what I was expecting to see inside this bathroom, but everything is spotless. Scrubbed clean. The marble floor, the tiled walls, the sides of the stone bath.

Cleo walks over to the basin. She looks at herself in the mirror, and then reaches up to straighten the black strands of hair that frame her face.

'The bleeding wouldn't stop,' she says. 'Mrs Beezley was home so I couldn't use the bathroom. I tried to stay under the covers and go to sleep. I just wanted it to be over with. I wanted to die along with my baby.'

Her voice catches in her throat and tears run down her cheeks, leaving behind black rivers of mascara.

I close my eyes because I am dizzy. Vivien lies on the grey tiles, on her side.

'Cleo, I can't be in here—'

'There was blood everywhere.' Cleo carries on, as if I haven't spoken. Her tears mingle with mascara and drip down onto her jumper. 'I saw blood smeared all over the walls. I could feel my blood soaking through the mattress, overflowing, slipping between the floorboards. I thought there must be a bright-red stain on the ceiling of the flat below.'

I lean against the door frame for support. I have nothing to say to her, nothing that can ease her pain.

'I thought I was going to bleed to death,' Cleo says. She picks up a towel from the towel rail. She stares at her desolate face in the mirror. 'And I wasn't sorry. I wanted to die. For so many years afterwards, I wished I had. But Mrs Beezley called her son over and he forced the door open. They told me later that she was trying to help me, but I went for her. She said I tried to strangle her. I don't remember any of it.'

Cleo sobs. She holds Vivien's white towel to her face to muffle the sound.

When the waves of grief subside, she drops the black-stained towel to the floor, turns on the cold tap and splashes water onto her face. She pats her skin dry, using another of Vivien's monogrammed towels, leaving behind more stains.

'So here I am,' she says. 'I'm alive.'

She turns to look at me.

'This is such a horrible place to die,' she says. Her black-ringed eyes are dull. They no longer glisten with tears. 'So hard. And so brutal. So many sharp edges.'

Chapter 22

Cleo's heavy footsteps are right behind me as I rush down the stairs to the first floor. She is still talking but I'm no longer listening.

I stop, in front of Lexi's closed door, and open it a crack, wincing as it squeaks. I lean in. She is still asleep, the room is peaceful. Behind me, Cleo's breath is ragged. I close the door, carefully, and I turn to face her.

She is determined to tell her story. Every last, sordid detail. Her speech is fast and pressured.

'I landed up in an acute psychiatric ward for a few days,' Cleo says. 'And finally, Ben came to see me. I told him, about his baby. I told him I wouldn't have done it if he'd just contacted me. Just once. I wanted to hurt him. Do you understand?'

'I do understand, Cleo. I'm sorry, about everything you've been through.'

I falter, as I hear my own voice. I don't sound sorry; I sound somewhat distanced and cold. I want to tell Cleo the truth: that Vivien and Ben wanted each other and loved each other and that's how life is sometimes. Cruel.

And that's the way I am sometimes, practical and rational. Unfeeling, at my worst. But this detachment helps me live my life. Unlike Cleo, who is at the mercy of her bitterness and her longings.

'Ben did feel guilty,' she says. 'Though not guilty enough to leave your daughter.'

I feel as though I can see right inside the woman in front of me, to where the seven-year-old girl who walked to school on her own still languishes. She is all alone. So little has changed for Cleo.

'Do you know what I remember so clearly about my stay in hospital?' Cleo doesn't wait for me to answer, her words pour out. 'Ben was wearing a new raincoat, one I'd never seen before. That raincoat, with its fancy checked lining, stank of Vivien. And so did he. He literally smelled different. Maybe it was a new aftershave, I don't know. But he stank of her. And the whole time he was with me, he didn't take that fucking coat off. He couldn't wait to leave me. He wanted to get back to her.'

I've heard enough. 'Please,' I say. 'Keep your voice down.'

Cleo takes me by surprise as she steps forward and reaches for the door handle to Lexi's room. I grab hold of her wrist before she can turn it.

'I thought I heard something,' she says.

'You didn't.'

'If the door's closed we won't hear her if she wakes up,' Cleo says. 'Ben asked me to watch over her.'

'For a few hours, maybe. But I'm her grandmother and I'm here now and I'm taking over. The door stays shut.'

Cleo looks a sight. Her eyes are bloodshot and ringed with black. If Lexi sees her, she will be terrified.

She pulls her hand back from the doork handle.

I need to get her downstairs. I manage to dredge up the last ounce of my compassion, and to speak kindly to her. I know she needs someone to acknowledge her suffering.

'I know what it's like to be lonely,' I say, 'and I'm sorry you went through so much pain. I'm sorry Vivien and Ben were selfish and cruel. I'm sorry I didn't contact you myself during all those years.'

'I made a terrible mistake,' she says. 'I lost my baby. But now things have changed. Not just for me, but for you too, Rose. Ben and Lexi need us.'

'Cleo, this is a fantasy.' I hear my voice rising, but I can't hold down my outrage. 'You cannot simply step in and take over Vivien's life. It doesn't work that way.'

'Ben needs me. I have a second chance to have a family.'

I take a deep breath to steady myself. I try again to make her see reality.

'Your closest friend stole the man you were in love with,' I say. 'And you lost your baby. That is all terribly sad, but it's also in the past. This is not your life and it never will be. Being here inside Vivien's house, with Vivien's child, isn't good for you, Cleo. It will only make things worse, seeing Lexi and coming face to face with all the precious things you cannot have.'

'All this was supposed to be mine,' she says, gesturing around her, at the family photographs lining the walls of the landing. 'And it would have been, if not for Vivien. Now Ben has asked me to wait for him. And I won't leave Lexi.'

I'm tired of talking. Sick to death of this insane conversation. There is no point trying to reason with her. I know full well Cleo doesn't understand what I'm saying to her, because she doesn't want to. She is unable to live with herself, unable to find her own path. She is still envious of Vivien. She wants everything that Vivien took away from her.

Without thinking, I grab hold of her arm. My fingers grip the cashmere jumper as I pull her with me, down the stairs. Cleo doesn't resist.

At the bottom of the staircase, I let go of her arm. She keeps one hand on the banister, as though she might rush upstairs again. We are wary of each other.

If Ben walks in on us, there could be a very ugly scene. The truth is I have no idea whose side he will take. It wouldn't surprise me at all if I was the one asked to leave. I doubt he will give me a chance to explain.

I'm out of breath and I feel myself losing control. I remember Yusuf's mother, the fear in her eyes. My need to protect Lexi has turned me into someone savage, someone with the potential for violence. I can feel this, I would do anything to protect her.

I take a few breaths as I collect myself. When I speak my voice is calm and strong, as though I'm on the ward again.

'Did Vivien know you were watching her? Did she see you?'

'I don't think so.'

'Was Vivien afraid of you?'

Cleo blinks. The ugliness inside her shows in her eyes, and on her kohl-stained face.

'No,' she says, 'Vivien wasn't intimidated by anyone.' She spits her words at me, like bullets. 'Vivien was the strongest person I knew. Your daughter, Rose, was a self-obsessed liar and a thief. She was always scheming to get something she wanted, usually something belonging to someone else.'

In a perverse way it's a relief to hear Cleo talking this way, to hear her admitting how much she hated my daughter, and how strong her desire has always been to take Vivien's life. I only wish Ben was here to bear witness.

I have to find a way to get him to believe me, to see what I see when I look at Cleo. Even if I am depriving him of his one last source of comfort, Ben has to see Cleo for who she is. A desperate woman.

Cleo's face is set rigid in anger. 'I wanted her to suffer,' she says. 'I wanted her to feel pain, the way I did.'

Any pity I felt for her has given way to something

else, something hard and cold. Cleo is not only a victim, she has a nasty side too. She frightens me.

'What did you do, Cleo, to make her suffer? Tell me.'

She glances upstairs, towards Lexi's closed door.

'Stalkers want to get close to their victims,' I say. 'They act out when their feelings aren't reciprocated. They become dangerous. You've been obsessed with this family for years. I'm going to make sure that Ben understands it's not safe for you to be anywhere near his child.'

I look around, peering under the mahogany hall table, trying to see where she's left her shoes and her bag but there's no sign of them. She'll have to leave barefoot. I don't care.

'I'm not a stalker. And Vivien was not a victim. I've never done anything to hurt Ben or Vivien. It was the other way round.'

Cleo seems to have calmed down, her anger has already dissipated. She takes a few steps forwards, so she's that much further from the stairs, further away from Lexi.

I move over to the front door and pull it wide open. I am strong enough to drag Cleo from this house and throw her out onto the street. A freezing, wet wind rushes in from outside. Cleo moves forward again and for a moment I think she's given up and she's going to leave.

But that would be too easy.

Instead, she leaves me standing at the open door and walks into the living room.

I start to sense defeat. Even if I force her to leave the house, she may stand outside on the pavement, pounding on the buzzer at the gate. She might sit on the steps, waiting until Ben gets home, ready to tell him some twisted version of what's happened here tonight.

I walk over to the doorway of the living room. I watch as Cleo opens a bottle of wine and pours herself a large glass with unsteady hands.

Something behind me catches my attention. A sound, perhaps, a rush of wind, or the creaking of a hinge.

I was so focused on Cleo, on watching her, that I didn't close the front door properly. Now it gapes wide open. I run halfway up the stairs and look up towards the landing. Lexi's door is open too.

Chapter 23

Lexi is gone.

Her bed is empty and the quilt with its little stars lies on the floor. I rush to her bed and run my hands over the rumpled white sheets, as if that might make her materialize. They are still warm to my touch, but she has vanished.

I try to think, to cling to my rational self. Could she have slipped out of the front door while I was watching Cleo in the living room? It's possible, but unlikely. And even if she did, she can't have gone far, the front gate is closed and securely locked.

Don't panic, I tell myself. *Do not panic.*

I rush upstairs, calling her name. I fling open the door to Vivien's bathroom. I flip on the light. There is only an empty, quiet space. I cannot help but stare at the floor, but no body appears.

I run down the passage to the master bedroom. I check Vivien's bed. I throw the duvet to the floor, I search under the sheets and underneath the pillows.

She is not here.

This is insane. Already, I have lost her. She might have overheard my argument with Cleo. She might be afraid. She might be hiding.

She could be outside, crouching down on the driveway.

I am panicking. I can feel what it would be like to lose her and I could not bear it.

Ben is going to kill me.

I run all the way down two flights of stairs, past the ground floor where there is no sign of Cleo, and I don't stop until I reach the basement. There, I stop dead on the bottom step.

I have found her. Of course I have.

Lexi is facing away from me. She's at the window, in front of the row of potted herbs. Soil is scattered on the limestone floor, all around her small, bare feet.

I stay still because I don't want to frighten her. I watch as she pulls out each and every plant in turn, wrenching them out by the roots. She moves along the row of evenly spaced pots until she has ruined them all: basil, sage, mint and coriander.

Soil spills onto her feet, onto the limestone floor.

Then, when she has finished destroying her mother's plants, she walks across the room, her steps slow and sleep-heavy. She stops in front of the sink.

'Lexi?'

She turns at the sound of my voice, but although her eyes are open, I'm not convinced she's fully awake. I think she hovers in that space between dreams and reality.

'Did you have a bad dream?' I say.

She looks confused, as though I'm speaking a foreign language.

'Is Mummy here?' she says.

I imagine I see sadness spreading through her eyes, but then I look again and I can't tell what it is she feels. She disappears inside herself and her eyes are dark and impenetrable.

'Lexi, let's go back to your bed.' My voice is gentle and soothing.

'Is Mummy here?'

'No,' I say. 'I'm here. Granny's here.'

'I saw Mummy.' Her bottom lip trembles.

I take a few steps closer, cautiously. 'Are you thirsty?' I say.

She nods.

There are so many drawers and so many cupboards and none of them have handles. I press my hand against smooth surfaces, which glide open. I find a pantry, filled with dozens of boxes of different teas and coffees, and next to that one, a cupboard full of different dinner services and a drawer with a set of copper pans. I leave all of the cupboards open behind me. Finally, I find the glasses. I fill one with tap water and I hold the glass to Lexi's lips as she takes a few sips.

She's looking down, at the drawer next to the sink. She presses her hand against it and it slides open. She reaches inside and takes out a pestle and mortar, made of heavy black marble. She begins to grind, looking down into the empty bowl as though she can see something there.

I begin to feel anxious. I grab the pestle and mortar out of her hands and shove all of it back inside the drawer. It closes with a metallic click.

Lexi stands like a statue in front of me.

I look around, at the carnage on the floor, the dying plants, the soil spread everywhere, and I know that something terrible is about to happen in this house.

Vivien

The day before she dies

Isaac won't tell me where we are going, because Ben wants to surprise me. But I guess anyway, since we're headed towards Farringdon. And I guess right. Isaac pulls up outside Kestrel's Antique & Vintage Jewellery.

I love Kestrel's. I love the windows crammed with diamonds and emeralds and rubies, all of them afloat on a sea of velvet. I love the hush inside, the thick carpets, the leather-topped desks and the crystal chandeliers. I love that each piece of jewellery is unique.

I also love the fact that antiques hold their value. A part of me is always focused on making sure I'm never, ever going back to that dank bedroom in Cambridge Court. The more diamonds I have, the further away I am from all of that, and the happier I feel. That is simply the truth.

Ben is waiting for me. He's standing outside, take-away coffee in hand, early as usual. He rushes forwards to open the car door. I step out and tilt my face up to his for a kiss. As he rings the doorbell, we reach for each other's hands.

Kestrel's is a father-and-son business and we are good customers. Mark, the son, rushes over to open up for us.

'Lovely to see you again,' he says. He is a softly spoken man in his twenties, tall and blond with a certain awkward manner I find endearing.

We follow him through to the back, past the matching father-and-son desks. Paul Kestrel, the father, is sitting at one of these and he glances up as we pass, still wearing his eyeglass. He smiles at us. He has the same shy demeanour as his son.

Mark shows us through to a private room, where we are seated in leather armchairs. Oil paintings of bejewelled Victorian women hang on the walls and the room has the musty smell of old money. In the corner there is a massive steel safe. Mark opens it, using one of those old-fashioned dials he has to turn back and forth. He pulls out a tray, then locks the safe again. Ben keeps hold of my hand. I sense he's nervous. He's been planning this.

'I know you don't like surprises,' he says, 'but I took a chance and picked out a few things I thought you'd like. The final choice is yours.'

With a flourish, Mark places a velvet-lined tray in front of us. Three pairs of diamond earrings are laid out in a row. Two pairs are studs, one set in platinum, the other in yellow gold. The third pair is set in rose-gold shepherd's hooks and I imagine they'll hang down a little below my earlobes.

Mark explains about the provenance of the stones, the cut and the colour. The carats. I reach for the platinum studs. I knew straight away these were the ones I would have. I lean forward so I can see my reflection in the oval standing mirror on the desk and I slip the earrings into my pierced ears. I make sure they're fastened tight, I tuck my hair behind my ears and then I turn to Ben, so he can admire them.

'Perfect,' he says. He reaches out to brush my cheek softly with the back of his hand. I notice he doesn't smile.

'You're sure?' I say.

He nods. 'Mark, could we have the room for a few minutes?' he says.

'Of course.' Mark leaves, closing the door behind him. The diamonds remain, strewn in front of us on their soft velvet tray.

Ben turns his green leather chair slightly, so it faces mine. I can see he's preoccupied, concerned about something other than jewellery.

'Are you worried about tonight?' I say.

He nods.

'Everything is going to be perfect. The caterers arrive at six. They're bringing extra tables and chairs and they're going to set up in the basement. We'll roll back all the sliding doors and open out all of the basement rooms into one large space. It's a bit early but I've chosen a Halloween theme, because the kids will love it. I've ordered Halloween crackers, Halloween witches' pumpkin soup and ghost cupcakes. I've bought dressing-up costumes for all of the kids. And a photographer's coming after dinner so we can send everyone pictures and videos afterwards. It's going to be spectacular.'

'You're incredible,' he says. 'Thank you.'

'So why do you look so unhappy?'

He reaches for my hands. 'Well, it's only a small matter of securing the multi-million-pound deal that's going to ensure my company stays afloat. But more importantly, it will mean I can cut back on the travelling. I can be home more to give you a hand with Lexi. I know you've practically been a single parent, the hours I've worked, the amount of time I'm away from home.'

'The investors adore you,' I say. 'And tonight you'll charm their wives and children and it will all work out.'

'Promise?'

'Yes, I do.'

He leans forward to kiss my lips, but there's a telltale crease in his forehead that I know means trouble. People always have an ulterior motive for buying excessively expensive gifts. Even my adoring husband.

'It's not Christmas and it's not my birthday,' I say, 'so why are you buying me jewellery from Kestrel's?'

He squeezes my hand. 'I wanted you to have a gift,' he says, 'not a birthday present, or a Christmas present

– but a gift purely because I love you. And I want you to remember I said that.'

'Now you're making me nervous.'

'I wanted to say thank you,' he says. 'I have everything I've ever wanted, you and Lexi. I want to make sure you know how much I appreciate you.'

Ben closes his eyes and presses my fingers to his lips. The sight of his gold wedding ring reassures me. He grows more attractive year after year; as he becomes more successful, so he relaxes into his own skin. People love him. I love him, more than I'd anticipated.

'Are you happy?' he says.

'Yes.'

'Our daughter is eight years old,' he says. 'She's not a baby any more.'

'I know how old our daughter is.'

'She . . .' He hesitates. 'She's smart and sensitive.'

I pull my hands away from his. *She's told him something.*

As long as I remember, I have always, always felt cold. Except when I'm with Ben, then it's as though I have a warm blanket tucked around me. I'm safe. But not today. Today I sense we are on dangerous ground.

'Viv, she says you put medicine in her milk, because she's overweight. She said you warned her to not to tell me.'

The temperature has dropped in here. I feel myself shivering.

'Is this true, Viv?'

'Yes. It's true.'

'Why would you do that to her?'

I draw my legs up on to the chair underneath me, I curl up, my arms folded.

'You don't understand, Ben. You have no idea what it's like to struggle with your weight every single day of your life.'

'Alexandra is eight years old. She's a separate person from you, Viv. You don't need to worry about her, she's perfect. You shouldn't be putting these ideas into her head. You're setting her up to be unhappy.'

'She's not perfect, Ben. You see only what you want to see when it comes to your family. She's ostracized by the other children. She's being bullied. I'm in the head teacher's office at least once a month. She has *no* friends. I managed to scrape together those four kids at her birthday party because I know their mothers and they took pity on me.'

'I phoned our GP,' he says. 'She has no record of prescribing any weight-loss medication for our daughter.'

'I consulted someone else. A specialist in paediatric obesity.'

I jump as he slams his hand against the desk. '*She's not obese!*'

I shrink further into the chair. I don't dare say anything. I don't like the way he looks at me. Like I'm shallow, or crazy, or not to be trusted with his precious daughter who can do no wrong.

He's shouting now, and the fury in his voice terrifies me. 'You shopped around until you found some arsehole who'd prescribe whatever you wanted them to if you paid them enough, didn't you?'

'Ben that's not true. He's a qualified doctor and it's a low dose. These days you don't even need a doctor, I could have bought anything I wanted over the internet. But I'd never do that.'

Ben looks away as he tries to calm himself down. When he speaks again, his voice is more measured.

'Mrs Murad phoned me a couple of weeks ago,' he says. 'She was worried you'd developed some distorted ideas about Lexi's weight. She told me you'd asked about medicating Lexi, and she was concerned, because Lexi is still so young. She was worried enough to break confidentiality. So I talked to Lexi. At first she refused to tell me anything, but I kept asking. A few days ago, she opened up.'

'You don't trust me. You think I'm a bad mother.'

'That's not true. But I'm devastated that you would ask my daughter to keep secrets from me.'

'I'm sorry,' I say. I lean forward, putting my feet down onto the floor, and I try to take hold of his hand. He pulls away.

'Viv, I know you're doing your best. We all know how traumatic the last ten years have been, all the doctors, all the failures, our lost baby. Mrs Murad worries about you and so do I. She's been your doctor for such a long time and she thinks you need psychiatric help. She says she's told you this herself, but she didn't think you were listening. I have to make sure you get the help you need.'

'Why here, Ben? Why are we having this conversation here? Are you trying to bribe me or threaten me? I can't tell.'

I start to loosen the clasp of one of the earrings, but Ben reaches out and takes hold of my wrist.

'Let go,' I say.

He won't. He takes hold of my other hand, too. We stay, frozen, staring at each other. There are tears in his eyes.

'I have no idea what we're doing here,' he says. 'I've been agonizing over this for days and I didn't know how to raise it with you.'

'What am I, Ben, some kind of witch you're afraid of?' Now I'm shouting. I imagine Mark and his father, eyeglasses on, raising their heads to listen to us argue.

'I know how sensitive you are,' he says, 'how you beat yourself up about not being a good enough mother. I wanted to take you somewhere you had to listen to me, somewhere neutral, somewhere you couldn't walk out before I'd finished. I wanted to show you how much I love you, to reassure you. It was a terrible, idiotic idea. But it doesn't really matter where we have this conversation. We have to talk about this.'

I look into his eyes and I see something has changed. Something is broken.

'I've been to see a psychiatrist,' he says, 'and I want us to go back and see him together.'

'You went to see someone behind my back? You spoke about me, without my permission?'

I try to rip my hands away from his, but he won't let go.

'If you don't let go of me,' I say, 'I will start screaming.'

Ben loosens his grip on my wrists. I pull away from him and grip the armrests. My eyes fill with tears, but mine are tears of rage.

'What did you tell him? He could ruin us.'

'No, Viv. You're being paranoid. Everything I talk to him about is confidential. He wants to help us.'

'Like Mrs Murad kept our conversations confidential?'

I'm in some kind of nightmare. The noise in my head grows louder and louder. I can't hear what he's saying.

'Ben, this psychiatrist could report me to social services.'

He looks shocked. He hasn't thought this through. 'Why? Viv, what have you done? What have you been giving her?'

Ben puts his head in his hands.

'We have a daughter,' he says, 'and she comes first. That's the way it is, Vivien. We're parents. We don't matter as much any more.'

'Fuck you, Ben.'

Mark is at the door, looking startled. He turns and makes a swift exit.

Ben sits back in his chair. His body is slumped, as though I'd punched him in the stomach.

'As soon as I get out of this place,' I say, 'I'm phoning the caterer. Every single thing for tonight will be cancelled. And don't you dare come home tonight. Don't you dare. You can go to a hotel and have a good long think about your cosy little chat with your new psychiatrist friend.'

I stand up. My rage gives me strength. I straighten my jacket and run my fingers through my hair. I adjust my posture, so my shoulders are back and my spine is straight.

'Don't come anywhere near us until I've calmed down. Or you'll be sorry. Do you understand?'

He nods, looking past me, not at me.

I walk, gracefully, like the ballet dancer I once was, through the front room of the jewellery shop. Mark and his father are behind their desks, pretending to look at their laptops. When I reach the door, Mark springs to his feet to unlock it for me.

I step outside, onto the pavement. I ignore Isaac as he gets out of the car. By the time he's come round to open the passenger door, I've already flagged down a passing cab. The driver is old and decrepit-looking, and I get a bad feeling about it, but I climb in anyway. As the taxi pulls away from the pavement, I remember I'm still wearing the diamond studs. But I'm not going back. Ben is going to have to pay.

Chapter 24

I didn't come to the house tonight intending to take Lexi away with me, but now it seems the only thing I can do for her. I hold her hand firmly in mine as we climb the stairs to the entrance hall.

I don't know if Cleo is still inside the house, or what she might be doing. I need to move fast, before she tries to stop me.

The cupboard next to the front door is packed solid with coats. I stare for a moment at Vivien's shiny black goatskin before choosing a waterproof for Lexi, one with a fur-lined hood. She allows me to put it on her without protest. I kneel down and fumble with the clasp, my hands are not as steady as they usually are, but I manage, zipping it right up to the top. I grab the smallest pair of Wellingtons. She holds on to my shoulder while I help her to push her feet into the rubber boots. I grab my own coat from the hall table.

Then I take hold of Lexi's hand again and I stop for a moment to smile down at her, to reassure her. Her strained face looks so small underneath her mussed up halo of hair. I can see in her eyes she is afraid.

'Everything is going to be all right,' I say. 'I'm going to take you home with me, just for tonight.'

I open the front door. The rain is coming down hard and I feel a flicker of foreboding. I am taking this child away from her warm bed and out into a dark, wet night. Ben is going to be furious. But this house is toxic and I won't leave Lexi again. I am the only one who can help her.

I press the buzzer that releases the front gate. Then I shut the door, grasping the slippery hexagonal handle with both hands.

Lexi pushes her hair away from her face and tips her head up to the sky. She opens her mouth to taste the rain. I cannot say if she is frightened or glad to be taken away from Blackthorn Road, but she is holding my hand and that's enough, for now.

We walk slowly down the stairs. I don't want her to slip and lose her footing on the wet marble. I push open the iron gate and lead her through. We're the only people out walking on Blackthorn Road. With a small child at my side, and the rain making it difficult to see, the journey to the end of the street seems to last forever.

I imagine the neighbours, peering out from every window we pass, watching me leading the child away. I adjust the hood of Lexi's coat, pulling it up to cover her hair. I'd rather not risk a cab, it might seem suspicious, a young child in pyjama bottoms under her coat, out so late at night. Alexandra might ask for her mother again, she might struggle or protest or ask to go home.

I imagine Cleo's footsteps behind us, masked by the sound of the rain.

As we cross the road, a group of four teenage boys is coming towards us. Hoodies conceal their faces, their elbows jut out, their hands are hidden in their pockets. I don't make eye contact; I grip Lexi's hand tighter. I am defenceless. I shouldn't have her out so late at night. I think about Ben and I imagine his reaction when he finds out I have taken his daughter. Lexi is his most prized possession. She is all he has left.

When we reach the Underground, a handful of commuters spill out of the station, their heads hunched over mobile phones. No one notices us. I don't look behind me because I am convinced I'll see Cleo, in her raincoat, determined to take Lexi away from me. I decide to hail a taxi after all.

The noise and the lights from the station seem to rouse Lexi, and she stops walking.

'I want to go home,' she says.

I try to pull her forwards, gently, but she resists. When I won't let go of her hand, she arches her body into a C-shape, leaning away and pulling in the opposite direction. A woman in a miniskirt with sky-high heels passes us, her eyes flicker between us from underneath her umbrella. She totters by. No one wants to get involved; people prefer not to see these things.

Lexi is looking up at me, she's pushing her hair away from her face with her free hand and trying to say something, but rain blows into her eyes and I can't hear her. I bend down closer and she whispers in my ear.

'Where is Mummy?' she says.

I kneel down and hug her tight. Her arms creep around me.

'I love you,' I say. I hold her as close as I can without crushing her. 'Everything will be all right,' I say. 'You'll see.'

I feel her body relax. I pull her hood further forward over her face. I stand up, taking hold of her hand again.

The sound of my blood churning in my ears is growing louder. I expect Ben to drive up alongside us at any moment and cause a terrible scene. I need to get away from this corner, it's too well lit outside the station and people and cars are passing all the time. I'm squeezing Lexi's hand; I try to relax my grip.

At the corner, the traffic lights change to green. We cross over to the other side. A taxi is approaching us, the yellow light on the roof shining. I'm about to hold out my hand to hail him when I feel a tugging at my coat. Lexi is pointing at something, at someone. Behind us, on the other side of the street, is a woman who looks exactly like her mother. A woman wearing a long black goatskin coat.

Lexi jerks away from me. Our hands are slick with the rain and she slides from my grasp.

The temperature of a body can change in a split second. Plummet. Break out into a sweat. I grab at the back of her coat, but she's already gone. She runs, across one lane and into the middle of the road. I fix my eyes on the back of her hood as though I could stop her, bring her back, with sheer force of will.

I run out into the road after her. A gust of wind drives the rain into my eyes as I scream her name.

She cries out as she slips and falls, pitching forward, her knees slamming against asphalt, hands outstretched to break her fall. Headlights bear down on her, the windscreen wipers of the taxi swish back and forth, the driver does not see the small girl with ginger hair and a grey coat lying in the road.

But Cleo sees, and she is closer. She runs, throws herself at Lexi, and there is a terrible, tearing sound as the taxi driver skids and cannot stop in time.

A terrible, dull thud. Two bodies in the middle of the road.

Chapter 25

It's one thirty in the morning and I'm sitting, zombie-like, on a vinyl-covered chair in a small cubicle-type room in Accident and Emergency. My coat lies across two chairs; it's muddied, black in places, from when I sat on the pavement with Lexi in my arms.

When I close my eyes, I can hear Vivien and Cleo chattering and giggling behind Vivien's closed door. I can hear the tinny sound of the tape recorder as the same song plays over and over again. 'Club Tropicana'. The girls are happy, I'm sure of it. There's no need for me to go inside and check on them.

Lexi shivers, a small and terrified animal. I hold her and rock her, but I cannot comfort her. She is fighting me. I turn her away, so she does not see the body. She screams for her mother.

Cars form a blockade on either side of us. People stop to help, and to stare. The taxi driver turns Cleo onto her side in the wet darkness. A man drops his briefcase and covers her with a long coat. Her body is very, very still.

The flashing lights of the ambulance arrive mercifully quickly. I am surrounded by familiar sounds and familiar smells. The buzzing of monitors, the sharp, clean smell.

I hear loud footsteps approaching. Wooden soles. I pray it's Ben, to give me news of Lexi, or even Ben with his daughter in his arms, saying she wants her grandmother. But of course it isn't Ben, because Ben wants nothing to do with me.

When I open my eyes, Isaac is standing in the doorway. His hands are shoved down into the pockets of his rain-stained mackintosh, his shoulders are tense and his expression is forbidding. I can hear his accusation in the way he looks at me. Ben looked at me the same way when he arrived at the hospital to find me at his daughter's bedside.

'How's Lexi?' I say.

'She's stable. They're keeping her in overnight.'

I exhale. 'I thought so. I knew she wasn't badly hurt. I had a look at her while we waited for the ambulance.'

Isaac doesn't move. He doesn't say anything comforting.

'Cleo's having a CT scan,' I say. 'They haven't been able to trace any next of kin, so I said I'd stay.'

I stand up, uncomfortable under his stare, and I go over to the water machine. I pull out one of the plastic cups, and several more fall out, dropping to the floor. I pick them up, balance them on top of the machine and pour myself a cup of cold water.

I find my nurse's persona, and I wrap it round me like a cloak before I turn to face him.

'What happened?' Isaac says.

'I went over to the house to check on Lexi. Ben wasn't home and he'd left her alone with Cleo. Cleo was unstable – crying one minute and angry the next. I couldn't get her to leave the house. She told me all sorts of things, about her past . . .'

I remember, then, what she'd said about Isaac, what she'd intimated about him and Vivien. But there's no point repeating her divisive accusations. Not now.

'It wasn't safe for us to stay in that house, I had to get Lexi out of there. I only meant to take her as far as my flat. But Cleo followed us and when Lexi saw her, she pulled away from me and ran towards her. You see Cleo had deliberately made herself up to look exactly like Vivien. Her hair, her make-up – she was wearing Vivien's fur coat, for God's sake – everything.'

My mouth is dry and stale. My head pounds and my neck and shoulders ache. I'm ready to sink under the weight of it all. But I cannot sink, because it would be selfish. I try to slow down, to sound rational.

'Isaac,' I say, 'Cleo had been stalking them for years. There's evidence in her flat. I've been to see the police about it. DS Cole told me Cleo has a history of violence. She assaulted someone. I know that in hindsight what I did seems reckless, but I was afraid for Lexi's safety.'

Isaac frowns. I'm not sure if he believes me, but

he is my last hope. With his support, Ben might forgive me.

'Ben has reported you to the police,' he says.

I want to say something, but no sound comes out. I clear my throat and try again. 'Reported me for what?'

'Child abduction.' His tone is grim. He's serious.

'That's insane. I'm her grandmother. You have to convince Ben to talk to me.'

'Ben is with Lexi. He won't let you anywhere near his daughter right now.'

My chest has seized up. The pounding in my head threatens to take me over, but I keep it at bay. I have to think.

'You took Alexandra out of her bed, in the middle of the night, without permission, and without telling Ben where his daughter was,' Isaac goes on. 'How the hell did you think he'd react?'

His voice is so cold.

'I swear, I was trying to protect her. Help me, Isaac, please. I know how much influence you have over Ben. This can be sorted out. Lexi is safe. She's unhurt.'

I see Cleo's body, lying limp on the wet tarmac. I see Lexi's palms, full of grit and blood. *I see Vivien, too.* All my fault.

'I am trying to help you,' he says. 'That's why I'm here. The police are looking for you and I think it's better if you don't talk to them tonight. You might say things you regret. Maybe you should find a lawyer, before you talk to anyone.'

'I can't leave Cleo here alone.'

'You just said she's dangerous.'

'I know. But she's also . . . I've handled this so badly. Cleo saved Lexi's life, too. Even though she caused the accident.'

I hear myself. I'm incoherent.

'Rose, stop.' Isaac walks forward and picks up my coat. He drapes it around my shoulders and then he puts his arm around me and guides me out. The nurses are busy, nowhere to be seen, and no one notices us leave. Outside, the car park is near empty. The rain has stopped.

'Where are we going?' I say.

'To my place. I've asked a friend to send through details of a solicitor.'

'Is that really necessary?'

'I think it's a good idea.'

As Isaac walks with me towards Vivien's car, I realize I don't care about the police. I only fear the damage I have done to my already fragile relationship with Ben.

His arm is heavy around my shoulders and it should be a comfort; at least I'm not alone. Yet the weight of it also feels like a restraint. I twist around, to look back at the hospital, and I shrug his arm away.

'I need to be here, at this hospital. I'm not leaving without seeing Ben.'

'For God's sake, Rose, leave him alone. Do you have any idea of the damage you nearly did tonight? He's barely begun to grieve for his wife, and if it wasn't for

Cleo throwing herself under that taxi, Alexandra might be dead too.'

'If it wasn't for Ben's relationship with Cleo, Lexi would have been safe in her bed. His judgement leaves much to be desired.'

'Ben's right,' Isaac says. 'You refuse to face reality.'

'Ben knows nothing about me.'

Isaac's patience has run out. He raises his voice, he's bellowing at me.

'Ben has been trying to hold himself together since Vivien died. He's doing his best to look after his kid and keep his business afloat and pay his mortgage and if you pull another stunt like this one, he could lose his sanity along with everything else.'

I can just about make out the shapes of tall trees against the sky, and behind them, flashes of light from the road. The sound of traffic is a comfort, for once. There are people nearby, just the other side of the trees. We've reached Vivien's car and I think Isaac might try to force me to get in. But he doesn't touch me.

'Ben's stability, financial and otherwise, is important to you, isn't it?' I say. 'Your own future depends on his success, on him keeping it together.'

'What on earth are you talking about?'

I stand with my back against the passenger door. 'Were you attracted to my daughter?' I say.

The car park is so dark, I can't see his eyes.

'Where the hell is this coming from?' He leans over me, his large hand pressed against the window.

Vivien used to look so tiny, so slight, next to this same car.

'Cleo implied that Vivien had some sort of leverage over you.'

'Have you lost your mind?' He bangs his hand against the roof, and I jump. Then he steps back. I can see he's trying to compose himself.

'Let me get this straight,' he says. 'When you're looking for an excuse for almost getting your grand-daughter killed, Cleo is dangerous and disturbed. But when it comes to what Cleo has to say about me, she's a reliable witness?'

'I don't know.' I stand completely still. 'Cleo hasn't actually lied about anything. She admitted to following Vivien without her knowledge, and to photographing her. She confessed to everything, to wanting Ben and Lexi, too.'

When Isaac speaks his voice is brittle. 'Okay,' he says. 'Yes. I found Vivien attractive. She was an attractive woman. I was fond of her. But I was her driver, that's all.'

'Did anything happen between you?'

'I'm starting to understand why Ben gets so frustrated with you,' he says. 'Why he doesn't trust you. I'm sorry you won't take any responsibility for your part in this. You still want to blame everyone else. First Cleo, now me. But Ben relies on me, and I won't let you hurt them.'

He keeps one hand in his pocket, with the other, he massages the back of his neck.

'I don't care where you go now,' he says. 'I'll drop you off wherever you like. Just stay away from Ben and Alexandra. Do you understand?'

'I can't do that. I can't stay away.'

'I'm serious,' he says. 'If you promise me you'll cooperate, if you leave them in peace, I'll try to convince Ben not to go ahead with a statement to the police.'

I hear the thudding of my heart.

'I'm not afraid of the police,' I say. 'They are never going to jail a grieving grandmother. I am afraid of only one thing: being separated from Lexi and not being able to watch over her.'

I pull my coat, Vivien's gift, tighter around me. It's cold out here.

'I'm sorry,' I say. 'You're right. I have no one to blame but myself. I do have to take responsibility. I'm guilty of so many things.'

I imagine Isaac's brown eyes might fill with a mixture of pity and impatience. He rubs the back of his neck again, as he wonders what to do with me. He must think me almost fully unravelled, but he is wrong.

'I'm not leaving this hospital without talking to Ben,' I say.

'I wish I could make you see sense.'

The cold is getting to me, and I shiver. A shadow flits across the edge of the car park. Stops. As does my heart. The eyes of a fox glint at me in the dark. He waits, poised and tense.

I understand now. Vivien was never happy, inside her

beautiful house on Blackthorn Road. Her wedding portrait shimmers in front of me in the darkness. Her eyes, behind the delicate veil, bear an expression of trepidation and excitement, as though she does not truly believe the life she stole from Cleo was real. As though she is waiting for something bad to happen. And in the end, she made sure it was so.

'Isaac,' I say, 'I need you to get Ben to talk to me. He trusts you. He'll see me if you ask him to.'

'I'm sorry Rose. I can't.'

I'm surprised to find that my head feels light and free of pain. The cold numbs my nerves and the violent thudding I have become accustomed to has relented. My voice, when I speak, is the one I use at the Weissman, the one I use to ensure that I am listened to, that junior nurses do not screw up in situations of life and death.

'Lexi is still at risk. There's something important I need to tell Ben. It could be a matter of life and death.'

'What do you mean?'

'I need to talk to Ben. Please, Isaac, if I mean anything to you, please trust me. Please listen to me.'

There is a silence and I know Isaac is trying to decide if I am unhinged. I reach out and take hold of his hand. I press my lips to his palm. I hope against hope that his feelings for me will win out over reason.

I know I have won when I hear him sigh.

'Promise me you won't do anything else crazy tonight?' he says.

'I promise,' I say.

I put my arms around him and I rest my head in the hollow of his throat. I stroke the soft place on his neck, between his hair and his collar. I inhale his scent, of cigarettes and aftershave. He puts his arms around me too and we stand like that, in the dark silence, just the two of us, and I pretend for a moment that we all might have a happy ending.

Chapter 26

I stand inside the doorway of Lexi's room in the paediatric wing. Ben is at his daughter's bedside, holding her hand and gazing at her. Lexi's eyes are closed. The starched hospital linen is pulled up to her chin and the white of the sheet matches the pallor of her skin.

I'm sure Ben heard me come in, though he doesn't acknowledge my presence. He looks fragile, shrunken somehow, as though he has withered over the last few hours. 'Have they sedated her?' I say.

He nods. He won't look at me.

'Ben,' I say, 'I'm so sorry about what happened. I would never, ever want to put Lexi in danger.'

'But you did,' he says. 'You nearly killed her.'

He keeps his eyes on Lexi. He's so enraged he cannot risk looking at me. Somehow, though, Isaac has convinced him to listen, because he isn't actually throwing me out.

I could try to explain, about Cleo, but this isn't the right time. I don't want to sound as though I'm trying to justify my own actions. And I don't have time. Instead, I am going to talk to him about the things that are truly important.

'Ben,' I say, 'I know you believe I'm a cold bitch who prioritized her career over her family. I know you think I didn't love my daughter enough. And you're right. Partly, you're right. When Vivien was little I missed out on so much that was important. I don't think she ever forgave me. Her father never even acknowledged her existence, and then she was abandoned by me, all over again. I sent her away. When I think about it now, I can see that all of this started so long ago. But it was so different when Lexi was born, so easy.'

Ben still won't look at me. He strokes the back of Lexi's hand with his thumb.

I venture a few steps closer. I stand at the foot of Lexi's bed, my hands gripping the metal bar. 'Ben,' I say, 'we both know that Vivien was not coping with mother-hood. I'm guilty for not helping her, and I blame myself every single day. But I think you knew too.'

Ben glances at me, briefly. Then he turns away again, back to Lexi. I keep talking.

'I'm sure you remember how weak Vivien was, physically and emotionally, after Lexi's birth?' I say. 'I helped as much as I could when Lexi was still in the Weissman Unit, but Vivien didn't visit much, did she?'

No response.

'I worried, at the time, that it wasn't just the physical

state Vivien was in, but that there was something more. Vivien didn't *want* to visit her baby. She'd been through so much with losing Lexi's twin, then the premature birth and the long hospital stay. There were so many risk factors, I should have seen she was at risk for not being able to bond with her daughter or even some kind of post-natal depression. But I convinced myself it was just a phase, that it would pass, with time, once Lexi was home and healthy.'

Ben nods and I feel a tiny bit of hope. My voice is steadier when I continue.

'When Lexi came home, after three long months, I moved in. Obviously I'm a neonatal nurse, so taking care of her was second nature to me, and she was such a lovely, easy-going baby. But after a week or so of being in your house, I started to worry. Vivien was becoming more and more dependent on me. She was doing less and less, leaving almost all of Lexi's care to me. It got to the stage where she insisted I do all the bottle-feeds; she was worried Lexi would choke if she fed her. She didn't want to change Lexi or bathe her on her own either. Vivien got this idea into her head that Lexi screamed whenever she touched her. She convinced herself that it was me Lexi wanted, that I was the only one who could soothe her.'

I stop to catch my breath. Ben doesn't say anything, but he's listening to every word.

'The longer I stayed,' I say, 'the less confident Vivien was. I was the one bonding with Lexi, while the two of them were growing apart. I truly believed that if I didn't move out, if I didn't step aside to give them some space, then Vivien would never have the chance to really be a mother.'

I clear my throat. 'Vivien didn't see it that way. She was furious with me for leaving. I didn't explain it to her either. I thought it was best if I kept my feelings to myself and simply removed myself from the situation. That was the way I'd always handled things. And it was a huge mistake.'

I pause. I watch Ben, hoping he might say something. I don't know if my words are having any impact, if he is softening towards me at all.

'Ben, I want you to know that leaving your house on Blackthorn Road was the hardest thing I've ever done in my life. I loved Lexi like my own child. But I thought I was doing the right thing for both of them. I thought I was coming between them. I thought that when I left, Vivien's maternal instinct would kick in. But it didn't, Ben, did it? Not really.'

He looks up, looks over at me and shakes his head. There is pain in his eyes, and sorrow.

'A bond between Vivien and me was severed a long time ago,' I say. 'Something important, a connection that was broken and never repaired. And because of our problems, I think there was always a little piece of Vivien that was missing. I think she struggled to love her own daughter. Because of me.'

I think there is a little compassion in Ben's eyes now.

'I swear to you, Ben, when Lexi was born I thought I was doing my best. If I could do it all over again I would. I would never leave. But did you really never notice anything? Something wrong between Vivien and Lexi? Something missing?'

'She was an attentive mother,' he says. 'She never neglected her own daughter.'

'But not a loving mother?'

He doesn't answer.

'I kept my distance, as you know. I was managing the Weissman Unit by that time and it wasn't difficult to lose myself in my career. Vivien was angry with me for moving out, abandoned once again, I suppose. I think she wanted to punish me. We had minimal contact, but because appearances were important to Vivien, she let me in, only to the extent where it wouldn't look odd. I was there at birthday parties, at Christmas. Over the years, I glimpsed what was happening out of the corner of my eye, but I pretended to myself I didn't see. I didn't ask questions because I didn't want to deal with the answers and I didn't want to interfere. But I know what Vivien was doing.'

Ben looks worried now. 'What do you mean?'

I walk round until I am standing opposite him, on the other side of Lexi's bed. She is in a deep, deep sleep. The tiny freckles scattered across her nose and the tops of her cheeks are the only bit of colour in her face. I lift her arm and I check her pulse.

Ben does not try to stop me, so I keep hold of her

hand. I've found my resolve and it resonates in my voice.

'I went to see Mrs Murad,' I say. 'She'd also picked up problems in Vivien's relationship with Lexi. She told me she'd insisted Vivien see a psychiatrist, because she was so concerned about her state of mind. She told me, Ben, that she broke confidentiality. That she'd shared her concerns with you.'

Ben stands up. He walks over to the door and closes it. He turns back to face me. 'Go on,' he says.

'Ever since the police asked me about the argument you had with Vivien, I've been trying to work out what you two might have argued about, what could have been so bad that you'd walk out on her.'

'I didn't walk out on her,' he says. 'She was furious with me and she told me not to come home.'

'It was because of Mrs Murad, wasn't it? She broke confidentiality because she was worried Vivien might hurt Lexi. And you were afraid, too.'

Ben hovers at the door. There are purple shadows under his eyes and his jaw tenses. He scratches at his upper arm. He still doesn't want to admit the truth.

I look down at Lexi's little face. 'That's why you and Vivien argued. Because you thought she was doing something to hurt Lexi.'

'I saw a psychiatrist behind her back,' he says. 'Vivien was furious. She was always so private, she hated the idea I'd been talking about her. She thought I'd betrayed her.'

'DS Cole told me that Vivien had a prescription for diet pills, for Lexi.'

'I didn't know,' he says.

Ben walks over to Lexi's bedside and sits down again, resuming his vigil next to his daughter. He grasps her hand. 'Do you believe me?'

'I do. Vivien wasn't just private, she could be secretive, too.'

'I had no idea Vivien was giving Lexi anything. I never dreamed she'd do anything like that. After Mrs Murad warned me, I talked to Lexi. It took some time for her to tell me what was going on, because I think Vivien had threatened her. But eventually, she said Vivien was giving her some sort of medicine because she was too fat. That Vivien would crush it up and stir it into a glass of milk.'

Ben begins to weep. His tears drip onto the white, white sheet. He lays his head down and his shoulders shake. I envy him. I haven't cried since she died, not once.

'We're all guilty,' I say. 'Vivien abused Lexi, physically and emotionally. I don't say she did it on purpose, but she did. And we both stood by while the damage was done. And now, Lexi needs someone to watch over her. Every minute of every day. And I want to be that person. I want to atone. I want to make up for all that my grand-daughter has suffered.'

Ben's shoulders become still. He looks up at me with red eyes.

'Do you really expect me to allow you to be around my daughter, after what happened tonight?'

'Yes.' My thoughts are clear and I know exactly what I need to say. 'Ben, I lied to the police.'

Alexandra

The night before she died

Alexandra could not sleep. She lay on her back, in her bed, worrying, because she had forgotten to do her maths homework. She felt for the corner of her quilt, the secret place where she had worked the stitching loose over many sleepless nights. She found the small hole she had made, and she poked her little finger through. She was careful to hide this damage from her mother.

She had left her maths folder at school and now it was really late and she had been playing on her iPad for too long and she couldn't tell her mother about the homework. Her mother had been crying.

And she didn't know where her father was.

Her stomach ached and her heart was beating too fast again, as though it might burst from her chest. Thoughts about her homework, her mother's tears, her father not coming home, sped round her head like cars round a racetrack, making her dizzy.

Alexandra knew she was fat. Her belly stuck out, her mother said, and it was true, she had to try hard to close the zip on her school skirt. But the pills made her frightened, they made her heart race and they made her full of wind, she felt like a blown-up beach ball about to burst.

Alexandra sat up, feeling ashamed. She had the runs, again.

She spent time in the bathroom, scrubbing herself and then the toilet, pouring in bleach, opening the window. She changed her underwear and her pyjamas, stuffing the dirty clothes into the bottom of the washing basket. She tried to make herself clean and to smell good, to please her mother.

Her heart was still going too fast. She didn't want to have a heart attack and die. She wanted her father. She thought about phoning him, she kept one of his business cards under her mouse pad, but it was midnight and she wasn't sure what her mother might do if she heard her using the phone so late at night. Her mother used to let Alexandra sleep next to her when her father was away working. But that was years and years ago. Before she was fat.

She couldn't lie still in her bed any longer. Her heart was a wild bird trapped inside her, flapping its wings so hard it might die of fright. She had seen that once on television. She had told her father about the medicine; she had broken her promise to her mother. Something bad was going to happen.

Alexandra slipped her feet into her velvet slippers. She walked out of her bedroom and quietly up the stairs.

The door to her mother's room was closed, but the light was on inside, it shone through the gap at the bottom. Her mother was awake. Alexandra knocked, waited a couple of seconds, then turned the door handle. As the door opened, she could hear the sounds of the television. At the end of the passageway she could see a dim, flickering light.

'Mummy?' she called out. She made her way along the passage, trailing her hand along the wall. She stopped at the end, when she could see her mother sitting up alone in bed.

'Where's Daddy?' she asked quietly.

'Alexandra, it's midnight. I'm never going to get you up for school in the morning.'

'My heart's going too fast, Mummy.'

'Nonsense. Stop worrying. The doctor said it's fine.'

'But—'

'*It's time for bed, Alexandra!*' Her mother's arm jerked up and her voice was loud and sharp.

Alexandra backed away, tears slipping hot and indignant down her cheeks.

She slammed the door of her mother's bedroom. She closed her eyes, but the image of her mother's anger burned on the back of her eyeballs. Her underwear was slimy again. The pills made her leak and she couldn't help it, she couldn't always get to the toilet in time. The worst part was when it happened at school.

She waited outside on the landing, under the picture of her mother on her wedding day, hoping her mother might come and find her. But she didn't. Her door stayed closed.

Alexandra decided there and then that she would take those pills and flush all of them down the toilet. The thought was half funny, half scary-exciting. She ran back down the passage and padded down the staircase in her slippers, all the way right down to the basement. Alexandra was not afraid of the dark.

She opened the top cupboard, the one near the window. She reached up on tiptoes to where her mother kept the medicines. She took out the box and popped all of the pills out of their plastic coats.

Then, she had another thought. An idea. A picture came into her mind. She saw her mother with frightened eyes and a mad beating heart and her bed covered in mess.

Alexandra opened the drawer next to the sink and took out the pestle and mortar. She took the pills and crushed them up until they were powder. Then she opened the fridge and took out the round glass jug full of the green muck her mother drank every morning. She placed it carefully on the counter and peeled back the cling film on the top, taking care not to scrunch it up.

She had watched her mother make this juice, out of spinach, beetroot and celery. Her mother had made Alexandra try it once but she had almost vomited.

Alexandra tipped the powder into the drink and stirred. She grinned to herself. Her mother would see. She would spend a day in the toilet.

Alexandra would tell her what she'd done, when her father was home and when her mother couldn't lose her temper in front of him. They would understand then that she was telling the truth, that the pills were making her sick.

When she had finished stirring and all of the powder had disappeared, Alexandra replaced the cling film and put the jug back into the fridge. She washed and dried the pestle and mortar and put them back inside the drawer.

She climbed all the way back up to the second-floor landing. The light under her mother's door was still on. She considered going inside and telling her what she'd done, and saying sorry, and asking if she might sleep in her bed. She was feeling very tired now. But Alexandra didn't want her mother looking at her in that horrible way again. So she went back downstairs and climbed into her own bed.

Something crackled in the pocket of her pyjamas. She reached inside and pulled out the crumpled-up medicine box and the empty pill packet and pushed them under her grey quilt.

In the night she had to get up over and over again, half asleep, because she needed the toilet. In the morning, her mother had to call up to her about a thousand times to get out of bed for breakfast.

When she went down to the kitchen, she got told off for staying up too late. As she ate her porridge, she remembered that her father had not come home the night before. She got up from the table and ran to the window. There was no sign of her father's car.

She looked at her mother's face and decided not to ask where he might be.

Her mother was already in her running clothes. On the way to school, she asked why Alexandra was so quiet, but Alexandra did not say that she was worried about getting in trouble because of the maths homework and worried about where her father was.

Her mother was the prettiest of all the mothers, by far, much more beautiful than the rest. Alexandra felt proud when she stood next to her at the school gates in her tight running leggings and her bright-pink trainers.

'Have a good day at school,' her mother said. Then, 'Love you.'

Her mother didn't kiss her goodbye. She turned and jogged away from her.

Alexandra remembered then, about the jug in the fridge, full of the thick, green juice. She wondered if it would taste funny, because of the pill powder she had added. She knew she was probably going to be in trouble later. Then she wondered if she had really crushed up all those pills and stirred them in to her mother's juice, or if it had all been a dream. She wasn't sure, she couldn't remember.

Chapter 27

My voice rings out, loud and clear in the silence of Lexi's hospital room.

'The day Vivien died, Mrs Murad's secretary phoned to tell me she hadn't arrived for her appointment. I had a bad feeling about it. It was so unlike Vivien, and I knew you were desperate to have another baby. At first, I didn't do anything, I carried on with my day. I told myself it wasn't really any of my business and that Vivien wouldn't want me to get involved. But something nagged at me. Maybe a mother does know. Maybe my maternal instinct wasn't completely numbed after all. Something made me go over to your house. I let myself in.'

Ben drops Lexi's hand. He sits back in his chair.

'Ben, she was already gone when I found her.'

'Oh my God. How could you be sure?'

'I've been a nurse for over thirty years. I know when it's too late.'

'Did you try mouth to mouth, CPR?'

'It was too late.'

'What about her head, the injury?'

'I don't know. I don't know how that happened. I assumed she'd fallen and hit her head. When I came into the house, I'd put my bag down on the hall table, and it had my phone inside it. So I left her, in the bathroom. I only meant to leave her for a few minutes, while I ran downstairs to get my phone, to call an ambulance.'

'But you didn't call anyone. Isaac did.'

'On my way downstairs, something made me stop, in the doorway of Lexi's bedroom. I stood and stared at her empty bed. Her pillow and her duvet and her quilt were all jumbled up, as though she'd been lying there only moments earlier. I thought about her little face, how devastated she was going to be. Then I saw something. A silver wrapper, sticking out from under her quilt.'

Ben turns a pasty shade of pale under his stubble. He rubs at his mouth, scrapes his fingernails against the stubble on his jaw.

'I went in there and I found the empty medicine packaging. The box was there too, on the floor under her bed. I recognized what it was – I know what those drugs can do to a person. The blister pack was empty, Ben. All of the pills were gone.'

I clear my throat. My nervous tic.

'I stood there, in her bedroom, and I remembered how unhappy Lexi had seemed at her own birthday party. I thought about how she'd refused to eat a slice of birthday cake, because it had too much icing on top. And Vivien didn't seem to find it strange, a child refusing to eat a piece of her own cake. And she'd asked Vivien for medicine, for a headache. I remembered the way she crushed up the Calpol tablet with the bottom of a spoon and mixed the powder into her hot drink. Lexi showed me, Ben. She showed all of us. She was begging for help, but none of us were paying attention. So whatever she did, she's innocent.'

'Rose, what did you do with the empty packaging?'

'I put it into the pocket of my coat. I went downstairs and picked up my bag and the set of spare keys I'd used to get in, and I left. I was in shock. I was trying to work out what I should do, the best way to handle it, for Lexi's sake. I went home and I had a drink. I realized there was no point in trying to hide anything. I assumed I would have been seen, or captured on camera or something, going into or out of your house. I assumed Lexi would tell someone about the pills, and what she'd done. But nothing happened. Absolutely nothing.'

I look down at Lexi. She is at peace. I stroke her hair.

'Has she said anything to you, Ben?'

'No.'

'I think she's forgotten, or she's blocked it out. Maybe she was sleepwalking when she did it.'

'Did what?'

'I don't know.'

But I'm not telling the truth, because I fear I do.

'Ben, I think Lexi might have had something to do with Vivien's death. I think she crushed up those tablets and put them into something Vivien was drinking. The same thing Vivien had been doing to her. I can't imagine Lexi understood what she was doing. Maybe she thought it was normal. I don't know.'

Ben is shattered. He's turned grey. He is immobilized in his chair.

'I thought if I kept quiet, if I didn't tell anyone,' I say, 'then I could spare Lexi from ever knowing what she'd done. And you, too. Do you understand? I wanted her to have a chance at a normal life.'

Ben nods. He's no longer looking at his daughter.

There's a knock on the door, a polite, soft tap.

He stands up. 'Have you told the police any of this?'

'No. And I don't want to, either. All I want, Ben, is to keep watch over Lexi so I can help her, if she needs me. Up until now they've treated me like a grieving mother, but if you accuse me of abducting Lexi, if they put me under pressure, I don't know what I'll say.'

There is another soft tap on the door. It opens and a young policewoman enters the room. She's wearing a black uniform. She doesn't have the sympathetic expression that DS Cole does.

I hold Lexi's hand while I listen to Ben talking to her. He says there has been a misunderstanding; that he asked me to take Alexandra to Cambridge Court for a sleepover last night because he had a meeting that was scheduled to end late. But then, because he's been so distracted since the death of his wife, and because he had a few drinks after the meeting, he forgot all about our arrangement. He went home and he panicked. He simply didn't remember he'd asked me to take Alexandra home to Cambridge Court. He apologizes for wasting valuable police time.

Finally, he reminds the officer how much stress he's been under since his wife died.

We all have.

Chapter 28

One month later

Like my daughter, DS Cole has good posture. She sits with her spine straight and her shoulders back on my grey-upholstered armchair. I sit opposite her, on the matching sofa. DS Cole has the look of someone who will go far. She reminds me of my daughter in that way, too. She has a certain air of confidence and of determination. I always admired those qualities in Vivien. I like to think that she inherited them from me.

'I'm sorry I didn't call ahead,' DS Cole says. 'I won't stay too long. You're probably on your way to work.'

'Actually,' I say, 'I've had to take some compassionate leave. I help Ben with my granddaughter most days now.'

Her eyes move to the small suitcase standing in front of the bar heater.

'I stayed over at the house on Blackthorn Road last night. Ben was in Cambridge, at a hotel near to the specialist unit where Cleo is being treated.'

'How is she?'

'She's doing better, I believe, but they don't know whether she'll ever make a full recovery. Her speech was affected by the head injury, and she has severe weakness on her right side, so her mobility is compromised.'

Ben and Cleo, I think, remain suspended in time. When they are together, they conjure up my daughter and neither of them is willing to let her go. I understand. Grief is a physical sensation, a pain that makes us want to search and search, until we find the person we have lost.

'We have evidence of her stalking behaviour,' DS Cole says, 'of the surveillance photographs she kept in her flat and on her laptop. If you're ever worried, we can take action to keep her a safe distance from your granddaughter.'

'I know. Thank you.'

The platinum blonde of DS Cole's hair emphasizes her bright-green eyes. She's wearing her usual outfit of tailored white shirt, black trousers and masculine brogues. The shirt is nipped in at the waist, the top buttons open.

I'm wondering about the reason for this latest unexpected visit. I'm not quite sure whether DS Cole is here in an official capacity.

I've set out a tray with a teapot and two teacups. The china is a matching set, white with a delicate silver stripe below the rim. An old Christmas gift from my daughter, I found it, still in its unopened box, and I decided it was too beautiful not to enjoy.

'I'm afraid there's no milk,' I say. 'I haven't had a chance to get down to the high street today.'

'Don't worry,' DS Cole says. 'I'll have mine black. With one sugar. Thank you.'

She crosses her legs and leans forward. 'You weren't at the inquest,' she says.

'I couldn't face it. I didn't want to have to sit there and listen to the details.'

I lift the teapot and pour.

Lexi is doing better, I think. She only suffers from her nightmares when Ben is away. I sleep lightly when I'm in the house on Blackthorn Road; a part of me is always listening out for her. Last night, sometime after midnight, I was woken by the softest pitter-patter of footsteps on the stairs. When I heard Lexi leave her bedroom, I felt along the floorboards with my feet until I found the blue velvet slippers that used to belong to my daughter, then I walked out onto the landing. Lexi's door was wide open. As always, I felt the familiar flutter of dread as I made my way down to the kitchen, to bear witness to her night-time ritual.

I always find her in the same place, at the island in the middle of the kitchen. She removes the pestle and mortar from the drawer and then she grinds her imaginary pills. Over and over. Time and time again.

I dare not interrupt her, or she will become distressed. She will scream and scream, as she did that night in Ben's arms. I have to let her finish.

Then, I walk over to her and offer her my hand. Her

skin, at night, still feels a little too cold. She lets me lead her back upstairs, back to bed. I tuck her in underneath her quilt and she hooks her little finger into the hole she has made along the edge.

By the time she falls asleep, I am wide awake. And I have my own ritual.

'I thought you might want me to explain the coroner's findings,' DS Cole is saying. She sets the delicate teacup down on the tray, and looks at me, waiting for my answer.

'Yes,' I say. 'I would. Thank you.'

I see myself as I walk up the staircase on Blackthorn Road, past Vivien's wedding portrait, and down the passageway that leads to her bedroom. I open the door to her bathroom, the one Ben always keeps shut. I step out of her slippers and onto the grey marble tiles.

DS Cole takes another sip from her cup of tea and then she begins to speak in her low, clear voice. 'Vivien had a fatal arrhythmia. But the coroner has given what we call a narrative verdict. He ruled there was not enough evidence to record Vivien's death as a suicide.'

'I see.'

Vivien is still there, waiting for me. She lies, crumpled, on her side, one arm flung out towards me as though she is trying to grab hold of me with her cherry-red finger-nails. I kneel beside her and I touch her cheek, but she is cold and she is empty. She has no pulse. Her pupils are fixed, dilated. Even so, I shake her, and I call her name. Like the parents on my ward, I understand, time and time again, that this is the end of my world as I have known it.

'Vivien didn't overdose on her antidepressant tablets,' DS Cole says, 'as you might expect a depressed person to do. But as you know, she had higher than normal levels of an amphetamine derivative, in her system. It's likely that she died because she took these pills on top of underlying, long-term damage to her body. It seems she'd been malnourished for a number of years. So, in a person of a different weight, with a different medical history, the outcome might have been different.'

'I understand,' I say.

The bone-china teacup, feather light, feels strangely heavy in my hands and I have to use all of my energy to lift it to my lips.

'We don't have enough evidence to determine Vivien's state of mind, her intention when she took the overdose.'

'You're saying it could have been an accident? That she didn't mean to kill herself?'

'We simply don't know.'

To my relief, DS Cole doesn't raise the issue of the missing medicine packaging. Ben told me that they assume Vivien took the pills while she was in the park. That she disposed of the empty packaging there. DS Cole is young and idealistic. I'm guessing she has no children of her own. Talking to a parent about the death of their child isn't a job one ever gets used to, and I think the young detective has done well. She never allows herself to become emotional, she retains a certain professional detachment, but at the same time she never comes across as uncaring.

I think she does care. And though we've met several times now, and she is not my friend or my confidante, sometimes I wish she was both. I long to confess. But that would not help Lexi. So instead, I concentrate on holding the lid of the teapot in place as I top up her tea.

'I also wanted to reassure you about the head injury,' DS Cole says. 'We had some concerns initially, but we now think the most likely explanation is that Vivien fell and hit her head against the side of the bath, when she lost consciousness.'

I remember holding Vivien and stroking her fontanelle.

I remember lifting her up, and then smashing her head against the side of the bath. I was in a panic. I wanted to do something, anything, to hide what Lexi had done. I wanted it to seem as if someone else was with Vivien when she died, as though there was someone else who wanted to hurt her.

I will never be able to explain what I did when I found her body. I acted on instinct, not logic. I was consumed with grief and with guilt. I had a primitive urge to protect Lexi. Perhaps DS Cole would see what I did as a crime. I don't know. I'm not proud that I've lied to DS Cole, or that I seem to have got away with it. I'm not proud that I left Vivien lying alone, in that bathroom.

But if I have saved Lexi from a lifetime of suffering, then I might have done something good.

My right hand is a little unsteady as I replace my cup in the saucer.

DS Cole looks thoughtful as she sips her tea. I think she understands me. 'There is one more thing,' she says. 'I thought you'd like to know what happened to Vivien's missing earrings.'

'You found them?'

'Yes. The waitress who works in the café at Regent's Park has come forward with more information. She wasn't entirely honest with us in her first interview.'

As I fold my hands in my lap, I notice that the bruises on the back of my left hand have all but disappeared. The headaches too are less frequent.

'This woman, Oksana, is from the Ukraine. She's been in the UK for three years, and she left her child behind, with her mother. She's the breadwinner and she sends money home to her family. She said that she and Vivien would talk sometimes, and that she'd told Vivien about her daughter. On the morning she died, Vivien came in to the café and gave Oksana a pair of extremely valuable diamond earrings. She told Oksana she wanted her to have them, to sell them, so she'd have enough money to bring her daughter over here to live with her.'

I don't wipe away my tears. I enjoy the feel of them against my dry skin.

'Vivien wrote her a note, on a serviette, saying the

earrings were a gift. We believe Oksana is telling the truth.'

'Will she be allowed to keep them?'

'That's up to Ben. I've got a feeling he'll say yes.'

DS Cole picks up her bag and opens it. She pulls out a tissue and reaches over to hand it to me. I pat my cheeks dry.

'Thank you,' I say. 'It's so kind of you to come and tell me in person.'

DS Cole nods. She leans forward to put her teacup down onto the tray, then she crosses her legs and relaxes back into the chair. She waits, as though she knows there is something more I need to ask.

'I do have one more question,' I say.

'Go ahead.'

'Did they ever catch the person who killed your sister?'

'Yes.'

'Did this person go to prison?'

'Yes.'

'And did that help you, with your heartache?'

'No,' she says. 'Not with that.'

She is very still as she speaks. I recognize that stillness, the lack of expression. It's a stillness I too have perfected, as though if I keep my body quite still, I can stop the pain, keep it buried in my core.

'We have to be careful,' I say, 'not to allow ourselves to become prisoners of grief. Do you agree?'

'I do.' She looks directly at me with those clear green eyes and she does not flinch.

'It might sound strange,' I say, 'but I'm going to miss talking to you.'

DS Cole smiles, as though she feels the same way.

'Thank you for the tea,' she says. And then she rises from the armchair in one fluid, easy motion.

When she is gone, I stand alone in my living room. Vivien's wedding photograph is still on the mantelpiece and next to it, Lexi's latest school photograph. It's stuffy in here. The windows are shut and the net curtains are drawn. This flat, where I've lived for so long, has begun to feel alien to me, while Blackthorn Road feels increasingly like home. It turns out Cleo was right. I do like being on the inside.

Epilogue

Lexi and I are holding hands. This graveyard is a peaceful place, a square of green grass enclosed by an old stone wall. Vivien's headstone is beautiful; Ben chose a white marble that glows in the sunshine. Bluebells have begun to spring up around the wooden benches.

Lexi has sprung up, too. She's grown taller since her mother's death; all of the hems of her trousers have had to be let down. She's flourished in these past few months, like a plant deprived of water and sunshine in a too-small container that now basks, replanted in a large and sunny corner of the garden.

I am holding a bouquet of flowers that Lexi and I made together, in the kitchen of the house on Blackthorn Road. I watched over her as she used scissors to trim the stems of the gardenias. When she had finished, I added forget-me-nots to our arrangement. The gardenias I bought, but the forget-me-nots grow in Vivien's garden. I noticed them one spring morning, as I stood in the kitchen, preparing Lexi's breakfast: bright patches of

296

violet blue emerging from between the cracks in the wall, on either side of the lion's head.

Alexandra reaches over and prises the bouquet from my fingers. She runs forward to her mother's grave and kneels down to arrange the stems. Her tongue pushes at the side of her cheek and she is deep in concentration. When she has finished, she begins to trace the gold lettering: *Vivien Kaye, beloved wife, mother and daughter.* The brief time between the dates of her birth and death speaks for itself.

I feel a shifting of air, a crackling, as Isaac walks up behind me.

Lexi is on her knees, tracing the years of her mother's life. Her hair shines coppery in the sun. I have let it grow long and beautiful. It is her lion's mane, her courage.

I feel the pressure of Isaac's hand on my waist as I lean back into him. Happiness flutters behind my ribcage, but at the same time, there is also a soft stirring of apprehension. I'm used to this sensation. It has become my constant companion.

I don't know what my granddaughter is thinking, as she traces the inscription on her mother's grave. Nor do I know what she intended, the day her mother died. She has never spoken about what she did, or what I found, hidden underneath her quilt.

I am always careful to make sure that any medicine in the house on Blackthorn Road is securely locked away. We do not speak of what happens at night.

Lexi comes back to me. She runs and throws herself

at me and she buries her head and her soft curls in my middle. I hold her and rub her back.

Then we say goodbye to Vivien, once again.

Isaac takes us for hot chocolate, with marshmallows and cream on top.

This is our ritual.

Acknowledgements

It has been my privilege to work with my editor, Harriet Bourton, on this story. Harriet helped me through several drafts, challenging and encouraging in equal measure and at all the right moments. Harriet accepts only the writer's best.

Beth Kruszynskyj has worked side by side with Harriet for much of this process and I am most grateful for all of her enthusiasm and assistance. My thanks go to the entire team at Transworld.

My agent, Madeleine Milburn, continues to support me with expert advice and guidance. Thanks also to Cara Lee Simpson and all at the Madeleine Milburn Literary, TV & Film Agency.

A number of experts gave generously of their time while I was writing this novel. Malcolm Fried, Steve Andrews and Wendy Wong spent several hours talking to me while I researched the background to the book. Callum Sutherland explained police procedures and pointed me to articles about forensic investigation. Sam

Lewis, the finest GP I know, and also my brother, helped with aspects of toxicology and the practicalities of finding a dead body. Professor Michael Patton kindly answered my questions about genetics. Ultimately though, this is work of fiction and any errors are mine alone.

Thanks as always to Jake and Joseph for their patience and for putting up with less attention than they deserve while I am distracted and in another world entirely. And finally, I'm so grateful to Rachel Tucker, Sarah Fisher and Emma Smith for all their support.

Read on for an extract from
Luana Lewis's chilling first novel:

DON'T STAND SO CLOSE

Hilltop, Friday, 7 January 2011, 3 p.m.

At first, she ignored the doorbell.

The sound rang out, echoing through the entrance hall, crashing through into the living room and clattering and bouncing inside her skull.

She stood at the window looking out at her garden, at a world that blazed white. A layer of snow coated the ground and the tangled arms of the trees and the Chiltern Hills beyond. It looks like Narnia, she thought, as though Aslan might stride out from the forest at any moment.

The quiet was unnatural. Unnerving.

The snow had begun to fall at nine o'clock that morning. The newspapers carried warnings: *A Wall of Snow*. Airports cancelled flights. Her husband had left for work as usual.

The doorbell rang again. Longer, louder and more insistent.

She felt exposed, in front of the wall of windows stretching across the back of the house. Her home was a white concrete edifice, a modernist triumph of sharp angles and tall windows. Nobody should be able to get past the entrance to the driveway without the intruder alarm sounding an ear-splitting warning. And yet someone had. The snow was the problem: it must have piled up so high that it had covered the infra-red eye of the sensor.

She pulled at the neck of her jumper. It was too tight and her throat itched. Her mouth was dry and her palms moist. It was three o'clock and darkness would come soon. Her husband would not be coming home. Inches of snow had turned to ice, had made the steep approach impossible.

She checked the locks on the patio doors. A draught whistled around the edges of the black steel doorframe, as if the cold was trying to force its way inside. The house was Grade II listed, nothing could be done, the doors and the windows could not be changed. She tested the locks once more and then pulled the heavy drapes closed.

The doorbell rang again. And again.

She paced the living room. A half-empty bottle of wine stood open on the coffee table. She breathed. In for three, out for three. She pressed her hands against her ears.

A normal person would go to the front door and see who was there.

Stella walked through to the large square entrance hall. A chandelier with myriad round glass discs spiralled down above the staircase. She flicked a switch and light bounced off the pale-grey walls and shimmered, everywhere, too bright. She was disoriented, as though she had stepped inside a hall of mirrors and could not get her bearings. She would not panic. Nobody had ever tried to harm her at Hilltop. People intending to do harm did not announce themselves, or wait to be invited inside. But she could not think of a reason why someone would ring her doorbell in the middle of a snowstorm.

She checked the monitor mounted on the wall next to the

front door. A young woman was outside. She stood on the doorstep, her arms wrapped around her chest, shifting from one foot to the other. A beanie hat was pulled down low over her long fair hair. A short leather jacket, covered in studs and zips, barely covered her midriff.

Stella lifted the handset. 'Yes?' she said.

'I'm freezing. Can I come inside?' Snowflakes churned around her as she shouted at the intercom. She shivered with cold and she didn't look like much of a threat. 'Could I use your phone?'

She looked up into the camera. Her face was lovely on the screen, with cat-like eyes and high cheekbones.

'I'm sorry,' Stella said. 'No. Try one of the neighbours.' She placed the receiver back on to the cradle.

She waited until the screen faded to black and the person outside disappeared and then she returned to the living room and took up her place at the window. But she was uneasy and the spell was broken. The snow that covered everything – the lawn, the trees and the hills beyond – no longer seemed magical. She hated being alone. The daylight hours were difficult, the nights almost impossible.

The air shattered as the doorbell rang again.

The police would hardly be impressed if she called them out to complain that a young woman had rung her doorbell. And she didn't want to disturb her husband. But she so wanted to call him and ask him what to do. Her BlackBerry was right beside her. She picked it up. Ran her fingers across the keypad. Put it down again. She would not call him, she would deal with this herself. She was getting better. Of course, she wasn't. She was alone and helpless and useless. She wanted Max. If she had her way, she would have him home all day.

Max deserved a better wife. He had rescued her and then it had all predictably gone to hell.

She returned to the front door, a rising anger competing with her nerves. The intercom screen showed the same young woman, with her beanie pulled down almost to her eyebrows and the absurdly short leather coat that provided no warmth.

'*What is it?*' Stella said.

She babbled as she looked up into the camera: 'I used to live here,' she said. 'I came up from London to see my old house. I didn't know the snow would be so bad. It's all frozen and it's really steep going back down the hill. Can I *please* come inside?'

Stella realized that the girl outside was very young. She couldn't be more than fifteen years old. Fourteen, maybe. A child.

'I'll call a taxi to take you back down to the station,' Stella said.

'You can't. They've shut down because of the snow. *Please*. The tube isn't running either, I'm stuck here. I can't go back down the road or I'll break my neck.' Her voice was rising with outrage and distress. 'Can I just come inside?'

The girl was shaking with cold. Her lips were a purple gash, startling and dark against the pale skin of her face. She looked as though she was about to cry. Stella felt sorry for her. Not sorry enough, however, to risk opening the door.

'No,' Stella said. 'Go and try one of the other houses. You've got an entire street to choose from.'

'Please,' the girl said, 'I'm so cold. Why can't you just let me in?' She pouted at the camera and she stomped her white trainers on the black marble tiles.

Stella slammed the receiver back against its white plastic

306

cradle. She watched as the girl tried in vain to keep warm. She paced up and down, leaving a haphazard pattern in the snow around Stella's front door. She wrapped her arms around herself and bounced, up and down. At a certain point, she stopped fighting. She sank to the floor, her head on her knees.

The cold must be unbearable, like torture.

The minutes passed as Stella sat in front of the fire on her grey linen sofa. She pressed her bare feet into the soft, Chinese deco rug. She stood. She walked around the navy border, placing one foot in front of the other as though she was on a tightrope. She stopped at the yellow and orange parrot embroidered in the right-hand corner. She did not understand why the girl insisted on waiting outside her door.

Her thoughts came fast and fragmented. One day it would be different. She would be free of her chains. But she was losing time. She found it harder and harder to remember what she had been like before.

The house was silent.

Almost forty minutes had passed since the bell had rung for the first time. The girl at the front door must have decided to brave the steep hill that was Victoria Avenue. She was right: if she tried to make her way down, she might slip and fall. But after all – and here Stella tried to make herself feel less guilty – what was the worst thing that could happen to her? She might end up with a wet backside. And once she made it down the hill – wet backside and all – she could walk along the High Street and she would be inside the cosy inn within minutes. The Royal Oak: good wine, an open fire-place and exposed beams. The television above the fireplace had sort of melted along the bottom but no one seemed to notice it was a fire hazard. Stella could feel the soft sheepskin throws against her skin. She could taste the Bloody Mary – poured from a jug on the counter, slices of lemon arranged on the wooden board next to the glass pitcher. Max had described it all. He often walked down there alone on a Sunday evening. Stella had never walked with him, but maybe she would go, for the first time, when he came home to her the next day. He must be desperate for her to leave the house, though he hid it well.

The silence had become a pressure, pushing against her eardrums, and the darkness drew closer.

Max would not force her back into a world that terrified her. But she had been hiding a long time. More and more often she feared it was too late. Whichever way she looked at it, she was a recluse.

With any luck, the girl had gone to pester the neighbours, families with children of varying ages whom Stella had never met.

Or she might still be outside, waiting.

The silence and the waiting became unbearable.

Hilltop was her home, she was safe inside. If she went down the road paved with paranoia and self-pity she knew where it would lead – into a padded cell, most probably. She *was* safe. Nothing had changed; no one could get in. It was just a girl.

Hilltop was her own private kingdom, her palace and her prison.

Stella returned to the entrance hall. She tilted the shutters and peered out into the silvery-grey landscape. Heavy snowflakes swirled everywhere, as though a million goose-down pillows had been sliced open in the sky. With each passing second, the light grew weaker. The girl sat with her back to the polished steel front door, her knees pulled up to her chest and her head down. She was a child: helpless and cold.

A part of Stella was excited, the part she usually kept locked down tight. A little of her old self stirred in her chest. She needed to take a risk, to shatter the invalid's life she had created for herself before it was truly too late. She needed to know that she could still be of use, to someone. She was tired of being inside, immobilized, waiting for something to happen, tired of waiting to get better while other people went on with their lives and her husband stayed away. She punched in the code, turning off the motion sensors. She rested her left hand on the door handle. There was a human being outside, alone and suffering. With her right hand, she reached for the deadbolt. She opened the door.

The blackened sky was shot through with violet. Icy air raged inside and heavy snowflakes blew through the open doorway then melted as they landed on the heated floor.

The girl was covered in white. Ice crystals had settled everywhere, in her hair and on her shoulders, and they clung to her leggings and her shoes.

She blinked up at Stella. 'It's fucking freezing out here,' she said.

Her blue eyes were defiant and full of mistrust. She stayed where she was, unsure whether she was to be allowed inside. She made no sudden movements and she did not try to force her way in. She waited to be invited.

Stella took a step backward and nodded. With stiff, frozen fingers, the girl picked up her bag and scrambled to her feet. She stepped across the threshold.

Stella shut the front door behind her, locked it and then

turned to get a better look at her uninvited guest. The girl was like a frightened deer. Strands of damp hair clung to her face. Her jacket hung open, revealing a cropped T-shirt and a hint of pale, goose-pimpled flesh. Bony knees protruded through tight black leggings. She held on to the strap of her rucksack and rocked back and forth on her grubby white running shoes. The girl pulled off her hat, her fingers still angry and red. She shook out her long wet hair and, as she did so, she caught sight of the colossal chandelier. She stared up for a moment, wide-eyed.

At five foot four, Stella was not particularly tall, and the girl was a head shorter than she was. And that was with the extra inch she gained from the running shoes. Stella felt foolish for being afraid.

'My toes are burning,' the girl said. 'And I can't feel my fingers.' She glared at Stella as if she were responsible for her pain. She curled her fingers into a fist, then released them; watching her hands as though they belonged to someone else. Her eyes glistened and Stella thought she might be about to cry.

'Why don't you take off your shoes,' Stella said, thinking about frostbite.

The girl bent down and tried to undo her laces, but her fingers were rigid and it took ages before she managed to loosen the double knots. As Stella waited and watched, the girl pulled off her trainers and placed them side by side on the front door mat. She wasn't wearing socks and her toe-nails were painted black.

'You should take that off too.' Stella pointed at her jacket. Up close, she could see it was no more than thin plastic.

The girl shook her head; no.

'Come inside, there's a fire – it's warmer,' Stella said.

She walked towards the living room, pointing at the doorway, as if encouraging a timid animal to follow. She felt energized, or perhaps she felt anxious, it was hard to tell the difference. The girl followed, barefoot and still clutching at the strap of her bag. She didn't look as though she felt at home in her old house. She stood motionless next to the sofa with her damp hair and her damp clothes.

Stella felt bad for leaving her outside so long. She lifted the tartan blanket from the back of the couch and shook it out. She ventured a step closer, holding the blanket out in front of her. When the girl didn't back away, Stella draped the blanket around her shoulders and wrapped her up tight. The girl's stiff fingers took hold. Stella saw it again, the suspicion in her eyes, and she backed away.

'Sit in front of the fire,' she said.

The girl sat, perched on the edge of the sofa, her back to Stella, staring at the small flames. The shivering went on and on. Stella hovered behind her, unsure what to do next.

'I should phone your parents and let them know you're here,' she said.

'My toes *really* hurt.'

Stella wondered if she might end up having to find a doctor for this strange, reckless girl who wandered about half undressed in the arctic conditions. She walked round and sat on the opposite end of the sofa. She noticed how beautiful the girl was. Exceptionally so. Her deep-set eyes were the colour of the sky on a clear, sunshine-filled day. Her hair had begun to dry, forming soft golden waves that caressed her cheeks. Her skin was velvety smooth. Her top lip was a shade too thin, but her bottom lip was fuller, pouting. She was so young.

'Why are you staring at me?' the girl asked.

'I'm Stella. What's your name?'

'Blue.'

Blue was the colour of her eyes. Blue did not sound like a real name.

'Is Blue your nickname?'

'It's my real name.'

'And what's your surname?'

She rubbed at her dry lips, tinged blue with cold, and hesitated, her eyes flickering around the room from left to right. 'Cunningham,' she said.

Stella had no way of knowing if she was lying.

'We need to get you home,' Stella said. 'We need to let someone know you're here.'

'I'm not going home.' The girl spoke with a certain determination that concerned Stella.

'Why not?' Stella asked.

'I had a fight with my mother. She won't let me back in.'

'Blue, even if you had an argument with your mother, she'll still be worried about you.'

No response.

'Well – I still need to call someone to let them know you're safe. Is there someone else I could call, besides your mother?'

Blue shook her head, not looking at Stella, staring at the fire. The shivering had lessened, but now and again a small quiver passed through her shoulders.

'We do need to find a way to get you home,' Stella said. Her words sounded empty, repetitive, lame.

'I didn't really use to live here,' the girl said. 'I made that up.' She turned to look at Stella. The colour of her eyes seemed to shift, so that the blue was deeper and more intense, the colour of cold, hard tanzanite.

Stella tilted her head from side to side, trying to release the muscles that had seized up in her neck and across her shoulders. 'Then why have you come here?' she asked.

If she panicked, if she breathed too fast, if she allowed her heartbeat to thunder out of control, she was lost. She should have gone upstairs when she heard the doorbell, shut the door of her bedroom, swallowed a sleeping pill, ignored the goddamn noise. There was a tightness in her chest, it was impossible to take in enough air.

'I came because I need to see Dr Fisher,' the girl said.

'My husband?'

'Yes.' Blue's mouth set in a stubborn line and she began to scratch at the skin on her forearms.

ABOUT THE AUTHOR

Luana Lewis is a clinical psychologist and author of two non-fiction books. *Forget Me Not* is her second novel.